RESTLESS HEARTS

YAHRAH ST.JOHN

OLIVER HEBER BOOKS

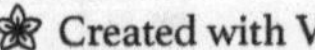

PROLOGUE

Present Day

"It can't be," exclaimed Addison Walker as *he* walked in. The man so startled her, she almost dropped the glass of champagne she'd been drinking at the Dallas Country Club charity event.

Addison's best friend, Collette Edwards, reached for and steadied Addison's wavering hand. "Can't be what?" asked a concerned Collette.

"Caleb."

Collette's head immediately perked at the name that had caused Addison so much heartache four years earlier. "What about him?"

"He's here."

"In Dallas?"

Addison nodded. "Not just in Dallas. He's at the party. Over there." She inclined her head.

"Are you sure?" The words died on Collette's lips as she spun around and indeed saw Caleb Hart—the one and only man Addison had truly loved. He'd walked in with an older gentleman wearing a designer tuxedo.

"Very," Addison stated. "What the hell is he doing

here?"Collette shook her head. "What are you going to do?"

"Do? I'm not going to *do* anything. I haven't seen the man in four years since *he* broke up with me. What I am going to do is go find my boyfriend."

"So you're going to act like Caleb doesn't exist, after everything he once meant to you?"

"Shouldn't be that hard," said Addison, "since he did the same thing to me." She turned to leave, but Collette touched her arm.

"Addy, are you sure you want to leave things this way. Don't you want to go over there and have it out with that son of a bitch, tell him how he broke your heart?"

"And give him that kind of power over me? Absolutely not. I made my peace with what happened between us years ago. I've moved on with Raphael."

Seconds later, Addison was walking away, leaving Collette to wonder if she'd truly gotten over Caleb.

CALEB TRIED to remain present in the conversation his uncle, businessman Duke Hart, was having with an investor in his new oil refinery project. But that didn't stop Caleb from staring at Addison as she walked away from Collette. It had been four years since he'd seen her last, and she was just as beautiful if not more so than she'd been all those years ago. Her usual straight hair was in a sophisticated updo, allowing a clear view of her delicately carved oval face, doe-shaped eyes and temptingly curved mouth. But there was something different about her. She was wearing makeup. When they'd been together, he'd preferred the natural look and had told her she didn't need it. And she still didn't.

And her body ... she'd matured into it even more. She wore a long lavender gown that hugged all the right curves. He could only catch a peek of her feet in the sparkling sandals, and it instantly reminded him of the night they'd first met when he'd removed her sandals one by one and had kissed his way up to the heaven between her thighs. And heaven it had been. She'd had her first orgasm thanks to his expert fingers.

He'd been a fool when he'd pushed her away, but how could he have allowed her to stay by his side as a paralyzed man? Had he known that a delicate high-risk surgery and rehab would give him the ability to walk again, he would never have let her go. But he didn't have a crystal ball to predict the future, and at the time he felt he had to let her go, for his sake as well as for hers.

"Caleb, did you hear me?"

Caleb blinked several times. "I'm sorry, Uncle Duke. What did you say?"

"Seems like someone has their head in the clouds," Duke commented.

"Sorry, Uncle. What was the question?" Caleb's mind was scrambled. How could he think straight when Addison was the one who got away?

~

"Hey, baby brother." Rylee came toward Caleb a half-hour later and gave him a long overdue hug. She was attending the event with her husband, Amar Bishop, who had been invited by a business associate. "It's so good to see you."

"You too, sis." Caleb squeezed her back. "It's been too long."

"And whose fault is that?" Rylee asked, putting her hands on her slender hips.

Caleb smiled sheepishly. "Mine." He had been MIA of late at most family events at the Hart family ranch in Tucson, Arizona. He just hadn't had the courage to visit Golden Oaks after his accident. The thought of getting back on a horse or anything with the ability to throw him would make him break out into a cold sweat.

"Yeah, it is," said Rylee, punching him square in the shoulder.

"Ouch!"

"You deserve it," she admonished. "Amar and I had to fly nearly two thousand miles just to lay eyes on you. And I must say, you're looking good." A broad smile spread across her face. "How the heck are you?"

"I'm good, I'm good." Caleb smiled back. "And look at you," he said as he grasped her small hand and spun her around. "Married life agrees with you. Or shall I say, being filthy rich agrees with you?"

Rylee blushed. "Thanks, I guess."

Caleb knew it had taken her awhile to become accustomed to Amar's lavish lifestyle of limousines, private jets, designer clothes and fancy cars. After nearly four years of marriage, she hadn't quite embraced it, but Rylee was starting to dress more like the wife of a billionaire husband with holdings in Internet, publishing and television, rather than a veterinarian at a small dude ranch. He'd heard that Rylee was now in charge of Amar's stable of Arabians that he'd inherited from his late father, Sheikh Abdul al' Mahmud, as well as freelancing her vet services to high profile clients.

"I'm sorry, sis, I don't hate on you. I'm happy for you and Amar. He's a good guy."

Rylee glanced over at her husband, who was entrenched in another conversation nearby. "That he is." She turned her attention back to Caleb. "Working with Uncle Duke agrees with you." She sized Caleb up in the designer suit he wore. It was very stylish and worlds away from his glory days in jeans and a T-shirt riding bulls at the rodeo.

Caleb nodded. "Yeah, well, I had a lot to get through."

"I know." Rylee's eyes misted just thinking about the terrible period that Caleb had endured to walk again. She'd wanted to be there for him, but he'd pushed everyone in the family away.

"I'm sorry for how I was back then."

"You're my brother, and I hold no ill will," said Rylee. "Anyway, that's in the past. Your future is bright now. I mean, who would have thought you'd be an oil executive?"

"Not me, but Uncle Duke did." Caleb stared over at his uncle, their mother's brother. "He gave me a new lease on life."

"Then perhaps it's time you reclaim it," Rylee said.

"What do you mean?"

"Addison."

Her name made him blush. "Yeah, I saw her."

"And? Are you going to go talk to her?" Rylee asked.

"How can I? You do remember how I treated her?"

"I do, but so much time has passed and she's probably moved on, but you should clear the air. If I learned anything from the death of Amar's father, it's that you can't leave words unsaid. Don't wait. Go talk to her."

"I don't know."

"Trust me. How bad can it be?"

~

ADDISON COULD NOT FIND Raphael anywhere, even after searching the country club, where guests were milling all around. Dammit! She didn't want to go back in there without reinforcements. She would just stay outside on the patio until she got ahold of herself.

Caleb Hart. *How can he be here?* It was just too surreal that after four years he would pop back into her life just as quickly as he'd disappeared from it.

Why did he have to show up now when she'd finally figured her life out, when she'd finally found a way, or should she say someone, to help her get over him? Raphael had been a godsend three years ago when they'd met in Paris, a sojourn she'd taken away from Dallas to forget Caleb. They'd started out as friends, with him listening to her pain over losing Caleb. But eventually that friendship had turned into something more, something deeper. And one night over a year ago, they'd given into the passion that had been steadily building between them.

Had it been fireworks like it had been with Caleb, her first lover? No, but it had been memorable, and they'd fallen into an easy relationship.

Addison didn't hear the footsteps approaching until they were behind her. She didn't need to turn around to know who they belonged to. She could smell *him*. He still wore the same cologne as he had all those years ago and probably still had the same swagger that went along with it. Taking a deep breath to gather her strength and willpower, she slowly turned around.

"Addison."

She exhaled and then finally spoke. "Caleb."

"It's been a long time."

"Not nearly long enough," she muttered.

"What was that?"

"Oh, nothing." She shook her head to clear the memories. "Why are you here, Caleb?"

"Isn't it obvious?" His dark-brown eyes roved over her.

"No, it isn't."

"I'm here to win you back."

1

Four Years Earlier

"This weekend is going to be unforgettable," Caleb Hart said to all the guys as they boarded his soon-to-be brother-in-law Amar Bishop's private jet. "It'll make you all regret ever giving up the bachelor life."

Along with Caleb and Amar were Caleb's brother Noah, Amar's right-hand man Sharif Khoury, and a family friend, Lucas Kingston; they were all headed to Vegas for Amar and Lucas's bachelor party. The two men were having a double wedding in Tucson.

"I couldn't ever regret meeting your sister," Amar said, glancing in Caleb's direction. "She's an amazing woman."

"Even if it meant dealing with her overprotective brothers?" asked Noah.

"Well, that certainly wasn't a walk in the park," Amar snorted, "especially when you clocked me in the jaw the first time you met me."

Noah's head fell back as he roared with laughter. "I'd forgotten that."

Amar moved his jaw around in remembrance. "I did not."

Caleb patted Amar's shoulder. "You're lucky it was Noah and not me. Considering how upset Rylee had been after she'd returned from the Kentucky Derby last year, I might have pummeled you."

"Then I will consider myself lucky. But the start of our relationship was nothing like Lucas's and Kenya's." Amar inclined his head toward his fellow groom.

Lucas nodded in agreement. "Very true, but I'm thankful Kenya and Chynna decided to switch places. Otherwise we would have never met."

"Ah, yes." Caleb rubbed his goatee. "You two did meet auspiciously. If you don't mind my asking, how did you ever get past the betrayal?"

Caleb wasn't sure he could have gotten over it. Kenya and Lucas met when she traded places with her twin, pop superstar Chynna James Hart. At the time, Kenya had been a low-rate actress hiding in the shadows until she'd expertly fooled everyone, including Lucas, into believing she was actually Chynna. And now look at her—she was an Oscar-winning actress. She'd won the award for the movie she'd been filming while imitating Chynna.

"I wish I could say it was easy," Lucas replied, "but it wasn't."

"What got you through it?" Caleb asked.

"Love," Lucas and Noah answered at the same time. Both men turned to each other and laughed aloud.

Lucas gave Noah a fist bump. "He knows what I'm talking about."

Caleb shrugged. "Must be some powerful shit if it can convince two otherwise sane men to shackle themselves under the bonds of matrimony."

"What's your beef with marriage?" Amar asked.

"Your parents have been married for years. I would think you would want the same for yourself."

"I love my parents," Caleb responded. "But I don't know ... I get restless ... I need my freedom."

At twenty-eight, Caleb was the youngest of the Hart brood, and he wasn't content on settling down into married life anytime soon. Life as a bull rider on the circuit guaranteed that he would never stay tied down to any one woman. Variety was the spice of life, and he loved variety. And to keep it coming, he had to keep all of his six-foot frame in prime condition for the ladies, and he had the six-pack abs, bald head and a touch of mustache and goatee to prove it.

On the other hand, there was his brother, Noah, the eldest and most stalwart of the family. He manned the Hart family's dude ranch, Golden Oaks in Tucson. It had surprised Caleb when Noah managed to snag Chynna James. But his brother was a smart man. Within their first year of meeting, he'd married Chynna and made sure she had a bun in the oven. Chynna was expecting their first child in a few weeks.

Meanwhile his older sister, Rylee, a veterinarian, had gone to the Kentucky Derby six months ago and fell right into the arms of a sheikh's son, the billionaire playboy Amar Bishop. Hell, they'd only been together a short time before his firecracker of a sister had convinced the interminable bachelor to put his player's card on the shelf.

"Eventually, you'll have to settle down," Noah said to Caleb.

"Says who?"

Amar gave him a sly grin. "I promise you, Caleb, when the right woman comes along, she'll knock you off your feet and you'll gladly get down on your knees and beg her to marry you."

"We'll just see about that."

~

"Girl, this suite is phat," Collette said to Addison as they admired their accommodations while their other friends, Emma and Violet, oohed and aahed over the surroundings.

"Yeah, well, Daddy has no idea I used his name and clout to get us this room," Addison replied. Even though she was twenty-three, she still lived at home and her father treated her like a child and gave her an allowance. But this weekend, she intended to spend what she pleased, which is why she'd taken her father's credit card when she'd left the house earlier that day.

"And here's hoping he never finds out." Collette popped the top off the champagne that had been waiting in an ice bucket for them when they arrived to the suite.

Addison rushed over to the pantry to pull out two champagne flutes so Collette could pour the drink. When the glasses were full, she handed one to her best friend and took the other for herself.

"Hold up, don't we get some too?" Skylar, her friend from finishing school, replied with a pout and her arms folded across the new breasts her father had just paid for. They boomed in the Bebe mini-dress she wore.

"Of course." Addison handed Skylar her flute and walked back to the pantry to fish out two additional ones.

Collette rolled her eyes at Addison as she held out the flutes.

Addison was sure Collette was wondering why

she'd invited Skylar, but it wasn't like she had exactly. At the Dallas Country Club, Skylar had overheard the three of them talking about their trip during Sunday brunch and had insinuated herself into an invitation like she always did. Meanwhile, Addison wished she could be more spontaneous. She hoped this trip would do just that for her. She was determined to do something daring and outside of her comfort zone while in Vegas.

As all the women held up their flutes for a toast, Addison cheered, "Let the fun times begin!"

"I know it may not appear to be enough bedrooms," Amar said when the men arrived to the elegantly decorated, three-master-bedroom duplex with floor-to-ceiling windows, "but the Wynn Hotel has put double beds in two of the rooms, per my request."

"Doesn't matter to me," Lucas said when he saw the billiards room enhanced with a flatscreen high-definition LCD television.

"Do you see this bathroom?" Caleb yelled from the first- floor master bedroom. "It's sick!" It featured a steam shower, whirlpool deep-soak tub, dual sinks and a separate water closet. He could picture a woman enjoying it all with him. Who knew what the weekend would bring?

Caleb came out from the master suite. "Do you mind if I have this room?"

Amar raised a brow. "Because it has a king-size bed?"

Caleb chuckled. He *was* known to be a ladies' man. "Well, you won't have much need for it."

"Caleb!" Noah admonished. "Amar arranged this

entire weekend, and he's one of the grooms. He should have the main room."

Amar held up his hand to Noah. "It's okay. Caleb's right. I don't intend on sowing my wild oats this weekend, so if he can put it to better use, by all means ..."

Noah shook his head, but Caleb didn't care. It meant that whatever happened tonight, he wouldn't be alone.

"What's on tap?" Lucas asked, walking over to the wet bar. He poured himself a Scotch.

Caleb rubbed his hands in glee. "Well, I have dinner and then cigars at Caesars Palace, followed by poker, then an exclusive invite to one of the best gentlemen's clubs in Vegas, and who knows ..." He purposely let his sentence dangle. They had no idea what he had in store for them.

"And can we assume there will be strippers at this gentlemen's club?" Amar inquired.

Caleb shrugged. "You know the old saying ..."

"What happens in Vegas, stays in Vegas," the men all chimed.

A COUPLE OF HOURS LATER, after they'd had time to get settled and showered, a stretch Hummer limousine pulled up for them outside the Wynn. There would be no party bus. Caleb thought that was played out and overdone. They were grown-ass men who'd been around the block and should be treated as such.

"Thanks," Caleb said to the driver, who held open the door so they could hop in. He slid into the seat and looked across at Amar and Lucas. As was their style, they were expertly dressed. Amar had finally lost the suit and had replaced it with trousers and a silk shirt, while Lucas had opted to play it cool. He wore all black, from his suit jacket to his pants.

Caleb shook his head. All this sophistication was overrated. He'd dressed comfortably in jeans and had opted for a chambray shirt instead of his usual plaid. Noah was similarly dressed, then there was Sharif. He had a style all his own, in a linen trouser outfit that looked like he'd come straight out of the Sahara Desert, but then again he was from Nasir, Amar's native homeland somewhere outside Dubai.

Caleb reached for the bottle of Dom Pérignon in the ice bucket, then poured each man a glass and held it. "Men, let's turn up!"

~

THE NIGHT WENT EXACTLY as Caleb had planned. The group started with an amazing dinner at the chef's table at Guy Savoy's at Caesars Palace and the most expensive wine he'd ever imbibed, courtesy of Amar. And if that wasn't enough, they'd retired to an exclusive gentlemen's club where they partook in poker and cigars.

Poor Noah had been completely out of his element and chose to watch along the sidelines with Sharif, while Amar and Lucas, the sharks they were, went in for the kill at the table with professional gamblers and, in Caleb's opinion, other suckers. He'd never seen such a meeting of the minds before as the two men went toe to toe.

Lucas and Amar couldn't be more different. Lucas was imposing at six-foot-five with his football player build and midnight eyes; on the other hand, Amar was nearly as tall as Lucas—he had an athletic build and a fair to olive-toned complexion and looked like he was of Mediterranean descent, but it was his bushy eyebrows, a broad nose and full lips that spoke of his African ancestry.

Caleb wasn't much of a gambler, but he wanted a front row seat to see the standoff between the two men. His cards were on Amar, but then Lucas surprised him and Amar when he bluffed his way to a win with a flush over Amar's Four of a Kind.

Amar was not fazed. He turned to Lucas and offered his hand. "Good game. Not many people can beat me or at least not any that I would agree to spend time with."

Lucas returned the handshake and then reached for all the chips to cash out. "I was a hustler on the streets of South Central before I was the owner of R & K Records."

"Ah, I will have to do my homework a bit better the next time I enter the ring with a worthy opponent." Amar turned to give Sharif a knowing glance.

"As entertaining as it was watching you guys get your guns off," Caleb said, "how about we turn up this evening and go party with some dancing and—"

"You mean strippers?!" Sharif said, aghast.

"Is this a bachelor party or are we having girls' night out?" Caleb said.

"Strippers it is," Lucas stated with a grin. "Where to next?"

THE LIQUOR WAS STARTING to get to Addison. She was feeling more loose and carefree than she ever had in her life. It had started with the two bottles of bubbly she and the girls had polished off before leaving their hotel suite. Once the liquor had spread through her veins, she'd allowed Collette and the others to fancy her up in one of their party dresses that barely reached her thigh and to curl her hair until it hung in spiral waves down her back.

Addison hadn't even recognized the sexpot in front of her. If she were a man, she'd want to do her! She smiled back at the reflection in the mirror of one of the nightclubs that had been one of many they'd frequented that evening. Collette had expertly done her makeup. Addison was staring at herself so hard, she didn't see Collette watching her.

"Are you okay, girl?" Collette asked. "You're not about to hurl are you? Just let me know, because I don't want any accidents, but I'll hold your hair back."

"No, I'm okay," Addison replied, turning around to better admire her backside in the dress.

"If you're done looking in the mirror, are you ready to get back out there?" said Collette. "I'm dying to see if this club has any better hotties than the last club, because the last two spots were sorely lacking."

"I am. Let's go." Addison grabbed her clutch and followed Collette out of the bathroom.

In this getup, Addison was ready to meet a hottie. Matter of fact, she was ready to do all sorts of naughty things with one. She was determined to rid herself of her virginity and her squeaky-clean image. Only Collette knew of her status, which she'd always kept quiet even when Emma, Violet and Skylar were regaling the group with their sexploits. Usually the women were so caught up in their stories that they never seemed to notice that Addison didn't contribute any of her own to the mix.

Addison had decided that tonight was the night. There was no reason for her to keep waiting for a Mr. Right who might never come along. If nothing else, losing her mother at four years old had taught Addison that life was too short. But it had been pretty hard to have a social life much less a sex life when her overprotective father kept a watchful eye on her; but now she was in Vegas with the opportunity to finally cut loose and live life on her own terms.

Addison followed Collette under the flashing lights through the throng of scantily clad female and male bodies. They arrived at the VIP section, where the rest of their group had congregated.

"Hey, girl, where have you been?" asked Skylar.

"Just freshening up," Collette answered. "I didn't realize you had a stopwatch."

"Jeez, Collette, chill out!" Skylar said. "I was only asking because a six-pack of sexy men just walked through the door, and I wanted everyone in attendance before I call first dibs."

"Where are they?" Addison spun on her four-inch heels and scanned the crowd.

"There!" Skylar pointed to six men of various shades and colors walking up the stairs to the VIP area.

Addison swallowed hard. They were all fine as hell. Some of them were dressed suavely in suits or linen ensembles, while two others had on jeans and button-down shirts. But there was one in particular, the bald one who was scanning the room, who caught her eye, and vice versa. He gave her a wink as he made his way up the stairs to the VIP lounge.

"Oh, Lord!" Collette fanned herself. "You ain't lying. Where have *they* been all night?"

"Who cares?" Skylar replied. "I'm just glad they are here now. And I call first dibs on the chocolate brother in all black."

"Says who?" asked Emma, one of the African-American girls in the group.

"Just because I'm vanilla don't mean I don't like chocolate milk," Skylar said. Seconds later, she was boldly sashaying across the room and walking toward the men.

"Well, don't just stand there and let her have all the fun," said Collette, grabbing Addison's arm. "We have to get in there, especially if you intend on changing your status this evening."

"Wait, wait, wait," Addison said, reaching for her drink on the table. She chugged nearly half the Lemon Drop martini before joining Collette and giving her best sexy walk across the room.

CALEB SMILED as he saw the group of women approaching. There were two African-Americans, two Caucasians and one Asian—the variety he liked. He wished the men with him could appreciate the bounty, but they were either chained in the bonds of matrimony or about to shackle themselves in a few weeks. He didn't intend to be one of them anytime soon.

Caleb rose from the couch he was sharing with Lucas and Amar to greet the women. "Ladies." He grabbed the hand of the bold blonde and kissed it. "How are you this evening?"

"We'd be better if you asked us to join you," she replied.

Caleb turned back to glance at his posse. Amar and Lucas were giving him several looks and hand signals that they'd had enough fun for the evening. Spoilsports. There was still much fun to be had and these ladies certainly looked like they could supply it. "Come join us," Caleb entreated and smiled, then he turned to give the men a "knock it off" look.

They complied and made room on the couch for several of the women. The blonde immediately zeroed in on poor Lucas while the redhead went for Amar.

Caleb watched with amusement while the other ladies chatted with Noah and Sharif. Sharif, the only other single man in the group besides Caleb, looked quite at ease having two attentive females at his side. Maybe it was the accent they loved.

Caleb, meanwhile, was focused on the sweet creature in front of him who'd stayed a few feet back from the melee. He didn't have a foot fetish, but her spiky shoes were killer and the spandex dress, well ... ah, what could he say ... it looked like it had been sprayed onto her body. He could see every curve of her lithe form. Not to mention she was tugging up the bodice of the strapless confection, bringing his attention to her cleavage. She was an attractive woman for sure, but his reaction to her was all gut.

"Hello," he said as he came toward her.

"Hello." A smile spread across her lips, and Caleb felt a tightening in the lower region of his body. He could just picture having those full lips on another part of him as she took him deep into her mouth. "Would you like a drink?" He noticed her empty hand.

"Love one," Addison replied. "A Lemon Drop, please." She knew she should cut herself off and begin her water regimen after having champagne and a couple of martinis, but she was having too much fun. She especially liked the way this man was looking at her as if she were a chocolate fudge sundae with a cherry on top.

"I'll get on it." He walked over to the waitress

who'd just returned to VIP and quickly placed an order, but not for her Lemon Drop. That was a girly drink, and he wouldn't be caught dead ordering it. He ordered a bottle of Patrón for the entire table. It was time to turn this party up. Way the hell up!

~

HOURS LATER, the entire group, from Caleb's brother to the soon-to-be grooms to the ladies who'd joined their festivities, were throwing back shots of Patrón like there was no tomorrow. Even the normally tame Sharif had joined in the mix and was dancing with the redhead and the Asian woman, who'd latched onto him.

And the beautiful female who'd caught Caleb's eye … well, she had balked at his change of drink, but she too was throwing back shots with him and flirting.

Caleb didn't protest when she *accidentally* fell in his lap on the couch after the crowd had descended upon the VIP area and was dancing all around them.

"I'm sorry," she apologized and tried to right herself, but the more she squirmed, the higher her spandex dress kept riding up, giving him a nice view of her toned thighs.

"Don't be." Caleb looked her square in the eye so she would not misunderstand him. He watched her swallow and sensed her nervousness, but she tried to disguise it and asked, "Care to dance?"

"Sure." Caleb held out his hand, and she lightly placed hers in his. He helped her to her feet, but not before he got a nice look at her ass in the dress. When he turned he saw Noah staring at them and giving him a wink. Instead of staying in VIP, they headed to the main dancefloor.

"There goes Caleb," he heard Noah say from behind him, but he didn't care. He couldn't wait to get his arms around this woman and see if she felt as good as she looked.

Once they were on the dancefloor, he tugged her closer to him, curving his arm around her waist. The close contact caused her breasts to graze his chest, and her doe-shaped eyes looked up at him in alarm. But as soon as he started moving their bodies to the rhythm of the music, he felt her relax.

"Do you always pick up women at nightclubs?" she whispered in his ear.

"Only if they look like you," said Caleb, pulling her even closer. He knew he was flirting shamelessly but didn't care. He brought her arms to circle his neck and then leaned in closer so he could sway their hips together to the reggae sounds.

"You're a good dancer," Addison told him.

"That's not the only thing I'm good at."

ADDISON PULLED BACK. Arrogance. Here was a man who knew what he wanted and wasn't afraid to say or act on it. She wished she could be more like him and not be afraid to act. Coming out on this weekend jaunt to Vegas was her first attempt at stepping out of her father's shadow to be her own woman. But was she ready for more? Was she ready to become intimate with a man for the first time?

It wasn't like she'd been waiting for a grand love affair. She'd just wanted it to be special. Memorable. And she'd never seemed to find it in her college relationships or the few short- term ones she'd had since then. And well, the men at her father's oil tanker company were well, boring if she had to admit it. None of them inspired any desire in her. She doubted they even knew how. Sleeping with this sexy stranger may not be special enough to write in her journal, but it would certainly be memorable. If his confidence was anything to go by, he would know his way around a woman's body ... and hers was already affected by his touch.

When he brought his hips into closer contact with hers, Addison *felt* him through her flimsy dress. There was no mistaking it, he wanted her and she was woman enough to take him up on it.

She hazarded a glance up at him and when she did, undisguised passion stared back at her through his long lashes and dark-brown eyes.

She was about to answer, but his friends were approaching them. One of them whispered something in the stranger's ear, and the stranger shook his head. Seconds later, the friend was walking away.

"What's going on?" Addison asked.

"My crew is packing it in and going back to the hotel."

He was leaving? Addison was forlorn. She wouldn't get the opportunity to act on her impulses. Her disappointment must have shown on her face, because he leaned down and said, "I'm not going anywhere."

"You're not?" She tried to mask her happiness. She obviously didn't do a very good job of that, because he gave her a large sexy grin.

"No. I told them I was having too much fun and to take the limo and leave me here. But what about you?" He glanced around. "I don't see your friends."

"I'm sure they're around here somewhere."

"Don't worry. I'll take care of you tonight, all night

if you need it." He stood so close to her that the heat from his body penetrated through to her breasts and she could feel them pucker.

Addison raised an eyebrow. "Is that right?"

"Yes." And to prove it, he bent his head and teased lightly at the seams of her lips until she parted them slightly. He took the cue and captured her lips in his, kissing her passionately. Addison had never been kissed in such a way, let alone right in the middle of a packed nightclub.

She surrendered to it, curling her arms around his neck. When he slipped his fiery tongue inside her mouth, she thought she might melt in a puddle right there on the dancefloor. While his tongue delved inside, his hands moved over her form, unfurling a desire she didn't even know she had or was capable of.

When he pulled away, Addison felt bereft. Her heart was pounding hard and her pulse was racing. The stranger had just made it clear that he wanted to spend the night with her. Could she act on it? Could she live in the moment?

"What do you say we get out of here?"

Several long moments passed as Addison warred with her body's desires and her conscious. Her body won out. "Let's go."

2

It was well after three a.m. when Caleb led Addison to the main living area of the penthouse at the Wynn. The place was dead silent; the guys must have all retired to their rooms upstairs.

"How about a drink?" Caleb asked as he headed toward the wet bar. He watched Addison walk over to the floor-to-ceiling window and look out over the Strip.

"I don't know. I've already had so much," she answered with her back to him.

"Then one more can't hurt." He turned on the lamp, and it bathed her in such a soft light that Caleb forgot about the drink and instead rushed over and spun her around.

Her face registered surprise just as his mouth descended on hers. And this time, he didn't hold back as he'd done before at the club. He allowed himself full access. His tongue dipped inside her delicious, sexy mouth, and he savored the taste of her as his tongue explored every inch. He might have stunned her at first, but she responded in kind to his urgent, exploratory kisses.

As if she weighed nothing, he lifted her into his

arms and carried her into the master bedroom. He brushed his lips across her sweet, ripe mouth as he laid her across the bed. He rose long enough to rid himself of his chambray shirt. He opened the first button, and she undid the rest. Her eyes were heavily lidded, but he could see her drinking him in. He leaned down and reached for the strap of her sandals and removed each one. He placed love pecks on each of her ankles as his hands moved upward to stroke her legs. He couldn't wait to reach the treasure that lay between her thighs and bring this woman and himself to a satisfying conclusion.

ADDISON TREMBLED as the stranger's expert hands rubbed her legs. When he reached her thighs and went underneath her mini-dress, Addison's breath hitched. He wasn't the first man to reach the promised land, but it had been awhile. Usually she stopped once she got this intimate with a man. She reminded herself to be calm. It wouldn't do for him to know that she was a virgin. Some men were turned off by her lack of experience, and she didn't want tonight to be one of those occasions.

She retained her composure until she felt his hands ease her thong to her ankles and off. Then he began caressing the soft petals of her womanhood. "Oooh ..."

"You like that?" he asked, looking up at her.

Powerless to speak, she nodded.

"Good, it's just the beginning."

She closed her eyes and felt a light tug of his teeth on her bottom lip just as his fingers made their way past her outer petals to find her opening and slide *in-*

side her. She was wet and slick, and he easily eased in and out, circling her, slow and steady, heightening her passion. Then he went faster and faster until she became a bundle of aching nerves, desperate for more. Of what, she wasn't sure, but she knew she wanted whatever he was offering.

She gasped as pulsations began to overtake her. "Oh, God!" She hadn't been prepared for this. Sure, she'd known they were attracted to each other, but this was so much more than she'd ever expected.

"Yes, baby," she heard his murmur seconds before a rush of nausea overtook her.

With no time to spare, she jumped from the bed and made a dash for the bathroom, slamming the door behind her.

~

CALEB FELL BACK on the bed in disgust as he heard the sounds of his sexy siren becoming ill. This was not how he envisioned the evening ending. He'd dreamt of how good they would be in bed together. She'd been so open and expressive during the start of her orgasm that he could only imagine what their lovemaking would have been. The operative word was *would*. There was nothing more of a buzzkill than having someone get sick in your bed. Thank God, she'd made it to the restroom. *But what now?* It wasn't like he could kick her out in her time of need. He wasn't that heartless.

Rolling his eyes, Caleb rose from the bed, walked to the bathroom door and knocked. "Hey, are you okay in there?"

There were several groans before he finally heard, "Umm ... yes, I'll be fine. Just give me a minute, okay?"

"Okay."

Several minutes turned into a half-hour. A worried Caleb anxiously opened the bathroom door to find the woman on the floor with her head in her lap and clutching a washcloth.

He scooped her up, and she protested but he calmed her fears. "It's okay. I've got you." He carried her back to the bedroom, and with his free hand pulled back the sheets and placed her inside.

"I'll be right back," Caleb said and went to the living room to pour her a glass of club soda. He returned with it and a bottle of Advil, and walked over to the lump on the other side of the bed. Clearly she was embarrassed and didn't want him to see her—she had covered her head.

He pulled back the comforter, and she turned her face into the pillow. He tucked back her wayward curls and looked into her strained eyes. "I have some club soda and Advil. You need to take these, or you'll be miserable tomorrow."

She shook her head. "I don't want them."

"I'm not taking no for an answer." And he didn't. He made her take a few sips of club soda and the pills before he tucked her into the bed and slid in beside her.

"I bet you didn't envision your evening ending up like this," she said, turning around to face him on the opposite pillow.

He smiled as he tucked his hand under his head. "No, I didn't. Get some rest." He didn't know what made him do it, but he brushed his lips across her forehead. He felt protective of her all of a sudden.

If she'd met any other man, who knows what would have happened? They might have tried to take advantage of her in this state, but Caleb wasn't that type of man. He liked his women sober and fully able to recollect a night spent in his arms.

ADDISON'S HEAD was pounding like it was ready to split open, and her eyes struggled to bring her surroundings into focus. When she was finally able to make out objects, she didn't recognize a thing.

She could, however, see that she was in an elegantly decorated room and that she wasn't alone. Turning to her side, she glimpsed the man sleeping next to her and quickly looked away. She immediately glanced down and saw that she was still wearing the sexy dress Collette had talked her into putting on yesterday. How did she end up here, and where was her best friend?

Just thinking made her head ache, and she quickly laid her head back on the pillow as images of last night began to waft over her—the champagne toast at the suite, followed by partying at several clubs and multiple cocktails. Then at their final destination, she'd met *him*. Memories of their sexy dance and make-out session at the club came swimming back, along with the stranger lying beside her, who'd made her orgasm on this very same bed. Had that really happened?

Addison looked over at him. He was sleeping soundly and hadn't caught the fact she was now awake and remembering every part of last night. She remembered how his fingers had made love to the lower half of her while his mouth had made love to her mouth and then ... "Omigod!" Addison clamped her lips shut and glanced at the sleeping figure again. He hadn't moved a muscle. Thank God. She remembered what happened next and was mortified.

After reaching a mind-blowing orgasm and when she should have been on top of the world and ready to take the next step in officially becoming a woman, she'd become sick ... and well-acquainted with the porcelain god. To make matters worse, the man sleeping beside her right now had had to pick her up and carry her to bed. Talk about a buzzkill. He must have been so sorry he'd picked her up at the club.

She had to get out of here, and quick, while he remained asleep. She was completely embarrassed. Slowly, she eased out of the bed, but she went too fast and almost lost her footing. She recovered and made it to her feet, looking for her sandals, but as she did she realized she didn't have on any underwear. Dear God! She was going to have to take the walk of shame without any underpants! Could this get any worse?

When she saw the sleeping stranger turn over in the bed, she ducked to make sure he couldn't see her, grabbed her sandals and sneaked out the door.

She thought she was free and clear once she hit the suite door, but then a male voice called out, "Do you need a ride back to your hotel?"

Addison stood straight up and glanced behind her to see a caramel-skinned man wearing a cowboy hat, plaid shirt and jeans sitting on the couch reading the newspaper. She must look a sight with her hair all mussed and wearing last night's dress. He must think her a hussy for sneaking out of his friend's room.

"Oh, I'm okay, thanks," Addison replied.

"I'll call downstairs to the concierge anyway and ensure a taxi is waiting for you. Tell them Noah sent you."

Addison gave a hesitant smile. "Thank you, Noah. That's awful nice of you."

"Be safe," he said as she closed the door behind her.

CALEB TURNED over and reached across the bed. His eyes sprung open when he felt only an indentation where the sexy siren with the doe eyes had lain the night before. Disconcerted, he sat up. Was she okay? Perhaps she was still sick.

Throwing back the covers, he walked half-naked in his boxers into the bathroom. It was empty. He scratched his head. Perhaps she was in the living quarters. He reached down for his jeans, slid them over his hips and zipped them up. When he opened the door to the master suite, he saw Noah holding a cup of coffee as he looked out over the Strip.

"Good morning." Noah inclined his head.

"Morning." Caleb barely looked at him as he made his way to the kitchen.

"If you're looking for the girl from last night, she's gone."

Caleb turned around. "How would you know? You guys were asleep when we got in."

"I saw her this morning when she tried unsuccessfully to sneak out the suite."

"Was she okay?"

Noah's brow rose. "You care?"

Caleb shrugged noncommittally.

"Must have been some night."

"You could say that," Caleb said as he padded with bare feet around the kitchen. He returned several minutes later carrying a mug of steaming-hot black coffee.

"I would have thought you would be bragging about your conquest," Noah said. "You're quite the ladies' man."

Caleb sipped his drink. "Wasn't much of one last night."

"What do you mean? What happened?"

"It was an utter bomb!" Caleb pronounced. "Not only did I not close the deal, but she got sick on top of it."

Noah laughed. "Are you serious?"

Caleb rolled his eyes. "I am. And if you tell anyone, I'll deny it."

"Deny what?" Lucas asked, coming down the spiral staircase.

"Nothing," Caleb answered. Not only was the night an utter failure, but he'd been so caught up in trying to close the deal and flirting, that they'd never exchanged names. Had she been like him and just wanted to have a night of fun in Vegas without any baggage? She must have been. It was too bad because he usually didn't give females a second thought, but there was something about her that made him interested in what might have been. Oh, well. He guessed he would never find out.

THAT MORNING, Addison crept into the suite, but her efforts at being undetected were fruitless; all the girls were sitting at the dining room table.

"Well, look at what the cat dragged in," Collette said when Addison closed the door behind her.

"Don't start, Collette. It's been a long night, and I have one helluva hangover." Addison headed toward the bedroom they were sharing to go take a much-needed shower.

"Oh, no you don't." Collette jumped up from the table, ignoring the stares of the other girls. To them it was no big deal that Addison had had a one-night stand, but Collette knew better.

Collette rushed into the bedroom behind Addison, closed the door and plopped down on one of the room's two beds. "Well?"

"Well, what?" Addison said as she sat on the opposite bed to remove her sandals.

"What happened? When you didn't come home I assumed you were, you know, doing the deed with the fine fella you picked up at the club."

"That was the plan," Addison said, kicking off one sandal and then the other.

"And?"

Addison undid the hidden zipper in the back of her dress and let it fall to the floor, then she reached for a robe on her bed to cover her nakedness and she put it on. "And then nothing," Addison said with a frown as she spun around to face her friend. "Your girl got so drunk that she got sick ... he had to put me to bed."

Collette's hands flew to her mouth. "Omigod! You're kidding."

"Nope. It's the truth. Right when things got heated, after he'd kissed and caressed my entire body, after he'd just gone down on me, I got nauseous and fled his bed."

Collette shook her head.

"I stayed in the bathroom so long, he feared for my safety and had to come in, pick me off the floor and carry me to bed."

"Addison, no ..." Collette couldn't believe it. She

was trying to keep a straight face, but that was hard to do when she'd just heard the funniest thing ever.

"Yup. I was so embarrassed this morning that the only thing I could do was hightail it out of his bed before he woke up."

"And did he?"

"No, thank God the universe was finally on my side, but I did run into a guy reading the paper in the living room. He was kind enough to arrange a taxi back to the hotel. Can you believe it? After I finally make the decision to lose my virginity and live spontaneously, fate throws me a curveball."

"Maybe the universe was trying to tell you something?"

"Which is?"

"That it wasn't the right time. He wasn't the one."

"I don't know, Collette. There was something about him that was different. I know he was there last night to get laid like most men are in Vegas, but he didn't have to take care of me. I mean, he brought me club soda and aspirin."

"Maybe he was trying to get laid this morning."

Addison's head whirled. "Really? Have you always been this jaded?"

"Of course not. I just don't want you to start acting like this guy was some sort of prince among men when he wasn't. He was meant to be a one-night stand, nothing more."

"Fine!" Addison said as she finally headed toward the bathroom. But she didn't really mean those words. No matter what Collette said, Addison was sure there was something different about the man she'd slept beside.

3

"Thanks for having me over for supper, Uncle Duke," Caleb said as they sat over plates of T-bone steak and baked potatoes the following weekend. It was a true man's meal. No muss. No fuss.

It was a week before Rylee's wedding, and Caleb was in Dallas for the rodeo events. He had been prepared to eat the slop that was called food in the arenas, so he was happy to have received a supper invitation instead to the interminable bachelor's mansion.

The mansion sat on nearly four hundred acres of prime west Texas real estate. His uncle, the oil man, had been drilling nearly three hundred acres on the land and making a killing but was starting to think perhaps he should start to consider other forms of energy.

"Is there something wrong with seeing my nephew?" Duke inquired.

"Of course not," Caleb said, cutting an enormous slice of steak and jamming it into his mouth. "Just unusual is all. Where's Bree and Jada?" Bree lived in Dallas, but Caleb knew his cousin Jada was flying in from

San Francisco for Rylee's wedding and making a pit-stop in Dallas to see Bree.

"Bree and Jada are both having dinner with their mother."

"And London?" Caleb referenced Duke's eldest daughter, who lived in New Orleans.

"She'll be flying directly to Tucson for the wedding."

Caleb wasn't surprised Duke's relationship with his eldest was tenuous at best.

"But if you must know, I do have an ulterior motive for the invitation," Duke said, interrupting his thoughts.

Caleb's head popped up from his plate.

"Your mama is worried that you've been at this bull-riding business for so many years and haven't settled down into a career or a family."

"Aww, Duke!" Caleb threw down his napkin. If this was the topic of conversation, he was starting to lose his appetite.

"Hey, hey." Duke stopped him with a raised hand. "Don't go getting your undies all in a bunch. I told her I would talk to you and see where your head is. I didn't ask you here to try and convince you one way or the other. Your life is your own."

"Thank God for that," Caleb said, resuming eating his steak.

"But that's not to say that it ain't time for you to put bull riding on the shelf. You're better than that, Caleb, always have been. You're not like my son, Trent."

Trent was the result of an affair with a Las Vegas showgirl that didn't end on a good note, which is why the woman didn't tell Duke he was a father until his son was nearly a teenager. Duke was none too pleased to find out he was the father, and Trent was angry he'd been denied a father and a better life.

"How's he doing?"

"In and out of trouble," Duke responded. "But what's new?" Duke shook his head in disgust. "I've tried to help the boy, Caleb, but I don't know. By the time I found out about him, I think the damage was already done. And no matter how much I do for him now, he still harbors so much anger and resentment because he feels the world owes him. He feels like his sisters, London, Jada and Bree, got a better break than he did because at least I knew about them and were a part of their lives, even if only a small part."

Caleb shook his head. Uncle Duke was such a rolling stone. He'd bedded countless women; his four children were with three of them.

"I'd be angry too if my mama had kept me away from my father," Caleb said, reaching for a bread roll and biting into it. He was finished after two hearty chomps.

"But how long am I supposed to pay for the mistakes of the past?" Duke asked wearily. "And it seems the more I try to help him, the worse it gets. So I've given up."

"That doesn't sound like you, Uncle Duke. You never give up on anyone or anything. Perhaps you guys just need some time apart."

Duke shrugged. "Let's talk about something else, like how we're going to get my sister off your back."

"I doubt Mama's going to give up her quest to get me to settle down, especially when Noah done gone and got himself married and Chynna's having their first grandbaby. And let's not forget Rylee's impending nuptials. I'm outnumbered there, Uncle Duke."

His uncle laughed and sat back in his chair, staring at Caleb. Duke understood the boy because he was much like himself. He wanted to live life by his own rules with no restraints. A man like Caleb couldn't be fettered, at least not until he was good and ready. "I understand that, son," Duke finally said, "but you can't ride bulls forever. What's your endgame?"

Caleb paused from eating to look into his uncle's brown eyes. "I've given it some thought."

"And?"

"I thought maybe I could come and work out here with you. Noah's got everything under control at Golden Oaks, so there's really not much for me to do unless I want to be a ranch hand, and other folks in the community could use that work. And I most certainly can't live off my mom and pop, but here," he said, glancing around, "I could be of some use here."

Duke nodded. He'd thought the very same thing himself. He loved his girls and knew Bree wanted to take over Hart Enterprises, but the oil business was no place for a woman. It was a dirty business, a man's business, and he'd hoped that Caleb would come to the decision on his own. And he had.

"How would you feel about that?" Caleb asked. His uncle was being awfully quiet. Caleb knew it was somewhat presumptuous of him to even suggest such a thing, but it had been on his mind of late, especially with Rylee about to move on from Golden Oaks. What was he going to do there now?

"I would love it, Caleb," Duke replied with a broad grin. "I could use a man like you on my team."

"Are you sure? I know I don't know a lot, but I'm a hard worker, and I'm willing to start at the bottom and work my way up."

"That's all I could ask for," Duke said. "When do you think you might come aboard?"

"It'll be a couple of months. I have to finish this rodeo circuit. There's a lot of money at stake, and I know I can take home some serious cash and put it in my nest egg."

"You got some savings?"

"Hell, yeah! You didn't think I was just out there blowing my hard-earned cash getting beat up by a bull on gambling, liquor and women, did you?" At Duke's dubious frown, Caleb continued, "I'm not saying I don't like the ladies. There was one in particular last weekend at the bachelor party that caught my attention, but I did finish a year or so of college and took some economics classes. I've invested my money wisely."

"That's good to hear. I doubt other riders are doing the same."

"I know everyone thinks I'm a knucklehead who doesn't have a good head on his shoulders, but that's the problem. Folks shouldn't underestimate me."

THE NEXT MORNING after insisting Caleb wear a hardhat and work boots, Duke took him to the oil rig, where the crew had started drilling operations at a new location.

"The geologist I hired seems to think this location has an oil reservoir we've yet to tap into."

"How did he figure that out?" Caleb asked.

"Wasn't a he, it was a she. After looking through seismic data to reconstruct the subsurface configuration, she was able to locate possible sites of oil traps.

She calculated the percentage of oil that could possibly be extracted from the reservoir, then she worked with the geophysicist who interpreted the seismic data and helped build a picture of the subsurface below that would help us locate the oil based on past changes in the structure of the land."

"Sounds complicated."

"It is," Duke replied, "but that's why I pay them the big bucks. Come on, let me introduce you around."

Before Caleb knew it, his uncle had introduced him—to the rig superintendent as well as the operations supervisor and lots of other roughnecks—as the next in line to help run the operation. Caleb had been equally surprised by his uncle's comments as were several men who assumed Duke's son would be next in line to run the business.

"Don't worry about Trent," Duke replied after several questions. "He'll get what's coming to him, but Caleb here has the heart and the passion I need to take this company to great heights."

"Just as long as you don't sell out to one of the mid-sized companies," one of the roughnecks murmured.

"I'm no sellout," Caleb said.

"Of course he's not," Duke defended his nephew, "and I'm not going anywhere anytime soon, so enough of this talk.

"Let's go, son." Duke led him away from the crowd.

"Daddy, you don't need to treat me like a child."

"Well, when you act like one by running up fruitless charges on my American Express, then you make me treat you like one."

"Then perhaps you should give me a company

credit card like you do with all of your other employees, rather than an 'allowance.'" Addison made air quotes with her fingers.

"Don't I pay you well?" her father asked.

Addison sighed. She couldn't believe they were having this same conversation. "You pay me an allowance, not a salary, and every other executive has a credit card."

"Which they wouldn't use to run up charges in Vegas."

"What's the big deal? It was a one-time thing."

"Don't talk back to me, young lady." He wagged his finger in her face. "I can still put you over my knee."

"Like you would even try," Addison replied with a smirk. She knew she was her father's world, had been since the day she was born and would be until the day he died.

"Sure wouldn't, baby." He smiled adoringly at her.

After Addison's mother, Lila, had died when she was so young, her father had clung to her like she was some sort of lifeline, and perhaps she was. Losing the love of his life had been hard for Benjamin Walker, and Addison knew it was why he'd never married again. There'd been other women, many of whom thought they could help the young widower and his young daughter get over the loss, but her father had wanted no part.

Addison had watched her father turn each would-be wife away after just a few months of dating. She hadn't wanted him to be lonely, but as the years went by, she began to get accustomed to it being just the two of them, father and daughter against the world.

But now, she was starting to feel stifled. She was a grown woman after all, but her father still treated her like a youngster. Addison wondered if he'd ever see her as an adult capable of making her own decisions. He'd even had a say in her choice of profession— she'd wanted to be a geologist out there in the dirt, helping to discover where the oil reservoirs were so she could be a help to him and his thriving oil tanker business, but he wouldn't hear of it. "It's not a profession for a young lady," he'd said. So she'd majored in Marketing and Finance and graduated summa cum laude from Texas A & M University.

"I'll agree that a weekend in Vegas was not an appropriate use of funds," Addison replied, "however, I stand by my request for a credit card."

"We'll agree to disagree on this. Are you still coming with me tonight to the Alzheimer's benefit?"

"Do I really have to?" She was not looking forward to being her father's date to one of the endless charity dinners he was invited to as a prominent businessman in Dallas.

"It's important."

"Aren't they all?"

"Don't sass me."

Out of respect, Addison remained silent. "What time shall I be ready?"

~

Two hours later, they were in the Lincoln Town Car being driven to the Fairmont Hotel. Addison had donned her usual charity event attire of classic sheath dress with a loose chignon and a few tendrils dangling on the sides of her face.

Whenever she was with her father, she had to dress older than her twenty-three years. When she'd been a teenager, she'd been happy to accompany him to such events because she'd felt like an adult, sitting at the adults' table and listening to adult conversation. But she'd long since become bored of these events and was not looking forward to tonight.

The driver opened the door, and Addison stepped out onto the red carpet as several local photographers snapped pictures of her for the society pages. Her father tucked her arm under his, and Addison smiled on cue. Seconds later, the doorman was leading them inside.

The hotel lobby and upper floors were already teeming with charity eventgoers. Benjamin Walker paused to speak with several guests while Addison went to make herself invisible. She made a beeline for the bar.

"Glass of Pinot Grigio."

"Sure thing," the bartender replied.

Addison turned to survey the crowd. She sorely wished Collette were here to offer her some comic relief. It was how they'd first met when she was thirteen years old. Addison had been on the sidelines of one of her father's endless social events, waiting for him to finish his business talk when the redhead with the freckles had approached her. She'd offered Addison a smile and a cigarette. Initially, Addison had been appalled, but eventually they'd snuck off to the balcony to indulge in Addison's first and last cigarette. She hadn't liked the taste of it, but she had liked Collette's ballsy nature, and a friendship soon formed.

"Penny for your thoughts," a deep baritone voice said from behind her.

Addison didn't need to turn around to know the owner of that voice. She remembered its smooth tone from when she'd passed out in his suite and he'd told her to sit up for a bit to have some club soda and aspirin. Her hangover would have been much worse if it had not been for him.

Slowly, she turned around to stare at none other than her aborted one-night stand. She offered a bemused smile. "Hello."

"Hey, didn't mean to disturb you. You looked deep in thought."

"I was. Recalling a childhood memory."

"Good or bad?"

She grinned when she thought of Collette. "Definitely good."

He stared back at her for several moments, and Addison wasn't sure whether she should speak or wait for him to do so. He seemed just as uneasy and stuck his hands in his pocket. That's when she noticed he was wearing a tuxedo jacket over jeans.

She raised a brow. "Interesting attire for a formal gathering."

"Never cared much for formal."

"I can see that. If I recall correctly, you like to go against the grain."

"Good memory."

"Some things aren't easy to forget."

He flashed a devilish grin. "Would I be one of them?"

Damn! She'd stuck her foot in her mouth and walked right into that one. "It would be pretty hard not to when I got sick in your bed."

"A gentleman would never bring it up."

Addison cocked an eyebrow. "Are you a gentleman?" She would think not. Caleb struck her as a bad boy who liked to live life on the edge.

He laughed. "Wow, how you gonna call a brother out like that?"

Addison shrugged and smiled. "If the shoe fits."

"Well, try this on for size—you owe me another date."

"Excuse me?"

~

CALEB LOOKED at the beautiful woman he'd been thinking about since the day she'd snuck out of his hotel room in Vegas. He'd been disappointed to find out she'd gone, but fate had just given him another chance. What were the odds that two people hooking up for a one-night stand in Vegas would attend the same charity event in Dallas?

When they'd arrived, his uncle had been besieged by several women looking for a wealthy man, leaving Caleb to fend for himself. He'd never much cared for these sorts of events, even in Tucson when his parents had sponsored them. But just when he'd been ready to write the night off as a complete and utter loss, he'd spotted her leaning against the bar looking just as bored as he was. It might appear too good to be true, but he had decided to go for it.

"You heard right. If you recall, you conked out on me right when we were getting to the fun part and *I* think you owe me a raincheck."

"Haven't you heard what happens in Vegas, stays in Vegas," Addison responded coyly.

"Since nothing happened, I think we need to remedy that."

"Has anyone ever told you you're pretty cocky?"

"Mighta been told that the odd time or two, so what's it going to be?" He knew he was pressing her, but he had to find a way to spend more time with her. Something in his gut told him she was worth getting to know.

"Hmmm ..." Addison paused for several long beats before replying. "I could be persuaded, but perhaps it might not be a bad idea to start with your name."

Caleb rolled his eyes; he could have kicked himself. He'd been so busy trying to seal the deal that they hadn't exchanged names *again*. Why would they when it would have been a mysterious one-night stand? But now, she wasn't so mysterious. She was standing right in front of him, and he had a chance to find out if she was truly as special as he'd envisioned. "Caleb," he said, offering her his hand, "Caleb Hart."

"Addison Walker."

Caleb grasped her soft fingers. "Pleasure to meet you, Addison." He wasn't eager to let her go. She was just as beautiful and alluring as she'd been a week ago in Vegas, if not more now. And those eyes, so innocent. And the sparks ... they were flying off the charts at the slightest touch of her hand. He could only imagine the chemistry they'd have in bed. He was imagining just that when someone called her name.

"Addison?"

She blinked, breaking the spell, and spun to face an elderly African-American gentleman. "Dad?"

"What's going on here?" The man looked Caleb up and down suspiciously.

Caleb knew that look. It was a fatherly overprotective look and told him that Addison's dad was none too pleased to see her cavorting with him. He knew he didn't fit the bill of most men at the event, with his jeans and tuxedo jacket. He was a father's worst nightmare.

"Daddy." Addison walked over to him and curled her arm around one of his. "I'd like you to meet Caleb Hart. Caleb, this is my father, Mr. Benjamin Walker."

"Sir." Caleb offered his hand, which Mr. Walker shook while summing him up.

"What brings you to Dallas, Mr. Hart?"

"I'm here visiting Duke Hart, my uncle," Caleb replied. "You might know him?"

"Ah, yes, who doesn't know Duke in this community?" Benjamin Walker said with disdain. Clearly, Caleb's uncle wasn't high up on Mr. Walker's list of favorite people.

A glass clinked and everyone in the lobby turned to see the mistress of ceremonies beckoning everyone inside the ballroom.

"Time to go in." Addison's father began to lead her away, but she put a hand on his arm.

"Why don't you go on in," Addison said. "I'll find you—"

"Addison—"

She cut her father off. "Caleb and I haven't finished our conversation. It would be impolite."

Her father gave him the once-over again. "Of course. I'll see you inside, baby girl." Reluctantly, he walked away, leaving Addison and Caleb alone.

Caleb smiled. He liked that she was willing to stand up to her father for him. That told him she had some gumption despite her soft demeanor. "Thanks for that."

Addison shrugged. "My father can be a bit overprotective, seeing how it's only been the two of us for some time."

"Your mother?"

Addison's head lowered for a moment before she looked up. "Died when I was four years old."

"I'm so sorry," Caleb said. "Must have been difficult to lose her so young."

"It was." She removed the small purse she'd been

holding on her wrist to take out a business card to hand to him. "Call me."

And without another word, she walked away leaving Caleb standing there smelling the sweet scent of her perfume and admiring her rear-end as she sauntered into the ballroom.

4

———

Benjamin Walker waited to bring up the subject of Caleb when he and Addison were in the car on the way back home from the event. "So where did you meet this young man?"

Addison didn't appreciate being questioned on who she was dating. It was none of his business. "Does it matter?"

"Don't be smart with me. Clearly you're on a quest to show your independence as evidenced by your Vegas weekend and now this young man. What is going on with you, Addison? Are you having some post-adolescent crisis?"

Addison counted from one to ten before responding. If she had spoken her mind just now, she would have been disrespectful, so she took a deep breath and reminded herself that her father was only looking out for her best interests, even if he was overbearing at times.

"I am not in the midst of a crisis," Addison said calmly. "I am, however, asserting my independence. Even you must know that I have to grow up eventually, but by God you have to allow it. Stop treating me like a child. I'm twenty-three years old and quite capable of making my own choices. Good or bad. And if I should falter, it's my," she said, pounding her chest, "my mistake."

Her father stared back at her, stunned. He'd been prepared for an outburst to prove that she still had a lot of growing up to do, but instead she'd given him a sound argument. She could see he was impressed when his stern facial features softened.

"I'm sorry, Addy. You're right. You're well past the days of needing my advice, but at least let me give it, then you can do with it as you will."

"Okay, speak."

"Duke Hart is a ladies' man. He's been breaking hearts all over Dallas for a long time now. If Caleb is related, the apple may not fall far from the tree."

"Daddy ..."

Her father held his left hand up. "I know they are not the same person, so my best advice if you intend to proceed down this path is to be careful. I don't want to see you get your heart broken."

"That's the thing, Daddy. That's a part of being an adult, and even if I do get my heart broken, I doubt it'll be the last. It's all a part of growing up."

"Has anyone ever told you you're grown beyond your years?"

She smiled as she leaned forward to take his hand and give it a gentle squeeze. "Umm ... I've been told it a time or two."

"I love you, baby girl."

"And I love you."

~

"WHEN ARE you going to be back?" Rylee asked Caleb from the other end of the line in Tucson. She was at

Golden Oaks watching their mother's last dress fitting, and Caleb was nowhere to be found. "You do realize my wedding is in a week."

"I have not forgotten," Caleb said. "How can I with the constant daily reminders?"

"Hey—"

"You know I wouldn't miss your big day for anything in the world, Rylee," Caleb interrupted, "but I do have a life of my own, you know."

"If you're talking about riding those bulls, that's not going to last forever. You've got to start thinking about your future. You're not as young as you used to be."

"Thanks a lot, big sis. But if you must know, that's why I'm here in Dallas with Uncle Duke."

"Oh, yeah? And?"

"And nothing. When I'm ready to talk about it, I will. In the meantime, I have to run. I have a date."

"A date? You've only been in Dallas for a hot minute, and you already have a date?"

"Don't hate, big sis. Just appreciate that your little brother has a way with the ladies."

"Don't go breaking no hearts over there."

"Me?" Caleb touched his chest in the mirror. "Never." Seconds later, he ended the call.

He was looking forward to his date tonight with Addison. When he'd phoned her, he hadn't known what to expect. He hadn't been sure if her father's disapproval might have swayed her against spending more time with him. He was so glad he'd been wrong.

Addison Walker wasn't his usual type. She was beautiful and sexy, but in an understated way. She didn't come across as flirtatious and bold like most of the women he usually spent the night with. He was used to women who told him what they wanted and how they wanted it. Addison struck him as much more reserved, even though in Vegas, she'd been fighting that impulse. He suspected her friends had dressed her up. He sensed the hip-hugging dress she'd been wearing didn't reflect the real her. The wisp of chiffon she'd been wearing at the charity event had suited her much better. It was elegant and regal, much like Addison herself, which is why he was choosing something Addison had probably never done and would make the evening all the more exciting.

He'd just finished shaving and showering and had donned his usual fare of jeans and cowboy boots when Rylee had called. Instead of his standard plaid shirt, he'd stepped it up a notch and was wearing a Bourdeaux cotton button-down shirt. Splashing on some cologne, he surveyed himself in the mirror. He cleaned up pretty good when he put his mind to it.

Grabbing his keys, he headed out the door. The drive to the Walker estate was about forty-five minutes from Duke's place, but that was just fine with Caleb. It would give him time to prepare to face Mr. Walker. He was sure Addison's father wasn't too happy about them seeing each other, but Caleb wasn't a coward by any means and would stand his ground with her old man.

~

BEFORE CALEB KNEW IT, he was in front of the estate. He was surprised tons of security weren't around given the amount of land. Caleb surmised it was in the neighborhood of a hundred acres or so. He parked the Ford Super Duty F-450 XL pickup he'd borrowed from Duke's stable of cars and trucks and stared up at the impressive mansion. It looked to Caleb like there had to be at least twenty rooms. What the heck did Addison and her father do with all that space?

He walked over to the door and pressed the bell. Instead of a butler appearing as he had anticipated, Addison was on the other side with a warm smile. Caleb smiled back.

"Hey there."

"Hi, yourself," Caleb said as he walked into the foyer. The house was as grand as he had expected and elegantly decorated. But none of that mattered now because the only thing he was interested in was Addison.

She was looking sweet yet sassy in some faded blue jeans, tank top and a tunic with the shoulders cut out. She was wearing some sort of shoes that weren't quite boots because her red toes peeked out of them. He especially liked her curly, unruly hair. He intended to run his fingers through it before the night was over when he finally cashed in on his raincheck.

"Are you done looking?" Addison said. "If so, we can go."

"No Spanish Inquisition?" Caleb asked, looking over her shoulder and behind him.

Addison smiled. "You were expecting my father to grill you?"

"Considering his less than pleasant expression when he met me, yes."

She chuckled. "We had a talk after the event, and we came to an understanding."

"Which was?"

"I'm an adult and will make my own decisions."

"Good for you. So you ready to get this evening going?"

"Absolutely."

～

"SO WHERE ARE WE GOING?" Addison asked, hazarding a glance in Caleb's direction as he drove. When he'd showed up to her doorstep, she'd lost her breath and nervous tension had filled her belly. The old Addison would have wanted to run and hide, but the new Addison was determined to face her attraction to this tall, sexy man. And sexy he was. It oozed out of his every pore, even though she knew he wasn't one of those men that spent hours in the mirror. He was a man's man, and it showed. He had a confidence and swagger that she'd never seen in any other man she'd ever dated.

"It's a surprise," Caleb responded.

"Really? Sounds like fun."

"I think you'll like it. So tell me, Addison, why hasn't some upstanding young man snapped you up?"

"You mean why aren't I married and settled down with a husband and starting a family?"

"Something like that."

"It's still a little early for that."

"You're what, twenty-three, twenty-four?" Caleb surmised. "I would have thought that most Southern girls would have been raised to go looking for a husband right outta high school."

"Ah, you think very highly of us Southern girls, do you?" Addison smiled. "Well, some of us have higher aspirations than just being a Mrs."

"I'm sorry if I offended you."

"You didn't because there are many Southern girls that go to college with that expectation. I just don't happen to be one of them."

"So what do you do, if you don't mind me asking?"

Addison was surprised that their conversation was

turning more personal. She'd expected with the chemistry between them that the evening would be highly sexual, but Caleb wanted to get to know her.

"I work at my father's oil tanker company. Been working there since I graduated. I'm working with his COO."

"Your father's in the oil business? Interesting. I bet you'll be there be in the COO's chair before long if your father has anything to say about it."

Addison chuckled. He was probably right. Although her father knew she understood his business like no one else, she suspected that he hoped her future husband might help her run it someday. "My father appears to know your uncle also."

"Is that right?"

"Told me your uncle is quite the ladies' man."

"And that I might be like him?" Caleb offered.

Addison nodded. "But I make my own choices."

"That's good to know. And we're here," Caleb said, pulling into a parking space in front of the rodeo.

"A rodeo?" Addison looked blankly at Caleb. Of all the places she'd expected him to take her, this wasn't one of them.

"C'mon, it'll be fun," he said, hopping out of the pickup. He walked behind it to come around and open her door.

"I don't know," Addison said as she stepped out.

Caleb reached across and grabbed her hand. When he did, a scorching current passed between them. He must have felt it because he looked into her eyes seconds before he pushed her backward against the truck and kissed her.

It wasn't the slow, languorous kisses he'd given her in Vegas when he thought he had all night to make love to her. This kiss was heat and passion and fire all balled up into one. He grasped the sides of her face, crushed her against him and claimed her lips. Addison was shattered by the hunger behind his kiss and gave herself over to the ripple of excitement that was churning inside her.

One of his thighs pressed forward, eager to be closer to her while his tongue coaxed her lips apart. Addison opened her mouth to his seeking full lips and succumbed to their domination. He thoroughly explored every inch of her tongue, stroking his back and forth against hers. Desire zoomed straight through her as he continued his ravishing. He sucked her tongue, and she moaned. Then one of his hands slid under her tunic and upward to caress one of her breasts. When he found his target, he caressed it with the pad of his thumb, and Addison felt her nipple harden underneath the tank top. She also felt herself becoming slick and her panties starting to moisten. *Dear God, is he going to make me come in the parking lot?!*

She'd never been kissed so completely, so passionately since, since that night in Vegas! It was thrilling, heady and intoxicating. Caleb must have felt the same way because the lower half of him had awakened and was pressing against her womanhood. Even in her jeans, there was no doubt of Caleb's obvious arousal. She was excited to know that she could make a man like him lose control and make out with her in the middle of the parking lot.

Eventually, he separated from her and took a jagged breath. "Wow! I, uh, didn't mean for that to happen so soon."

So he meant it to happen later? Addison wondered. Exactly what did he have in store for her? She was nervous *and* excited to find out.

"I think we should go inside," she murmured softly, righting herself.

"Good idea." Caleb offered her his arm instead of his hand. Was he too afraid that by touching her he'd lose control again?

~

INSIDE, the rodeo was in full swing. Fans were milling about the stadium, either chatting in groups or getting beer and popcorn at the concession.

"Wanna beer?" Caleb asked. He needed to get control of his equilibrium. He hadn't meant to kiss her like that in the parking lot with no warning, but she'd looked so delectable standing there all sweet and innocent. She had to have felt the crackling of attraction that had sparked between them when they'd touched. Kissing her had just been the beginning. He wanted more, and he intended to have it. Tonight.

"Love one."

"C'mon." He led her to the concession stand and ordered two beers along with a bucket of popcorn. Then they headed toward the steps and climbed them until they reached the view of an enormous arena. He was sure Addison was probably surprised at just how many folks came out to the rodeos. The arena was packed to the rafters.

There were half-a-dozen stalls that would have bulls coming through them any second. Caleb looked forward to showing Addison his world.

Once they sat down, Addison leaned over to grab a handful of popcorn and toss it into her mouth. "So why did you bring me to a rodeo?"

Caleb turned sideways. "Because ... it's what I do."

A blank expression registered on Addison's face. "I don't understand."

Caleb smiled affectionately. "I'm a bull rider."

"A what?" Addison nearly choked on a popcorn kernel.

"You heard right. I ride bulls for a living. It's one of my favorite pastimes."

Addison's eyes widened. "And are you riding tonight?"

"Wouldn't dream of it," Caleb replied, taking a swig of his beer. "Tonight is about you and me. I just wanted you to see this place. It's a big part of my life."

"I had no idea."

"What did you think I did?"

"I don't know. In Vegas, we didn't actually get around to talking ..." Her voice trailed off, and her mind instantly wandered back to being in that master suite when Caleb had slowly bunched up her mini-dress to her waist and removed her thong. She began to feel hot, and she blinked several times at the memory.

Caleb knew where her mind had drifted to because in that moment, he'd been right back there with her in that room. But there would be enough time for a replay of that later.

"How long have you been bull riding?" Addison asked, reaching for the popcorn bucket again.

"About four years now."

"That long?" She couldn't imagine willingly deciding to get on a bull each and every night knowing you could get thrown off and potentially injured.

"Yeah. You sound surprised."

"Can't you get hurt?"

"Sure, if you don't know what you're doing, but I've been on horses all my life. Riding is second nature."

"Being bucked off a bull is altogether different from riding a horse."

He laughed. "True, but the same technique applies."

"Wait a sec, you just said you've been around horses your whole life. Where'd you grow up?"

"My family owns a dude ranch in Tucson. It's not too far from that famous Canyon Ranch place."

"Oh, yes, I've heard of that." Several of Addison's girlfriends had gone there once for the weekend for a detox and quick weight loss program. "A dude ranch, huh? You don't strike me as the type to wanna deal with family and their kids wanting to go horseback riding or feed the rabbits."

"I'm here, ain't I?" Caleb asked, glancing her way.

She nodded. "It's like we talked about, going against the grain and not doing what's expected of you. Have you always been this contrary?"

"Always, but it's what makes me 'me.'"

"And I like you." The words slipped out of Addison's mouth before she could retrieve them.

"I like you too, Addison Walker. What do folks call you for short?"

"Addy."

"Addy." Caleb let the name roll off his lips. "I like it."

"I prefer Addison."

"Because it sounds more mature?"

"And what's wrong with that?"

"Because when I use it, it'll be an intimate moment and will sound completely different."

Addison swallowed hard and blushed. It happened whenever Caleb looked at her with those dark-brown smoldering eyes of his and spoke to her that way. She turned her head away and forced herself to watch the show, which was just starting as the announcer was riding his horse into the center of the ring.

"Just so you know, these events aren't just about the bull riding—there's bareback riding, steer wrestling, team roping, saddle bronc riding, tie-down roping and barrel racing. We cowboys take the sport very seriously."

She glanced sideways at him. "I had no idea."

"I know most folks think I'm crazy for what I do, but I do take what I do seriously. I'm part of the Professional Rodeo Cowboys Association, known as the PRCA."

"There's an association?"

"Yes."

They watched the cowboys ride and fall off the bulls while Caleb explained their techniques; but all Addison was noticing was Caleb's thigh casually brushing against hers and the masculine scent of his cologne.

"That about does it," Caleb said, rising to his feet.

"What?" Addison blinked several times.

"C'mon." Caleb grabbed her hand and hauled her up. "Let's get out of here and go have some fun."

Before they made it out of the arena, a Caucasian man in Wranglers, Justin Boots and a plaid shirt came ambling toward them.

"Caleb, man." He grabbed one of Caleb's hands and pulled him into a one-armed hug. "What the heck are you doing here on your night off?"

"Good to see you too, Josh," Caleb replied as he pulled away.

"You know I mean no offense."

Caleb laughed. "And none taken. I just want to show my lady here where I work."

"And you brought her here? Guess you didn't want to impress her." Josh laughed. "No seriously, you have yourself a good man here." Josh directed his attention toward Addison. "Known him for four years now, and if you ever need him in a pinch, he'll be there."

Addison smiled. "That's good to know. It's great to meet you, Josh."

"You guys take it easy." He tipped his cowboy hat at Addison, nodded to Caleb and walked away.

Once he'd gone, Addison turned to Caleb. "Your lady?"

"You have a problem with me claiming you as mine for tonight?"

Addison didn't mind a damn bit, but she would never say that to him. Instead she began walking backward, in the direction of the door. "Just for tonight?" she asked with a flirtatious smile.

Caleb laughed. He sure hoped not. He had a feeling that once he'd had Addison, she might become an addiction he couldn't shake.

5

The rodeo didn't signal the end to their evening. Caleb had a lot more in store for Addison Walker. He pulled the pickup into the driveway of a cowboy bar, known not just for the best steaks but also for the occasional woman dancing atop the bar table.

Caleb noticed Addison's wide-eyed look when they walked inside only to be immediately face to face with a large mechanical bull. Several women and men were standing in line ready to take a spin. He intended for Addison to take one too if he had anything to say about it.

The hostess led them to one of the many wooden booths surrounding the extra-large dancefloor that pretty soon would be filled with cowboys and cowgirls alike dancing the two-step and every other line dance imaginable.

A waitress came over several minutes later and asked them what they wanted to drink. Caleb looked at Addison.

"Umm ..." She paused.

"Two Coronas," Caleb filled in for her.

"Sure thing," the waitress said. "Be back with your beers."

Caleb noticed Addison looking around her. "Feeling out of your element?" he inquired.

She turned back around to face him. "Why would you say that?"

He shrugged. "I doubt your father would approve of you coming to a place like this. I bet you go to those martini bars that the rest of the yuppies go to."

Addison huffed. "If you must know, my friends and I frequent bars like this. We're not that square."

"Really?" The disbelief in Caleb's voice was evident, and he didn't try to hide it. He knew Addison was putting on airs.

"Yes, really and to prove it," she said, pointing behind her toward the doorway, "I'll get on that mechanical bull." She began pulling off her leather jacket.

"Really?" He hadn't seen that one coming. He'd thought he'd have to dare her to do it, but Addison was a spitfire and wouldn't go down without a fight. He liked that.

"Yes. Right now!" She slid from the booth to her feet.

"Are you sure?" Caleb said, standing up. "You don't have to prove anything to me, Addison."

"Like hell I don't," she said, stalking toward the entrance. "You think I'm some rich debutante that's led around the nose by her father and doesn't have a mind of her own. Well I'm not." When she reached the line and saw no one ahead of her, she asked, "How much?"

"Five dollars."

Before she could reach into her jeans pocket, Caleb already had his wallet out. He pulled a five from his billfold and handed it to the attendant. "Here you go." He started to follow Addison toward the bull, but the attendant put out his hand.

"All nonriders need to stand behind the gate."

"Alright, alright." Caleb walked behind the gate. "Addy, you don't have to do this." He was rethinking his great idea. What if something happened to her? He'd never forgive himself.

Addison held up her hand. "I got this."

ADDISON WANTED to wet her pants. Lord, if Collette could see her now, she would say Addison had lost her mind. But she really hadn't; she didn't know why it was so important, but she wanted Caleb to know she was a grown-ass woman capable of thinking for herself and making her own decisions.

She knew what was on the menu for the end of the night. Caleb intended to take her to bed, and she was fully on board. She'd wanted him since the moment her eyes had connected with his in that club in Vegas. The fact that they'd had to wait this long felt sort of anticlimactic. She just hoped that it lived up to her expectations. She'd waited a lifetime to give her virginity to the right man. And although she wasn't sure what would become of her and Caleb after tonight, she was sure of one thing: She wanted to *be* with him tonight. He was the one.

It's why she hopped onto the mat and hopped over to the mechanical bull to prove to him she was woman enough to take on *whatever* he had in store for her.

Another attendant was waiting for her by the bull. He gave her a lift up. "So the object," he said with a microphone to the crowd, "is to stay on the bull for as long as you can with one hand in the air. Ain't that right, everybody?"

Several cheers and whistles rang out.

"Do I win anything?" Addison asked, looking down at the attendant.

"Honey, this ain't the fair," he said. "Let's get this party started." He hyped up the crowd as he jumped off the mat and headed to push the start button.

Addison looked at the audience that had suddenly amassed to see her debacle and spotted Caleb giving her a thumbs-up.

"Oh, Lord," she whispered seconds before the ride turned on and she began flailing.

CALEB COULDN'T BELIEVE his eyes as he watched Addison stay on the bull with one hand in the air. When the ride started, he thought she was going to be a casualty at the first buck, but Addison was a bulldog. She came close to falling off several times, but she would not give up. She stayed on the bull for the entire ride, making a believer out of him. Addison might appear sweet and soft to some, but she was hard as nails when pushed. Not to mention, she knew how to ride a bull. He couldn't wait for her to ride him.

She jumped from the machine and onto the mat without the assistance of the attendant and then sauntered toward Caleb. "Well?" Her hair was tousled, and her eyes were bright from excitement. She was sexy as hell.

With one arm, he pulled her close to him and slanted his mouth over hers. The crowd around them went wild with cheers and catcalls. When he lifted his head, he wasn't the only one glassy-eyed. "The show's over, folks. Let's go get some food." He patted her behind and guided her toward the dining area.

Addison slid into the booth, and Caleb followed

behind to sit opposite her. "Don't underestimate me," Addison said.

"I won't make that mistake again."

She smiled broadly. "I'm ravenous and thirsty." She reached for one of the two Coronas that had been placed on the table in their absence and took a long swig.

"You're back," the waitress said.

"Yeah, we had to go take a ride on the bull," Caleb responded.

"How'd you do?"

Caleb pointed to Addison. "Wasn't me. She was the victor. Stayed on the entire ride."

"Awesome! So what can I get you folks?"

Not long after they placed their orders for cheeseburgers and fries, the food arrived and Caleb was learning a lot more about Addison. He found out she was an avid runner and usually ran several miles a day and had participated in several marathons for charity. He also discovered she had an aversion to hip-hop music, but a love of classical and country music, which were opposite ends of the spectrum. As they talked, they also shared a brownie sundae for dessert, which had both of them licking their lips.

"Would you like to dance?" Caleb needed to move after that sinful dessert. He rarely ate sugar and usually stuck to protein and a low-carb diet, but tonight was the exception.

"Let's do it," Addison said.

In seconds they were on the floor, where an instructor was showing everyone the moves to the line dance. Addison picked it up a lot quicker than Caleb. He didn't have two left feet, but he was usually in the corner talking to some curvy female when the dancing started. Tonight, however, he was enjoying being with Addison. They laughed as they stumbled through the steps, but soon they were both catching on and moving in rhythm to the music.

"This is fun," Addison said as she sashayed.

"It is." Caleb stared at her for several long moments. Their gazes locked.

She glanced up at him, and she must have sensed his desire because she stopped midstride and looked him directly in the eye before saying, "You wanna get out of here?"

"You read my mind."

He took her hand, and they walked off the dancefloor. It didn't take him long to settle the bill, but it was long enough to have him anxious to finally be alone with Addison. If he had his way, they'd be doing it right there in the truck, but Addison was not that sort of girl. She was a lady and deserved to be treated as such.

INSTEAD OF GOING BACK to his uncle's, where he'd been staying, Caleb finally drove to the hotel where he had a room for the week. He'd checked in on the first night, but hadn't been back since. He made a quick stop at the front desk to ensure there were no problems.

He glanced around and saw Addison nervously shuffling on her feet as she flipped through a magazine. She didn't see him watching her, but he was sure she didn't just decide to spend the night with just any man. Caleb considered himself lucky that she would spend the night with him.

He walked over to her and held up the keycard. "All set."

"Good." She half-smiled and walked beside him to the elevator. He pressed the button, and the doors opened almost immediately.

Caleb could feel some of Addison's resolve weaken despite her bravado. He knew she was attracted to him as much as he was to her, so he had to do something. He leaned down, cupped her chin so she could look at him and brushed his lips across hers. He claimed her mouth, slowly, tenderly and expertly.

His tongue traced her outer lip, and she tasted like the dessert they'd consumed earlier that evening. He took his time feasting on her mouth. As his tongue slid inside, he walked her backward until she was against the elevator panels and their bodies were flush. Then his mouth took hers in a series of slow, shivery kisses. He ran his hands over her backside to cup her ass, bringing her center in close contact to his erection.

She moaned, wrapped her arms around his neck and returned his ardor with equal intensity. He tangled his hands in her hair, angled his head and plundered her mouth.

Dear God! He hadn't wanted a woman this bad since he'd been a randy teenager about to have sex for the first time, but Addison made him feel just as anxious and just as needy. A need which only she could fulfill.

Bing!

The chime of the elevator signaled they'd made it to his floor and luckily without any interruptions, otherwise someone would have gotten an eyeful.

They pulled apart guiltily and without a word exited the elevator. Caleb was holding Addison's hand, not for fear she'd run away, but because he couldn't get enough of the sparks that were generating between the two of them. That kiss had ignited his entire body. It was like nothing he'd ever experienced. He wanted more.

When they made it to his room, he slid the card into the slot, and blessedly, the door opened. They entered the darkened room, and Addison thought they would have stayed in the dark, but to her surprise Caleb turned on the lamp by the bed.

She blinked and brought him into focus.

"I want to look at you," Caleb said, walking back toward her. "Taste you."

"Caleb ..." Her voice hitched as he approached.

When he reached her, he didn't speak. Instead he let his hands do the talking and removed her leather jacket and tossed it on a nearby chair.

"I want you, Addy," he murmured. "I want to make love to you, be inside you, make you come until you scream my name over and over. Are you ready for that?"

She nodded. He took that as an affirmation and lifted her tunic over her head.

"Good, because I intend to taste every inch of you, and when you come, I will be there to lap it up."

Her tank top was next. He took it off of her and flung it aside until she was standing in front of him in her jeans and bra. It was one of those front closure satiny confections and would provide easy access. He gazed into her eyes as he released the clasp, allowing the bra to fall open and reveal her beautiful yet ample breasts to his admiring gaze. He brushed her nipples with his fingertips and felt them harden. He smiled. Making love with Addison was going to be even better than he had imagined.

He felt his erection hardening in his jeans, but ignored how she was affecting him because he wanted to savor the moment. Without a word, he bent down and captured a nipple in his mouth.

ADDISON WASN'T PREPARED for the onslaught of his seeking tongue on her breasts, and she swooned. Caleb caught her, wrapped her legs around his waist and carried her to the bed. But instead of laying her down as she'd anticipated, he'd settled her in his lap and held her in his arms as his mouth ravaged her breasts, one and then the other with equal attention. He lavished her nipples with tender flicks of his tongue before taking one in his mouth and sucking.

"Oh, God!" Her back arched, and her eyes fluttered closed. She heard a groan and realized it was herself. It had escaped all on its own.

Eventually his mouth returned to hers, and he kissed her deeply as his tongue glided in and out, exploring her. She wanted Caleb in the worst way. She didn't know it was possible to feel the emotions he was evoking in her, but she was caught up. It didn't help that Caleb had unzipped her jeans with one hand and was working his way inside the waistband to fondle her between her legs. His hand skimmed past her panties until he found her core. She gasped when she felt his touch on her feverish skin.

Pleasure was starting to overtake her as he caressed her with his fingertips. A ripple of excitement surged through her at having his fingers inside. She felt herself getting wet, and they hadn't even had sex yet. Having Caleb touch her this way was incredibly erotic. His mouth moved from hers to the nape of her neck and higher to her ear. He placed his tongue inside, and she moaned.

Addison glanced up at him through glazed eyes. His gaze was just as heated as her own.

"You like that, baby?" Caleb crooned.

"Y-yes," Addison murmured as he continued to caress her intimately.

"What do you want now?" he asked.

"You."

"Me, where?"

Addison was embarrassed to say. She'd never been this vocal with a man about her sexual needs and desires, but Caleb was intent on bringing this side out of her.

"Tell me."

"I-I ..." She couldn't think because he was thrusting his finger in and out of her so rapidly. Her breathing was coming faster and faster as her desire escalated. "I want you inside me."

"Then let go," Caleb growled.

"I don't know if I can ..."

But she needn't have worried because Caleb was an expert lover with skilled hands. Before she knew what was happening, her body exploded. She screamed. Caleb held on to her, finally laying her on the bed as she convulsed.

When it was over, Addison's eyes remained shut. She couldn't believe Caleb had made her come like that just with his fingers. She was afraid to open her eyes, but Caleb wasn't having it.

"Look at me, Addy," he said, staring at her.

Nervously, she looked up into his dark-brown eyes.

"Are you a virgin?"

6

———

Embarrassed, Addison looked away, and Caleb knew he'd guessed right. To another man only interested in his own gratification, her inexperience may not have been obvious, but he prided himself on reading and responding to the woman he was sleeping with, and Addison's naïveté and her orgasm had told him all he needed to know.

When she finally opened her eyes, she said, "Is that a problem?"

Caleb glanced at her. Her eyelids were heavy and passion-glazed, and the answer to that question was a no-brainer. "No, it's not."

"Are you sure about that? Because it usually angers most men. They expect a woman who knows what to do in the bedroom."

"Yes, I'm sure. It just changes my approach to making love to you."

"You still want to?"

Caleb grasped her hand and placed it over his still hard-as-a-rock erection that was dying for release.

"Oh!"

"And I'm not most men," Caleb added. "I'm just glad I know, so I won't hurt you."

Addison smiled and shyly stood up bare-chested to stare into his eyes. "I know you won't."

"How?"

She shrugged. "I just know. Just like I know that I don't want this night to end." She slid off the bed and unpeeled her already open jeans and panties down her legs until she was naked.

Caleb swallowed at Addison's bold actions even as he couldn't stop his eyes from taking in all her curves, from her hips to her long legs and back to the patch between her thighs.

He was in trouble. His mind told him to run as fast as he could. A virgin! A virgin! He hadn't been with one since his first time in the barn at Golden Oaks. But since his first encounter with Addison in Vegas, he'd wanted the one who'd gotten away. Little did he know she was untouched and unspoiled. When he made love to her tonight, he would become her first lover. He would be the first, the only. As a man, it was oddly exhilarating to know he could teach her everything about the joys of lovemaking between a man and a woman. And oh how he would enjoy it.

"Come here," Caleb said.

Slowly, she walked until she stood in front of him. Her pert breasts were stunningly beautiful; he couldn't wait for another taste, but he wanted her to be comfortable. "Undress me."

She coughed. "Excuse me?"

He rose to his feet, grasped her hands and brought them to his belt buckle. He looked deep into her eyes and nodded. He could see her nervousness, but she complied, removing the belt and sliding it from the loop. It dropped to the floor, and she lowered her eyes.

"Look at me," Caleb said, "as you continue to undress me."

She smiled hesitantly and instead of going for his jeans, which he couldn't wait to be free of, she went for his shirt and pulled it loose. One at a time, she painstakingly released each button until he was finally bare-chested. He stroked her silken hair and brought it up to his nose for a whiff.

She was amused by his actions, but didn't stop undressing him. She unzipped his jeans and bent down to remove them from his narrow hips. He assisted her by toeing off the boots he'd worn and then stepped out of the jeans until he was in his boxers.

He didn't wait for her "what next" question. Instead, he grasped the back of her head and pulled her forward. His mouth moved slowly over hers at first and then harder to deepen the kiss. Their tongues found each other, mating in a slow dance as they circled. His hunger for her deepened, and he pressed her closer to him and then backward until they fell in a heap of limbs onto the bed.

"I'll make this good for you," Caleb whispered softly in Addison's ear. He delved inside her waiting mouth with his tongue and flicked it across the roof of her mouth, then, slowly, he pulled away.

She looked up at him in alarm, but he reassured her. "Lie back," he said and helped Addison lay against the fluffy pillows on the king-size bed. Then he began a trail of kisses from her breasts to her stomach until he came to the juncture between her thighs. Slipping his hands under her ass, he brought her to his lips and had his first taste of heaven.

His tongue traced her womanly folds until he dove inside to taste her sweet nectar. At his teasing, lapping and tonguing, she whimpered and bucked on the bed. He liked that she was enjoying his ministrations, and he didn't stop; he held her hips in place, picked up the pace and surged forward, flicking his tongue across her engorged nub and sucking on it.

Addison ran her hands over his head as her breathing began to come in rasps. She was trying to hold on to her equilibrium, but he wanted her to come again. He wanted her dripping wet for him so he could easily slide into her. He got his wish because she threw back her head and cried out as the full force of her orgasm hit.

"Caleb!" She fell backward against the pillows.

Caleb slid forward until he was inches away from her face. "Did you enjoy that?"

Addison could only nod. Now it was time for the main event. He slid his boxers down his legs then reached across to the bedside drawer for a box of condoms.

ADDISON WAS QUIVERING as the contractions from her orgasm flowed through her. Through the haze, she could see Caleb reaching for a condom to protect them, and she was glad for it, but her body was liquefied. She didn't think it was possible to feel this good.

She realized that he'd ensured she was completely satisfied by being careful to make her have two earth-shattering climaxes, but she'd done nothing for him. She reached for him, but he tapped her hand away.

"There will be time for me later," Caleb said as he sheathed his large member. "What I want right now is to be inside you. To feel you tight around me."

Caleb's wasn't the first penis she'd seen fully erect, but it was by far the largest. Could she take him inside of her? She would soon find out because Caleb was hunched over her. "Just relax, okay? I'll take it slow."

She nodded, but she could already feel herself tensing. Caleb must have sensed it because he kissed her once more with the same passion he'd shown every other time. His hot tongue flickered over her mouth again and Addison knew she couldn't, wouldn't deny herself or this moment.

"I want you, Caleb. Take me, take me now," she urged, grinding the lower half of her body against his. "Make me yours."

"God, you're torturing me, woman."

"But it's a good torture, right?" Addison said, spreading her legs so he could settle between them.

"God, yes."

She leaned forward to bite his neck and that was the catalyst. Caleb grasped her hips, and slowly the hardened tip of his penis grazed her womanly core. He kissed her deeply again, and she relaxed as he guided himself into her body. She couldn't believe it. They were joined together as one. The physical connection was incredible. Slowly, he eased inside, allowing her body to get accustomed to him. Any pain she may have felt was minimal as Caleb continued to love her mouth as his lower body thrust deeper inside her.

He plotted a course and navigated her body to meet his with a slow rhythm of in and out, in and out and then faster thrusts. The pleasure was intense, even more so when Caleb bent his head to suckle on a hardened nipple. He was making her weak with every movement, every kiss. Addison thought she would die from the pleasure, but instead, it built, reaching higher and higher until she didn't think she could soar any further. And then she reached the peak and crested, screaming out Caleb's name as she held him tight.

Caleb wasn't there yet; instead, he kept going, plunging deeper and deeper. She didn't know it was possible to come again, but shivers of pleasure began coursing through her and she exploded. This time, however, Caleb bucked and he tensed up as he hollered out her name when pure ecstasy took over them both.

"Addison!"

~

SEVERAL MINUTES LATER, Caleb slid away from Addison completely sated. He hadn't felt the kind of passion he'd shared with her, since—well, it had been a long time. He'd forgotten how intimate lovemaking could be when it was shared with someone he really cared for; and it surprised him that this late in the game, someone could make him *feel* again. Being on the road as often as he was, he'd become jaded from sleeping with as many different women as he could, but Addison wasn't like them. She was special.

How else to explain how a beautiful, vibrant, sexy girl like her could still have been a virgin at twenty-three? Rather than be angry that she wasn't as skilled as some of his other lovers, he took it as a challenge. He would use his prowess and show her just how gentle, caring and giving he could be.

He remembered Uncle Duke giving him some advice once when he'd been a young buck of fifteen and eager to get into one of the ranch hand's daughter's pants during a visit to his family's home one summer. Duke had told Caleb not to be in such a haste to satisfy his own needs, that a real man would ensure his woman was taken care of first before giving into his own desires. Caleb had never forgotten that priceless advice and had lived by it, which is perhaps why many of the women he'd bedded, although they may not have been happy to have only one night with him, could not complain he'd been a selfish lover. They could say that he'd ensured their every need was met. He'd done that tonight with Addison. He'd made sure she'd come multiple times before he'd finally allowed himself to let go.

And now, bless her heart, he turned to his side to peer at her. She'd fallen asleep. He leaned over, tucked several tendrils of hair behind her ear, and brushed his lips across hers before his head hit the pillow. Then he threw one large hand around her, tucked her into his groin and closed his eyes.

ADDISON WAS NOT ASLEEP. How could she be after what she'd just experienced? But she hadn't known what else to do after sharing such a huge moment with Caleb, her first lover! So she'd rolled over to her side and faked sleep so she could process the emotions going on in her head. She hadn't expected to feel so, so different, but yet so happy. Being with Caleb had been nothing like the romance novels she read when her father wasn't looking. It was better. A rush of sexual need had flooded through her when he'd swept her into his arms in the elevator and had culminated with them making love. He'd touched her and made her feel things no other man had. She'd allowed herself to be completely free and because of it, she'd come alive with him.

Now, of course, she wondered if their lovemaking had been as enjoyable for him as it had been for her. Caleb had been very giving, ensuring she was pleased in every way imaginable before he'd finally come. The feeling of having Caleb moving inside her had not only been erotic, but immensely pleasurable too. Their union had been hot, heated and urgent, yet he'd been gentle with her and she'd hardly felt any discomfort.

Caleb Hart was an incredible man, a man she could easily fall for if she wasn't careful. But for now, she would content herself with the fact that she'd finally become a woman. And she was determined to be more of a woman by being as giving with him as he'd been with her. She would let him sleep for now, but later, she would surprise him.

7

Caleb awoke with a start, stunned and aroused because he felt a hand traveling down his flat stomach and then covering his shaft. Seconds later, a warm, wet mouth closed around his shaft's base. He breathed deeply and let out a groan of pleasure. The licks and flicks were light, gentle and a bit unsure, but Caleb didn't mind. The fact that Addison was giving his already-anxious member some attention was the best wake-up present he could think of.

He peeked beneath the sheet to peer at her. She held his penis and was stroking him with one trembling hand while her tongue teased his tip. It was incredibly sexy.

Caleb smiled. "Good morning."

She smiled back at him. "Good morning," she said and then lowered her head again to bestow a kiss on the tip of his penis. The head strained to meet her mouth, but she didn't shy away from it. Instead she enveloped the whole thing, and Caleb nearly shattered as he fell backward against the pillows. Blood and heat surged through his entire body.

He loved the way Addison worked magic with her hands and mouth, and it made him horny as hell. It made him want to forget his uncle's directive on pleasing his woman first and just flip her over and pump away inside her. Instead he had to return the favor, and one hand clasped one of her thighs as he urged her to open her legs. She complied, allowing his fingers to travel lazily up her thigh, and when he reached her mound he slid one finger inside of her. She moaned, but didn't pull away, so he sank his finger farther. In and out. He stroked her clitoris surely but gently until he could hear her breathing become hard just as his was coming faster and more furious. He wanted her to come with him, but she seemed equally insistent that he arrive first.

Addison's mouth stretched, and she accepted all of him, sucking forcefully and taking him deeper and deeper. And then as he was doing her, she took him to the hilt and then pulled off of him.

"Addison—" But he never finished his sentence, because her mouth took him back in and sucked harder and harder as her hands softly explored his balls. Caleb didn't want to climax down her throat, but the little minx brought him to the edge and his orgasm slammed him.

"Shit!" he cursed as he let go and came.

She peeked up from underneath the sheet with a smile as she licked her lips. "Did you enjoy that?" she asked. He could see that she was proud of herself for having pushed him over the brink as he'd done her.

"You know I did," Caleb replied honestly with a satisfied smile, "but you know that wasn't fair. I-I was sleeping and wasn't prepared to put up a fight."

"Is that right?" she said with a wink. "What are you going to do about it?"

"Come here." He grasped her face and kissed her hard and deep. He could taste his own essence, but he didn't care. He crushed her breasts against the solid expanse of his chest and threaded his fingers through her loosened curls while his tongue slipped inside her mouth to plunge in and out just as he intended to do with his body as soon as he recovered from his orgasm. He felt Addison's breasts swell against him, and he reached for one. His fingers closed around one nipple, and he pinched it between his thumb and forefinger, tracing the smooth brown disc until it turned into a hardened bud.

It was time for him to have a taste of his naughty angel. His mouth moved from her lips so he could take her left nipple into his hot mouth. He swirled his tongue lovingly around it, and Addison's head flew back.

"Caleb—"

"Yes, baby …" He moved from the left breast to the right so he could suckle on the other nipple. "Has anyone ever told you you have beautiful breasts?"

Addison shook her head. She was unable to speak, which meant he was doing something right. He licked her nipple while his hands skimmed her belly and then lower. Her breath caught when he stroked her nether lips, but instead of tightening her thighs, she opened them wider.

"That's right, love, let me in," he whispered as he slid two fingers inside. He teased the walls of her vagina and her clitoris while his mouth moved from her breasts to return to her lips. He could feel himself coming alive again, and he was ready for another hit. He slid a condom on and then grasped her hips and moved her over his hardening shaft, easing inside her already wet heat so she could ride him.

"Oh." Addison's back arched as she began grinding against him.

"That's it," Caleb said, lifting his hips to fill her tight walls. "Ride me, baby. Ride me."

Addison bounced atop his hard penis. She was riding him like she'd rode that mechanical bull, and he loved it! He was enjoying seeing her relish their intimacy and not being afraid of it. She embraced it, rising up to meet his every thrust.

ADDISON STARED at herself in the hotel room mirror after she and Caleb showered together. She'd never showered with a man before, and that was if she could call what they'd just done showering. It had been more like washing each other's bodies as they made love again. She didn't look any different, but she *felt* different. Would anyone see it?

Her father!

Shit! After staying out all night, she would have to go home. She'd turned off her cellphone, and her father must be worried sick. But Addison wasn't sorry for spending the night with Caleb. It was everything she could have hoped for and more for her first time.

At that moment, Caleb walked into the bathroom. "Ready to go?" he asked.

She nodded.

After she'd grabbed her purse, they headed toward the door. Addison didn't know what to expect on the morning after as she'd never gone to bed with a man casually before. But she needn't have worried, because Caleb reached for her hand and they walked together to the elevator. Once inside, he leaned over to brush his lips softly over hers.

Addison sighed. No awkwardness. Thank God.

When they made it to his truck, Addison reluctantly turned on her cellphone, and moments later, she heard the chimes of missed voicemails and texts. She glanced down and saw she'd missed six calls from her father and three from Collette.

Where are you? Collette's message said. *Your father is worried.*

Addison rolled her eyes. If her father had the foresight to call Collette, she was really in for it.

"Is everything okay?" Caleb asked when Addison remained quiet during the ride.

"Everything's fine." She put her phone on vibrate.

Caleb leaned over and grabbed her chin, forcing her to look at him. "Don't lie to me ever," he said. "Tell me what's wrong."

Addison lowered her head. "They're just some calls from my father and best friend."

"They're worried because you didn't come home last night?"

When she didn't answer, he continued, "I take it you've never done that before?"

Addison nodded.

"I'm sorry, Addy, if I caused problems by keeping you to myself all night, but I just couldn't help it." He grinned.

Addison glanced up. "Don't apologize. I enjoyed our night and morning together. I wouldn't change a thing. And as for my father, I'm sorry I worried him, but he's got to understand that I'm a grown woman."

"Yes, you are," Caleb said huskily.

The ride back to the Walker mansion didn't take long. When Caleb pulled up to the driveway, he leaned over and placed a long-dragging kiss across Addison's lips before jumping out of the pickup to come around and open the passenger door. As he did so, the front door of the Walker home swung open revealing Addison's father.

Caleb helped Addison out of the pickup and turned to see Benjamin Walker glaring at them. Caleb turned back around to face her and whispered, "Are you going be okay?"

Addison nodded.

"I'll call you later." Caleb bent down and brushed his lips across hers, walked to the driver's side, got in and kicked the pickup into gear.

Addison heard him drive away as she walked toward her father, who stood with his arms folded. "Good morning," she said.

"Don't 'good morning' me," he responded as she walked inside the foyer and he slammed the front door. "Do you realize what time it is?"

"Of course I do." Addison held up her left wrist. "I have a watch."

She could see steam escape her father's ears. "I was worried sick!"

"I know, and I'm sorry."

"Oh, so you *do* think I deserve some common courtesy?"

"Yes." Addison reminded herself to calm down, though she didn't appreciate the way he was talking down to her as if she were a teenager. "I understand you're upset, Daddy, and I'm sorry I caused you to worry as I would never want to do that."

"But yet you did," he spat, "because of that young man." He pointed toward the door. "I should have known he was no good. Look at who he's related to," he said as he stormed down the hall. "I mean his uncle is a notorious ladies' man. Has several kids up and down the coast."

Addison rolled her eyes. "For Christ's sake, Daddy, Caleb is not his uncle."

"No?" Her father spun around. "You could have fooled me. Didn't he keep my very naïve daughter out all night and bring her back the next morning? Sounds exactly like something Duke Hart would do."

"Listen, I apologize again for worrying you and Collette, but I won't apologize for making my own choices."

"Even when those choices can lead you astray? Trust me, that young man is bad news. He'll break your heart."

"You don't know that."

"Like hell I don't. Duke Hart has always been a ladies' man, bedding women in every county. I don't want to see the same thing happen to you, baby girl. You know nothing about this young man, and from what I can see he's just using you."

"You're wrong, Daddy."

"I hope so, Addison, because you're headed for heartbreak."

The truth was, Addison had been using Caleb. She'd wanted her first time to be with someone she desired and who knew his way around in the bedroom. She'd done exactly that. The one thing she hadn't counted on was that she'd enjoy it so much that she'd want another taste.

~

TEN MINUTES LATER, when Addison was alone in her room, she called Collette.

"Where the hell have you been?" her friend berated her from the other end of the line.

"Hello to you too," Addison replied.

"Oh, no you don't. Don't you dare try to turn this around on me. You were the one who had your poor father so worried to death that he called me. And you know I'm his least favorite person, so he must have been desperate."

"I'm sorry, Collette. Truly I am."

"The least you could have done was warn me so I'm prepared."

"Again, I'm sorry, and I promise I'll make it up to you, like maybe take you to that new boutique you've been wanting to check out." As a starving artist, Collette needed help with money, especially since her father had cut her off.

"Well ..." Collette paused. "I suppose you can bribe yourself back into my good graces. So tell me, what or should I say *who* had you out all night? And please make it good."

Addison chuckled. Trust Collette to be blunt. "Well ..." Addison paused for effect.

"Just spit it out! I'm dying to know."

"I am no longer a virgin."

"Get out!"

"It's the truth."

"Who did you do the nasty with? I mean, there isn't anyone in town you've been seeing. Or have you been holding out on me?"

"Of course not." Addison snickered. "It's not someone new, but someone old."

"Who?"

"Remember Vegas?"

"OMG!" Collette shouted. "The guy from the club in Vegas? No, it couldn't be. If I recall you didn't even know his name. Didn't you sneak out of his bed after your unfortunate illness?"

"That's all true, but I ran into Caleb at a charity

event a few days ago, and he mentioned we had some unfinished business. That's when we finally exchanged names and numbers. And well, last night, we sealed the deal and made love."

"Wow! Is that fate or what? I mean usually what happens in Vegas, stays in Vegas, but this shit was like fate. For you two to meet up in Dallas of all places? What are the odds?"

"I couldn't agree with you more," Addison replied, "and I have to tell you, Collette, it was well worth the wait. Caleb Hart rocked my world."

"He did, huh?"

"And then some," Addison added, lying back on the bed. She couldn't help but replay the moments they'd shared together the night before.

"I'm happy for you," Collette said. "You've finally joined the rest of us, and now look out world, 'cause you're about to get your freak on!"

"I'm no slut!" Addison responded. "But—"

"You wanna hit that again?" Collette surmised.

"How did you know?"

"When a man hits the spot," Collette said, "you want him to keep coming back to do it over and over."

"Which won't be easy with my father looking over my shoulder every five minutes. The man nearly had a coronary when I didn't come home last night."

"Girl, he was blowing up my phone something awful."

"I'm grown, and he's just going to have to deal with it. Otherwise, I'm moving out."

"Well, it would be about time. You're long overdue, my friend, to strike out on your own."

Addison sighed. "I know, but I would feel bad leaving him alone in this big house."

"But it's not your responsibility, Addy. I mean

you're not his wife, you're his daughter. And it's about time he recognized that."

"I suppose you're right. In the meantime, what should I do about Caleb?"

Collette chuckled. "Oh, you needn't worry now that Caleb has had you and broken you in. He won't want any other man to have you, at least not until you both have had your fill."

AS HE GOT DRESSED LATER that evening for his first rodeo event of the night, Caleb's mind kept wandering back to Addison and their lovemaking. He'd wanted her something fierce after the abrupt end to their night back in Vegas. Seeing her in Dallas had been a welcome shock and once he'd made their date, he'd been eagerly anticipating making love to her. Last night had surpassed his expectations even after he'd found out that she was innocent.

She'd been just as passionate as he'd known she would be. When he'd gone down on her, her responses had been honest and unrehearsed. She'd just opened herself up to the experience and beauty of sex and the excitement it could create. He knew he'd made her come many times because she would not only whimper, but her entire body shook. She was an open book and one he looked forward to reading over and over.

"Hart!" Josh called out, awakening Caleb from his daydream. "How many times are you going to keep tying down that calf?"

Caleb glanced at the calf underneath him and turned to his friend. "As many times as necessary." The rope had to be stiff enough for him to maintain a loop but flexible enough to bend around the head of a charging calf. He'd chosen a new poly rope made of synthetic fibers because it was more durable and resistant to water and grime than natural ropes that some of the other cowboys used. He was hoping it would give him the edge he needed.

"Naw, man, that ain't it," Josh said, coming over to Caleb's side. "You were staring off into space and looking all dreamy-eyed."

Caleb laughed. "You're a load of shit!"

"I speak the truth. I bet you were thinking about that sweet young thing you had the other night. Man was she fine. I would love to—"

The words didn't even get out of Josh's mouth before Caleb had grabbed him by the collar of his plaid shirt. "Don't you talk about Addison like that, ya hear?"

Josh's eyes widened. "Yeah, man, I'm sorry. Okay?" Josh pushed at Caleb until he released him. "Damn! What's gotten into you? Or should I say what have *you* gotten into?"

When Caleb lunged for him again, Josh sideswiped him. "Okay, okay, man, I'll lay off. It's clear I can't tease you about this girl."

"She's not a girl. She's a woman."

"And off-limits?"

"That's right. She's mine."

Josh held up his hands in defense. "Understood. I was just joking anyway. I've never seen you this way about a woman before. You usually love 'em and leave 'em. What's so different about this one?"

That was a good question, Caleb thought. For a reason he couldn't quite pin down, he cared deeply for Addison. And despite opposition from her father, Caleb knew he would be seeing her again real soon.

8

─────

The next morning, Caleb decided to stop by his uncle's mansion. He'd made up his mind over his morning coffee that he would stay on a few days before returning to Tucson for all the wedding festivities. It wasn't like he had to do much. He was a groomsman and only needed to walk one of his cousins down the aisle. How hard could that be?

So Caleb had more time to stay in Dallas, which meant he'd find a way to spend a few more nights with Addison. Of course, it wouldn't be easy letting the doe-eyed beauty go at the end of the week, especially after he would have taught her everything she knew in the bedroom. He wasn't thrilled with the prospect that she would lend her skills to another man, but he also wasn't the sticking-around kind.

Addison was the type of girl you married and raised kids with. Caleb knew it was wrong that he would take all she had to give and then leave, but better she learn about heartbreak first from him than some other guy. Caleb truly thought she was a spectacular girl and didn't mind staying a couple of extra days to get to know her.

When he finally made it to Duke's mansion, he didn't bother ringing the doorbell. He just walked right in, right into an argument Duke was having with his estranged son, Trent, on the phone.

"I'm sorry you had to hear that," Duke said after he hung up.

Caleb shrugged. "Fathers and sons argue." He could recall some moments with his father, Isaac, when they'd gone head to head.

"Not like that," Duke responded. "Trent is just so angry at me because he had a hard life. I don't know how to reach him."Caleb nodded. "He's your son. You have to keep trying."

Duke was deep in contemplation for several minutes. "So, why are you here? I wasn't expecting you."

"Perhaps this isn't a good time to take you up on that offer," Caleb said. "I was thinking about putting in my notice once this circuit is finished, but—"

"No buts," Duke interrupted. "I meant what I said. When do you want to start?"

"Right after this circuit is finished, but I thought maybe during the day I could shadow some of the team and get a head start."

"That sounds like a mighty fine idea. Let's make it happen."

~

AS SHE SAT and looked over the monthly figures for Walker Trucking in her twenty-fourth-floor office, Addison was wired. She hadn't heard from Caleb all day, and she was beginning to wonder if the night they'd shared meant nothing to him. For her, it had been life-changing, but perhaps for him it had been just another roll in the hay. After all, it was obvious that Caleb was a robust man with a hearty sexual appetite.

After lunch, Addison was going over figures with another accountant when her assistant, Maggie, popped her head into the conference room where they were gathered. Maggie was much older than Addison, and Addison felt strange giving her orders considering Maggie probably had more work history in her pinkie finger than Addison had, but her father had insisted on it.

"What is it, Maggie?"

Maggie walked into the conference room and closed the door.

"Well." Maggie glanced behind her. "There is a man here asking to see you. He didn't have any appointment but was insistent that you would want to see him."

Addison wasn't expecting anyone and slid her chair over so she could glance through the conference room's glass doors. There was Caleb, standing in the reception area.

Addison jolted and tried to keep at bay a big smile that was struggling to overtake her face. He was here, which meant she was more to him than a fling. But how did he know where she worked? Oh, right, she'd told him during dinner, and it wouldn't have been hard for him to find Walker Trucking's address online. She just wished he would have called. She wasn't looking at all sexy in a simple black skirt suit.

"Excuse me for a moment," Addison said, rising to her feet and smoothing down her skirt.

She walked toward Maggie, who whispered, "He didn't seem like someone you'd associate with, so I wasn't sure if I should show him in."

"I'll take it from here," Addison responded softly and opened the conference room door.

Caleb noticed her the minute she exited and offered her his signature sexy smile. Addison's heart hammered as she looked him up and down. He was wearing faded Wrangler jeans, a plaid shirt and a cowboy hat. He looked completely out of place amongst the modern décor of Walker Trucking's offices, but she was excited to see him.

She smiled as she approached. "What are you doing here?"

"I thought I would surprise you for a late lunch."

"I'm sorry. I can't get away. I have a meeting in an hour."

"Damn, I was hoping you could sneak away and spare a few minutes."

"I could spare a few. Let's walk to my office. Follow me." As she led him down the corridor, she could see several workers staring at them. It was unusual for her to have guests let alone someone like Caleb.

"I have a better idea," Caleb said, and before Addison knew what was happening, he was opening a door labeled "Utility Closet" and yanking her inside. It was dark except for a patch of light shining underneath the door.

"Caleb, what are you doing?" Addison whispered.

"I'm going to live out one of my fantasies." He locked the door. "Now no one will disturb us."

"Wait ..."

Caleb shoved her back against the door, grasped the sides of her face and kissed her long, hard and deep. He'd startled her, taking her breath away momentarily, but it didn't take her long to recover. She wound her arms around his neck and pulled him closer.

"I want you right here," he said, moving his mouth from her lips and down to her neck. "I want to make you come."

Addison was at a loss; she'd never been spoken to this way before. No man had dared, considering who her father was, but Caleb didn't seem to care. He was about to make love to her right here in the utility closet!

It was outrageous and completely exhilarating. Her head leaned back as Caleb began nipping her neck with love bites before going higher. She moaned when he reached her ear and his tongue flicked inside. While he teased it, one of his hands caressed the curve of her breasts while the other began removing her suit jacket. She didn't hear it fall to the floor because Caleb was fondling her breasts over her silk shirt. Her nipples puckered at his touch.

"Oh, yes, babe," Caleb said when he felt them turn to nubs. Addison hadn't known her breasts were that sensitive. He had a way of coaxing a response out of her even now in such a heated inopportune moment.

And he wasn't stopping there. He lowered his head and moved from her ear to her breasts. She gasped when he suckled her nipple right through her shirt.

"Dear God!"

"You like that," he said, swirling his tongue over her covered nipples.

"Y-yes," Addison eked out and grasped his head so he could stay right there. While his mouth had her moaning softly, Caleb's hands were roaming down her hips to grasp her thighs.

"What else would you like?" He slipped his palms underneath her skirt and bunched up her shirt. Then she felt him caressing the inside of her thighs and reaching for her bikini panties. She held her breath.

"Tell me what you want," he said, pushing aside the flimsy satin of her panties and sliding a finger inside of her.

"No." She shook her head. She couldn't ask for it, but she didn't have to. His finger slid in and out, and Addison knew she was already slick. Caleb was tapping into a sexual need that she hadn't known existed until he'd brought it out in her.

"Yes," Caleb said, leaving her breasts and returning to her lips with an open-mouthed kiss. His tongue stroked hers softly while his fingers stroked her below with quick flicks.

Addison couldn't think about anything but the sensations that Caleb was evoking. All thought to where she was flew out the window. She could only think of Caleb and this moment. He was going to have her crying out if he didn't stop soon. He must have sensed that she was near because Caleb removed his fingers and took control. She heard the tear of foil and then Caleb grasped one of her thighs.

Caleb pushed aside Addison's panties and surged inside her.

"Oh ... yes," she began to moan, but he didn't let her get out another word. In order for this to work and not draw attention to them, he needed her to be quiet. He covered her mouth with his while the lower half of his body began thrusting inside of her. God, yes! He slowed down the pace to make the moment last. He grasped ahold of her butt and began grinding against her.

~

CALEB KNEW he was wrong coming to Addison's office like this, but he hadn't been able to help himself. He hadn't seen her last night because of the rodeo event, which was usually a late evening for him. His body had craved Addison, and he'd woken up this morning wanting more of his sweet angel. He'd told himself that he would just stop by and see her, maybe even take her out for lunch. Then she'd been standing there in the doorway of the conference room looking so sweet, so innocent and so damn sexy. He'd lost all rational thought.

He was corrupting her. Making love to her in the utility closet of her office was wrong, but it felt so right. She felt so good. He was caught up and wanted to pound into her, but instead he walked over to the wall farthest from the door and ordered, "Bounce on me, baby."

"I don't know how."

He lifted her butt and rocked her several times against his hard erection. "You like that?" he asked.

She picked up the rhythm and began bouncing on him like he was an exercise ball. "Oh, yeah, babe. Like that? Give it to me!" he groaned softly.

And she did. Her body erupted first, and she whispered loudly, "Caleb!"

"Yes, babe, I know," he said and climaxed right along with her. When the eruptions subsided, he lowered her to the floor and turned away to take care of the condom. Turning back around, he saw Addison leaning against the wall looking slightly dazed. Her hair that had once been nicely coiffed was slightly mussed, and her makeup ... well, her lips were swollen from his kisses.

"Are you okay?" he asked, pulling up his jeans.

"I-I'm okay," she said, slightly out of breath. "I think."

Caleb smiled. "You think?"

"I mean, I'm not sure what just happened."

"Would you like a repeat?"

Addison shook her head. "No, I think making love with you once in the utility closet is quite enough." She pulled down her skirt and began straightening her blouse. "What are you doing to me, Caleb Hart?" She walked away from him long enough to pick up her discarded suit jacket lying on the floor.

"I think I could ask you the same question."

"Excuse me?"

"I didn't come here with the intention of taking you in a closet."

"Then how did we get here?"

Caleb shrugged. "Chemistry. Passion. It's off the charts."

"Has this happened to you before?"

"No, not to this degree," Caleb replied honestly. He'd had good sex before, but this was different, and he wasn't at all sure what to do about it. "Let's just go with the moment until it burns out."

"And what if it doesn't?"

Addison's question was valid. What if it didn't? Caleb was in unchartered territory and offered his best guess. "We're just two hot-blooded young people. It'll fizzle, and when it's over we'll go our separate ways."

"Because you're not the commitment kind of guy?"

"That's right. My lifestyle as a bull rider doesn't permit it." He knew this was a copout. It wasn't his lifestyle. He'd seen other bull riders that were family men, but it just wasn't right for him. He'd never seen himself as a married man. And despite how special Addison was, he wasn't about to change anytime soon.

Addison nodded and began slipping on her jacket. Caleb could see the sadness in her eyes at his words, so he walked over and helped her finish putting the jacket on. "How about dinner later tonight at my uncle's place?" he asked.

"Aren't you getting on the road soon," Addison inquired, "for another event?"

"Not just yet."

"Then dinner sounds good."

"I'll pick you up at seven p.m.?"

"How about I meet you instead?"

He figured she probably didn't want her father in her personal affairs. "You're on. I'll text you later with the address."

Caleb walked over and unlocked the door. "I'll go out first," he said. "Wait five minutes and then come out after me."

~

ADDISON WAITED, but left the closet nearly ten minutes later. She would be totally embarrassed if anyone had seen her come out after Caleb.

When she exited, no one was around, thankfully. She made it back to her office without anyone seeing her, not even Maggie, who was away from her desk. It gave Addison enough time to close the door and sink against it.

What had she just done? Had she really just had sex with Caleb in the utility closet of her father's business? She must be losing her mind if he could make her behave so recklessly. Had he put some sort of spell on her? She had no idea sex could be so addictive.

And tonight, there was dinner at his uncle's place? She was excited that she would get to meet a member of Caleb's family because it told her he took her seriously. But her mind couldn't help but wander to later, after dinner. Should she pack her overnight bag? Her stomach curled, and the place between her legs still tingled from where he'd fingered her in the closet and made her come without barely breaking a sweat.

Oh, yes, she was most definitely packing an overnight bag.

9

"Where are you headed?" Addison's father asked her several hours later in the foyer at home.

"Out."

"That's cryptic."

"I meant it to be," Addison replied and then took a deep breath and said, "I'm going out for the evening, Daddy. You shouldn't expect me home."

His brow rose. "Excuse me?"

Addison knew he would be stunned, but he'd asked for her honesty and that's what she was trying to deliver. "You heard me correctly. I have plans for tonight." She wasn't going to elaborate anymore. Her father was a bright man. She didn't need to paint him a picture.

"So you're not going to heed my advice?" He folded his arms across his chest disapprovingly.

"I heard what you had to say," Addison replied, "but ultimately, this is my decision."

He pursed his lips. "Very well, Addison. Do as you wish." He turned on his heel and without another word, stalked away.

Addison stared at his retreating figure. She hated

to be at odds with her father, but he had to learn that he wasn't going to run her life. "Have a good night," she called out after him as she closed the front door behind her.

~

"I really appreciate you having Addison over," Caleb said to Duke.

"A friend of yours is a friend of mine," Duke replied.

Just then Caleb's cousins Bree and Jada stepped into the living room. Jada was the fashionista of the two, in leather pants, a see-through silk sweater over a tank top and some pumps that looked like they cost more than several weeks' salary. She was petite with a curvy build that fit her lifestyle as an anchor on a San Francisco morning show, and with her café au lait skin and perfect makeup, she was never without a date.

Meanwhile, Bree was dressed more simply in distressed jeans and a chiffon tunic and wore some weathered cowboy boots. She was an outdoor person, and her caramel skin was shiny bright from the natural air. Her hair was cut in a stylish bob, and she wore just a touch of gloss on her full lips. Bree was content with her career; Caleb couldn't recall the last time he'd heard about a date.

"Caleb!" Jada rushed over to greet him with a warm hug. "It's so good to see you."

"We were thrilled when Daddy told us you were coming for dinner *and* bringing a guest." Surprise was evident in Jada's voice.

"Yeah, I thought you liked the single life like Daddy here." Bree came around to kiss her father on the cheek and then sat on the edge of his chair. "What gives?"

"Does there have to be a reason for me to want to spend time with my favorite cousins, the prettiest girls in the world?"

"You charmer," Bree said. "And good deflect, but I want to know who she is."

Just then the doorbell rang, and Caleb was thankful for the reprieve. He was not anxious to be the subject of Bree's inquisition. She could be one helluva ballbuster when she wanted to be.

Caleb walked to the foyer to open the front door, and there Addison stood before him looking as ravishing as the last time when he'd had her backed up against the wall of the utility closet and banged her within an inch of both their lives.

"Can I come in?" Addison broke into his lascivious memory.

"Of course, babe," Caleb said with a sexy drawl. His eyes roamed over her shapely figure in the Chianti-colored leather-seamed dress. The leather was strategically placed vertically and stopped at the short hem right above her knee. Addison had a killer pair of legs, and the dress and matching pumps highlighted them.

As for Caleb, his outfit hadn't changed much except he'd showered and changed into a fresh pair of denim jeans and replaced his usual plaid shirt with a deep-purple one.

He leaned down and swept his lips across Addison's, and that's when she whispered, "I-uh brought an overnight bag. I-I wasn't sure ... I hope I wasn't presumptuous."

He loved her innocence. "Absolutely, I want you in bed tonight so I can ravish you all night long."

Addison blushed and just then his cousins broke their moment as they entered the foyer.

Bree came forward first with her hand extended. "Hi, I'm Bree Hart, Caleb's cousin, and this is my sister, Jada." Bree motioned her over.

Addison shook Bree's hand, but it was Jada who leaned over and gave her a quick hug. "Welcome," Jada said. "C'mon in." She grasped one of Addison's arms and led her into the living room.

"Thank you," Addison said as she glanced behind Caleb, who followed them.

Caleb knew she would feel more at ease for the evening having his cousins around, though he doubted she really knew what he had in store for her once his cousins were gone. She was going to get very little sleep tonight.

ADDISON HADN'T EXPECTED SUCH a warm greeting or that she would be meeting so many members of Caleb's family. It told her he respected her.

"You must be Addison," an older gentleman said, coming toward her while the two women sat on a loveseat across from Caleb, who'd parked himself on the sofa.

"I am."

"I'm Duke Hart, Caleb's uncle."

"Great to meet you, Mr. Hart."

"There's no formalities in my house." He too offered her a hug. "Please call me Duke."

Addison smiled. "Duke it is." She accepted his hug and was somewhat shocked when Caleb pulled her toward him on the sofa and forced her to sit on his lap. Didn't he realize how inappropriate it was for him to behave this way in front of company? Caleb didn't seem to care. He just wrapped his arm around her waist.

"Addison, you look really familiar," Jada said.

"Really?" Addison wiggled in Caleb's lap, uncomfortable at his open display of affection.

Jada snapped her fingers. "Oh, wait, did you have your coming out ball at the Dallas Country Club? You're Addison Walker."

Addison nodded. "I did. How did you know?"

"My sister has an amazing memory," Bree responded.

"Addison Walker," Duke said her name again. "I don't suppose you're related to Benjamin Walker?"

Addison detected a note of concern in his voice. "He's my father. You know him?"

Duke nodded. "We go way back."

"Enough about the past," Caleb said, glancing up at her. "Would you like a drink before dinner?"

"I'm sorry, Addison," Duke replied, walking over to the wet bar in the room. "Forgive my lack of manners. What would you like?"

"Nothing right now. Perhaps some wine with dinner?"

"Wine?" Caleb scoffed.

"Yes, wine," Bree quipped. "Some of us are civilized and would like something other than a beer. Isn't that right, Addison?" She glanced in her direction.

Addison laughed. "I'm going to have to agree with Bree on this one. I can drink the occasional beer, but it's not really my thing."

"You didn't seem to mind much on our first date."

"Oh, leave the girl be," Duke replied. "Let's head to the dining room. It's about that time."

Caleb smacked Addison's bottom, and she rose off

his lap so he could stand up. When his uncles and cousins left the room, Caleb held Addison back for several minutes.

"What—" She never finished the rest of her sentence because he planted his lips on hers.

Caleb had to kiss her. He stepped closer, pulling her into his arms. His mouth descended on hers yet again, and her lips instinctively parted, allowing him entry. Addison tilted her head slightly, making her lips more accessible to his demanding mouth. Sitting on the sofa, every nerve in his body had compelled him to kiss her, ravish her until he couldn't remember his own name. And when she'd wiggled her bottom earlier in his lap, he could feel his erection springing to life at her innocent action, but that's the affect Addison had on him.

He was happy to have her on his turf tonight and away from her father and his restrictions, but he couldn't wait for later when it would be just the two of them alone.

She wrapped her arms around his neck and connected with him in an almost primitive way. The erotic foreplay of their tongues fusing was arousing all sorts of sensations inside of him. "If you keep that up, we'll forego dinner," he said throatily.

"I didn't start this."

"No, you didn't," Caleb murmured, "but I'm more than ready to finish it."

"Ahem." A loud cough sounded from behind them, and Caleb turned to see Duke standing in the doorway. "C'mon, lovebirds. Dinner is ready."

~

In Caleb's opinion, the rest of the evening went splendidly. Addison had a natural, easy way about her that anyone who met her was bound to fall in love with. And he saw that happening with his cousins and Uncle Duke.

After dinner, while the girls chatted across the table, his uncle leaned over and whispered, "That's a mighty fine girl you've got yourself there, boy."

Caleb glanced at Addison, who must have sensed him watching because she shot him a sideways look and winked. "I know that," Caleb said, turning to Duke.

"Are you sure you know what you're doing?"

"What do you mean?"

Duke shrugged and picked up his bottle of Bud Light. "That's not a girl you want to mess with, if you get my drift."

"Who says I'm messing?"

Duke gave him an incredulous look.

"Okay, okay," Caleb whispered, "but there's something about her that I'm drawn to. Trust me. I know what I'm doing." He knew Uncle Duke was warning him to be careful, but he was a man who liked to live on the edge. Ignoring his advice, Caleb grasped Addison's hand. "We're going to call it a night," Caleb announced to everyone.

"Oh, of course," Jada said with a smile. "It was a pleasure meeting you, Addison."

"Likewise." Addison reached over and squeezed Jada's hand, then nodded at everyone and wished them a good night.

Caleb rushed Addison out of the dining room and down the corridor.

"Where are we going?" she asked.

"You'll see."

When he made it to the indoor solarium that housed a large indoor pool and hot tub, Caleb flipped a switch. The room came alive with soft lighting.

"Wow! This is amazing," Addison said as she walked on the mosaic-tiled floor. She glanced up and admired the glass sunroof and the moonlight streaming in.

"Uncle Duke put it in years ago, but no one hardly uses it," Caleb said from the opposite side of the pool. He toed off one of his cowboy boots and then the other. "That's why we can take advantage of it tonight." He began unbuttoning his shirt, and once it was undone, he tore it off and flung it across the pool at Addison. She caught it.

"Caleb," Addison said, glancing at the door they'd just come from, "what if someone comes in?"

He unlatched his belt buckle, and it fell with a thud on the tile. "Are you scared?"

"I-well, I-" She stumbled on her words. He loved that he made her nervous and uneasy. He was going to open her up to a whole new world of sensuality, one she would never forget.

"I think you are." Caleb reached for his zipper, removed a condom from his pocket and unzipped his jeans until they too fell on the floor. He stepped out of them until he was bare-chested and wearing nothing but his boxer briefs. That's when he started toward her.

Addison began backing up, trying to head toward the door, but Caleb knew she didn't want to leave. She was just nervous at getting caught. When he was a few feet away and Addison's back was against the door, that's when he made his move.

He bent down and swiftly removed his boxers until he was naked in front of her.

"Oh, my!" Addison exclaimed.

In three long strides, Caleb reached her and he wasted no time ridding Addison of the unwanted clothes that were preventing him from reaching the promised land. He stripped every stitch of clothing from her body, piece by delectable piece, until she was just as naked as he. His first thought was to drop to his knees and go down on her right then and there, but he resisted the urge and instead grasped her hand. He led her toward the pool, and she followed him into it.

"Oh, it's warm," Addison said, sounding surprised as she sank deeper into the water.

"I made sure of it," Caleb said, spinning around to face her.

Addison smiled wryly. "You sneaky devil. So you had this idea in mind?"

Caleb laughed devilishly. "If I said yes, would that surprise you?"

"Everything you do surprises me, Caleb Hart."

"Happy to hear it." Caleb pulled Addison toward him and kissed her passionately.

He wanted so badly to *taste* her. He pushed her backward toward the pool steps. He laid her against them, and her hair fell in swirls. He lifted her lower body to his mouth. He kissed her inner thighs until he found the place he ached to taste. That's when he placed heated kisses there. Addison lifted her hips, arching off the steps.

Addison was beside herself. The need for modesty or inhibitions vanished as Caleb made love to her with his mouth. She unabashedly opened her legs so his lips could cover the center of her as his tongue delved in and out with delicious sweetness. "Caleb!" she screamed.

He didn't stop, instead he nipped and licked and

teased her relentlessly. Addison didn't care who heard her because Caleb was feasting on her like she was his next meal. When he dove in again with sweeping thrusts of his tongue, a moan struggled to escape her mouth. He was doing all sorts of wicked things to her, and her thighs began to quake as an earth-shattering climax rocked her.

She was still trembling when she felt Caleb's hardened tip at the juncture of her thighs, and when he thrust inside her, she rose and met him. She hadn't quite recovered from her orgasm, and Caleb was already sliding in and out. He chartered a pleasure cruise for them both, and Addison wasn't going to just lie back and let him lead. She wrapped her legs around his waist and took him in deeper.

"Oh, yes, babe, like that," Caleb urged.

He navigated her by squeezing her butt, and soon Addison was feeling her muscles spasm as yet another mind-bending climax hit her. Caleb began to buck wildly, and Addison felt his release and he yelled her name.

10

"Caleb, when are you coming home?" Rylee asked the following morning. He'd just left Addison in his bed at Uncle Duke's and was on his way downstairs to fetch coffee for them both when Rylee had called. Not that he didn't love his sister, but she was the last person he wanted to talk to right now. "I thought you were returning today, but Amar told me that you told him not to send the jet."

"That's right," Caleb replied as he padded into the kitchen. Thankfully, it was empty and his cousins and uncle were nowhere in sight. As he walked toward the coffeemaker, he noticed that someone had graciously made a pot that was still on the warmer.

"You promised."

"I know," Caleb said, holding his cellphone in the crook of his neck as he walked over to the cabinet to remove two coffee mugs, "but I have a few loose ends here, and I will need a couple of more days. Don't worry, sis. I'll be back in time for the rehearsal dinner and your big day."

"Why the delay? I called and your event ends tonight. There's no reason you can't come back to Golden Oaks after."

"Wow! Were you checking up on me?" Caleb walked back to the coffeepot and poured himself a mug.

"No, of course not." Rylee sounded like she was insulted by the comment. Then she said, "What are you hiding from me, Caleb?"

"Nothing," he replied hastily. "I just have some things I need to take care of here first."

"Like what?"

"Has anyone ever told you that you're nosy?"

"Yeah, but as I recall when I was dating Amar, you wouldn't let the matter rest, which could only mean ... this is about a woman, isn't it? You're staying in Dallas because of a female."

Damn her, thought Caleb. How was it that Rylee could read him even when he wasn't in person? "If you must know, I am spending some time with a woman."

"I knew it! You were being too sketchy with details. So give it up, who is she? How did you two meet?"

"I'm not getting into all the details with you, Rylee, but suffice it to say I'll be here a bit longer than anticipated."

"Bring her to the wedding."

Caleb nearly choked on his coffee. "Excuse me?"

"You heard me correctly," Rylee said. "You should bring her to the wedding as your plus-one."

"No way."

"Why not? It is common practice to bring a date to a wedding."

"Yeah, but women get ideas at weddings."

"It's just a date, for goodness sake, Caleb," Rylee huffed. "And who knows, you might have more fun. I mean we'll all be coupled up, me and Amar, Noah and Chynna, Kenya and Lucas. You don't want to be the odd man out."

Rylee had a point. His siblings *would* be coupled up, and he would be trying to find the nearest watering hole to put himself out of his misery. But if he brought Addison, he wouldn't feel left out and she would maybe make the event more tolerable. They'd been having a spectacular time together, in *and* out of the sack. Having her in his bed for a few more days before their relationship inevitably ended would be an added benefit.

"Alright, Rylee. I'll ask Addison."

"That's her name—Addison?"

"Yes." And that's all Caleb was going to offer, otherwise, his sister would sic Amar's right-hand man Sharif on them and have him compile a dossier on Addison before she even walked onto Golden Oaks soil.

"Excellent. Well, I look forward to meeting Addison, and I will add her to the guest list and adjust the seating arrangements. See you soon."

"Later." Caleb rolled his eyes. God help him. What had he just agreed to and what had he gotten himself into?

ADDISON AWOKE to an empty king-size bed, much to her chagrin. She sat up and let the sheet fall from her bosom as she spread her arms out. She couldn't believe how comfortable she felt in spite of being completely naked. Caleb had a way of making her feel at ease. Whenever she was with him, it was like her feet barely touched the ground. She supposed that was his easygoing nature, but deep down she knew she was starting to develop feelings for him. It wasn't a smart move considering he was a bull rider and they were known for not staying in one place. But she couldn't help it; she was falling for him.

Just then, Caleb walked into the bedroom, bare-chested and holding two mugs, which she could only assume held coffee. He came toward her, bent down and brushed his lips across hers before sitting and handing her a mug. "For you, my dear."

She smiled. "Thank you." She bent to take a sip, but he stopped her.

"I warn you, it's black. How I drink mine."

"That's fine," Addison said, sipping the coffee. She hated it black, but could live with it if it meant she had her morning dose of caffeine. She glanced up and saw Caleb staring at her. "I must look a sight." She pushed her curls out of her face. Usually she had time to straighten her hair before he saw her.

"Don't." Caleb stroked her cheek. "You're beautiful."

"Now, I know you're lying." She attempted a laugh. "I have bedhead, and I could use a toothbrush."

He grinned and put down his mug on the night-stand before reaching for hers and placing it next to his. Then he pushed her backward against the pillows and lay atop her so he could look into her eyes. "I like you earthy."

"Earthy, huh? You have high expectations."

He looked at her again with a funny expression, and it made her nervous. "What? What is it, Caleb?"

Instead of answering, he moved off her and leaned against his side. "What are you up to this weekend?"

Addison shrugged. "No real plans. Collette and I might do some shopping. Why?"

"Well—"

She leaned over and tilted his chin so she could see his eyes. "Well what?"

"I was wondering, if you didn't have any plans, if you-you'd be my plus-one at my sister's wedding this weekend. It's at my family ranch in Tucson, so we'd have to fly there, but I could bring you back in time for work on Monday."

Addison smiled as Caleb rambled on. When he stopped long enough to take a breath, she asked, "So you want me to be your wedding date?"

His dark-brown eyes peered into hers, and Addison's heart began beating loudly. "Yes, I want you with me. Th-that's if you want to come."

Addison nodded. She couldn't believe he was asking her to his home, where she would meet his entire family. This was a huge step, but one she would totally take with him. "Of course I'll go with you."

"You will?"

It was the first time Addison had heard the normally confident Caleb unsure of himself. "Absolutely, it'll be fun. When do we leave?"

"Day after tomorrow, if that's okay with you."

She inclined her head. "It will give me enough time to take care of a few things before we go." She started to get up so she could get on the road, but Caleb pulled her back down onto the bed.

"Oh, no you don't," he said. "You didn't think I was finished with you, did you?"

~

AN HOUR LATER, after they'd showered and dressed, Caleb was walking Addison to the car when she heard gunshots.

"What was that?" Alarmed, she looked around at the house and surrounding land.

Caleb smiled. "Oh, that? Probably my cousins on

the gun range. C'mon," he said, grabbing her hand, "I'll show you." He walked around the back of the mansion to the opposite side of the property. There, his uncle, Jada and Bree stood holding rifles.

As Jada loaded her rifle with ammunition, she looked up. "We didn't wake you, did we?"

"Of course we didn't," Bree answered for them and glanced at her watch. "It's nearly ten o'clock."

"So?" Caleb asked, cocking a brow. "Some of us *do* work long hours."

"Bullshit!" Bree snorted.

"Thanks a lot, cuz." Caleb frowned.

Bree laughed, turned around with her rifle, unlocked it and then cocked it again. "If the shoe fits." Then she fired. She hit the target dead-center.

"Good shot!" Caleb said.

"You'd be good too if you practiced."

"I'm good enough," Caleb replied, "but Addison here could learn how to use a weapon." He pushed her toward his cousins. "Why don't you guys show her a little something while I talk to Uncle Duke?"

"But ..." Addison tried to shake her head, but Jada and Bree weren't having it and pushed her toward the table where the weapons lay. They began going over the different weapons from the handgun to the Glock to the rifle to the AK-47 that their father owned.

"We prefer to stay away from that," Jada said, eyeing the AK-47, "but if you want to try it, by all means."

"No thank you," Addison said.

"C'mon, don't tell me your Daddy didn't teach you how to shoot," Bree teased. "You're a Texan. It's like a rite of passage."

"Much to Caleb's surprise, I'm no novice," Addison said, reaching for the rifle and reloading it with ammo. "I know my way around a weapon." She turned back toward her target and fired off several rounds.

When she was finished, she handed the rifle back to Jada.

She and Bree were both staring back at her in shock. "I may be a Southern lady," Addison responded, "but like you said, I'm a Texan, through and through."

"WHAT'S WRONG, SON?" Duke asked when Caleb pulled him several yards away from the women to talk.

"I think I made a mistake."

Concern was etched on Duke's weathered face. "What did you do?"

Caleb leaned his head toward Duke so he could whisper. "I asked Addison to come with me to Rylee's wedding."

"And that's a mistake?"

"What if she gets the wrong idea? You know how women get around weddings. They start getting ideas." Caleb didn't want to send mixed messages to Addison. He was looking for fun, nothing more.

Duke chuckled. "Yeah, but you and Addison have had the talk, right?"

Caleb nodded.

"So you've made it clear to her that you're not looking for a commitment."

"Yes, sir."

"Then you've been upfront and honest with her. If she chooses to come with you, it's her decision. She knows the rules of engagement."

"I know that," Caleb replied, "but Addison's young and innocent, if you get my drift. I don't want to hurt her, but by the same token, I don't want to let her go. You know what I mean?"

"I do."

"So, was it like that with you and Jada and Bree's mom?"

Duke nodded. "Yeah, but I lost her by not being honest, by trying to be a player. You've done the exact opposite. So give Addison a little credit. She may be stronger than you think."

LATER THAT AFTERNOON back at home, Addison was blissed-out as she danced around her bedroom listening to Ariana Grande on her iPod docking station, so much so that she didn't see Collette standing in her doorway until she spun around.

"Collette!" Addison clutched the dress she'd been holding. "What are you doing here?"

Collette smiled broadly. "I came here to catch up with you since you've been hard to reach this week, and look at you," she said, motioning to Addison. "You're as giddy as a schoolgirl. I would ask what's gotten into you, but I know *who*."

Addison blushed at Collette's forthrightness, but then again that was her friend—she had no filter. She quickly sauntered toward Collette, grabbed her arm and pulled her into the room, but not before looking down the hall to make sure no one was listening. She could only imagine her father had spies, especially when she'd informed him last night not to plan on her return that evening.

"Why so secretive?" Collette asked, sitting on Addison's bed after she'd closed the door. "Your father knows you're seeing Caleb, right?"

Addison nodded. "Yes, but I don't have to rub it in his face when I know he disapproves."

"Ah, yes." Collette nodded her understanding. "Caleb is exactly the type of man our fathers warn us about. He's the ultimate bad boy, but that's the appeal. Is it not?"

"No, not at all," Addison said, coming forward to sit beside Collette.

"C'mon, Addy, this is the first time you've gone against your father's wishes. You've always done what was expected of you. Your father must be going batshit crazy that you're standing up to him."

"He's not happy with me, but it's *my life*."

"Damn right it is. So, bring me up to speed. What have I missed?"

Addison exhaled. *Oh Lord, where should I start?* "Collette ... Caleb has me spinning."

"Oh, does he?" She raised a brow. "And where does he have you doing this position?"

"Collette," Addison said, reaching across and swatting Collette's thigh, "you're incorrigible, you know that?"

"And that's why we make great friends. We're yin and yang. So stop stalling and spill the beans."

"He's so hot and sexy, my God! We can't keep our hands off each other. We're like two dogs in heat."

Collette laughed. "Do tell."

Addison glanced at the door, making sure it was closed before looking Collette right in the eye. "Caleb showed up to my office."

"And?"

Addison smirked and stared hard at Collette.

Collette's eyes grew large as saucers. "No, you didn't!"

Addison shook her head. "We did, but not in my office. We did it in the utility closet."

"Get the hell out!"

Addison laughed, throwing her head back. "Girlfriend, it was the hottest and most thrilling experience I've ever had. I thought when we snuck out of the all-girls school to go smoke pot on the roof that that was the most dangerous thing I'd ever done, but this—this was different. It was ..." Her voice trailed off.

"Illicit?" Collette offered.

Addison pointed her index finger at her friend. "Yes, that's it. It was illicit, which made it all the more exciting, knowing that someone might walk in or find us at any minute."

"I take it no one did?"

"That would be correct. Then I had to go back to my office and act like nothing had happened after Caleb had just—"

"Banged you in the utility closet."

"Don't be crass, Collette."

Collette grinned. "I'm sorry, but the fact that he can make you act completely out of your prim and proper character is an amazing feat. I have to give Caleb his props. Any other juicy tidbits you want to share? This is better than any soap opera or reality television show."

Addison couldn't resist a chuckle. "I'm so happy I can amuse you."

"Don't be so touchy. I want the dirt," Collette urged.

"Well, if you must know, he had me over to his uncle's place and I met his cousins before we snuck off and ended up in the solarium, where," she whispered, "the man made me come over and over again in every possible location before taking me upstairs and making me ride him. Jesus, I can barely walk." She laughed.

"I wish I had those sort of problems." Collette chuckled. "So, you guys are going at it like rabbits until what, he leaves for his next event?"

"I would have thought the same," Addison replied, "if he hadn't invited me to his sister's wedding this weekend."

"He did *what*?"

Addison grinned broadly. "That's right. He asked me to her wedding, where I'll get to meet *all* his family. So he must want something more, right?"

Collette shook her head. "That is very surprising, but Addy, I don't want you to get your hopes up that this might end in something other than a great weekend."

Addison stood up angrily and stalked over to the closet to hang up the dress she'd been thinking of taking with her on the trip to Arizona. Then she spun around. "But why else would he have invited me?"

"Because he doesn't want to go alone and clearly he enjoys your company."

"So you think I'm making too much of this?"

"Listen." Collette rose from the bed and walked over to Addison. She reached down and grasped one of her hands. "I don't want you to get your hopes up that this relationship will end up being anything other than casual. I don't want you to get hurt."

Addison snatched her hand away. "Now you sound like my father. I think I can figure out Caleb's feelings toward me. I am the one sleeping with him."

"You are," Collette admitted. "But he's also your first lover."

"So that means I know nothing? Give me a little credit, Collette."

"I do." Collette touched her chest. "I'm just cautioning you to be careful with your heart."

Addison turned away and began pulling more clothes off hangers. She couldn't face Collette because she was right. Deep down, Addison knew she was playing with fire, and if she got too close she knew she would get burned.

11

"We're here." Caleb turned off the engine of his red pickup and looked over at Addison.

She smiled and glanced out the window at his family's home. They'd just arrived to Golden Oaks after a two-hour flight from Dallas. He'd picked up his truck from the airport, where he usually parked for an extended trip, and had driven them to the ranch.

"Don't be nervous," he said right before he jumped out and walked behind the truck to come around and open the passenger door.

Addison slid down. She looked incredible. She'd chosen to wear her hair wavy, just the way he liked it, instead of straight as she did for work. He leaned down and brushed his lips across hers.

"Damn, Caleb, the girl just arrived. Give her some air," Caleb heard Noah say from above them.

Caleb turned around and saw Noah and his wife, Chynna, on the porch's front steps. Chynna was rubbing her very pregnant belly as she watched them.

"Shut it, Noah," Caleb replied, pointing his finger at his brother and giving Addison a wink. "I believe I've caught you and Chynna necking a couple of times." He left Addison's side and unhooked the latch on the bed of the truck so he could remove their luggage.

Noah bounded down the stairs in several quick steps toward Addison. "Hi, I'm Noah. Caleb's brother." He stopped short when he got close to Addison, then stared at her for a long moment before giving her a quick hug.

"Couldn't tell," she said with a smile, which Noah returned with a smirk.

~

BEFORE CALEB COULD EVEN ASK for any help, Noah was right there beside him picking up the luggage. When it was all out of the bed, he gave Caleb a fierce hug. "It's good to see you, bro."

Caleb grinned. "You too. Where's Ma and Rylee?"

"Ma's running around making sure everything is perfect for tonight's rehearsal dinner. Especially with Amar's brothers coming over, she's beside herself."

Caleb was surprised. "Both his brothers?"

Noah nodded. "Yeah, I wouldn't have thought so either, since he didn't come to the bachelor party, but apparently Tariq and Khalid will be here."

"This is definitely going to be one heck of a wedding," Caleb said. "And Rylee?"

"Where else would our sister be?"

"In the stables," Caleb answered. He walked toward Addison. "C'mon, let's get you settled in my wing."

"Your wing?" Addison asked with surprise.

"Oh." Caleb paused on the steps. "I know I may appear to be just a poor rodeo schmuck, but I'm not." He grabbed one of her hands and led her up the steps before she could reply.

"I'm Chynna." His sister-in-law attempted to lean over and embrace Addison as Caleb showed her up the stairs, but Chynna's stomach prevented much other than a quick pat on the shoulders.

"Wow, I can't believe I'm meeting *the* Chynna James," Addison gushed. "I have all your music."

"Well, thank you." Chynna beamed. As much as his sister-in-law had become accustomed to the ranch lifestyle, she was still a superstar and loved the adoration.

"C'mon inside." Chynna grasped Addison's arm away from Caleb and led her to the foyer.

Caleb watched Chynna give her a tour, and as he and Noah headed up the steps to his wing, he could see she was impressed with the surroundings.

Once they were in Caleb's bedroom, Noah wasted no time giving him some heat. "You brought a girl home," Noah said. "I wouldn't have believed it if I hadn't seen it with my own eyes."

"Believe what?"

"That you would ever willingly bring a woman home," Noah responded. "But now I know why." He smiled knowingly.

"What?" Caleb was perplexed by Noah's behavior.

Noah walked to the bedroom door and shut it. "She," he pointed to the door, "is the girl from the club in Vegas, isn't she? The one you took back to the hotel but didn't manage to seal the deal with?"

Caleb frowned. "That wasn't my fault." He didn't appreciate having his manhood questioned. Joke or not.

"Never said it was, but there was something about that girl. You've mentioned her since that night and now ... you bring her to the wedding? Hell, how the heck did you reconnect? I thought you didn't even exchange names."

"We didn't."

"Then how'd you find each other?"

"We weren't trying. I went with Uncle Duke to some uppity charity event in Dallas and imagine my surprise when I saw her standing by the bar. It was like a wish come true and well, let's just say I finally sealed the deal."

"I bet you did." Noah grinned. "And now you're sprung."

"Sprung," Caleb scoffed. "I'm not sprung. In fact, it's just the opposite. Addison is a very special girl and didn't have a whole lot of experience."

"And you don't want anyone else to have her?" Noah said. "Sounds awfully sprung to me."

"Don't go reading things into this invitation. I needed a date for the wedding 'cause all you guys are all coupled up. Since we've been spending the week together, Addison was the logical choice."

"If you say so." Noah headed for the door.

"I do," Caleb said, following him out. "When the week is over, I will go back to being the playboy you've all come to know and love."

"Sure you will, Caleb. Sure you will."

～

ADDISON COULDN'T BELIEVE how breathtaking Golden Oaks was. On the way to the main house, they'd passed tons of cattle and horses grazing in the pasture on land that looked like it went on for miles. And well, the Hart family estate was especially homey with its grand foyer and staircase, hardwood floors and stone fireplaces ... even with the stuffed deer heads that adorned the walls.

As they toured, Chynna rattled on to Addison about the history of the ranch for nearly a half-hour. She explained how Caleb's parents had owned the ranch for thirty-six years and how when Noah returned from college, he'd come back and helped them make it into a dude ranch. The estate was impressive, from the fitness, game and movie rooms to the business offices, racquetball court and indoor pool with Jacuzzi, sauna and massage room.

Addison didn't know what she'd expected, but it certainly wasn't this. Caleb was right when he'd berated her for thinking him poor because he was a bull rider. He was so independent and determined to find his own way; she'd forgotten that his family was quite wealthy.

In the corridor, they passed several pictures and Chynna explained, "That's Madelyn and Isaac, Caleb's parents, whom you'll meet this evening."

"And who's that?" Addison pointed to a curly-haired woman in a photo with a very attractive man who appeared to be of Mediterranean descent.

"That's Rylee, Caleb and Noah's sister and my BFF and her fiancé, soon-to-be husband Amar Bishop."

"He-he's—"

"Gorgeous!" Chynna whispered, turning to her with a smile. "It's okay, we've all thought it. Rylee has done quite well for herself. But Noah," Chynna said, glancing at a picture of her husband on the wall, "is the only man for me." She rubbed her belly, a sign of their love for each other.

"I hope to have that kind of love one day," Addison commented wistfully.

Chynna smiled. "You never know, you could have already found it."

"What do you mean?"

"You and Caleb."

"Oh, we are definitely nowhere near what you and Noah share."

"No, but you can get there," Chynna said. "Noah and I didn't have an easy road of it. And some of it got to play out in the public spotlight."

Addison nodded. She was a huge fan, and she'd seen the press dog them in the early stages of their romance.

"I can tell you I wasn't looking for love when my car crashed on this ranch a little less than two years ago, but I did and in the process I found a great love. I wish the same for you and Caleb."

"Thank you," Addison said, but she doubted it would be that easy. Caleb had made it very clear to her where they stood before they'd left Dallas. After she returned home and weathered her father's stony, silent disapproval, she'd gone back to Duke's with her packed bag, wherein Caleb had informed her that he was having a great time, but that he didn't want her to get the wrong impression.

"I enjoy spending time with you, Addison," Caleb had said. "But I'm not looking for commitment, okay?"

She'd tried to put on a brave front when she'd replied, "And what makes you think I am?"

He'd stroked her cheek and said, "Good, I just don't want to send you mixed messages. This wedding is a big deal for my sister and for my entire family, and I'm happy to have you share it with me because we mesh. But after it's over ..."

His voice had trailed off, and Addison had gotten the message loud and clear. After the wedding, their weeklong fling would be over. He'd effectively dashed her hopes that there might be more to their relationship than just great sex. Her first thought was that she wanted to leave and go back home, but the other part of her—the part deep down that she didn't let anyone see—wanted to be here with Caleb even if it meant that time together was short-lived.

"Addison!"

Addison blinked several times and noticed that Chynna was looking at her strangely. "What?"

"Are you okay? Did you hear a word I said?"

"I'm sorry, Chynna. I guess I'm a bit jetlagged."

"Oh, forgive me," Chynna said. "You're probably hungry too. Come with me to the kitchen because I could sure use a snack. This baby has me hungry all the time."

Addison stared fondly at Caleb's picture one more time before following Chynna.

"WELL, look at what the cat brought home," Rylee said when Caleb poked his head into a stall in the stables.

"Hello to you too." Caleb grinned when he saw his big sister. Though he was the youngest, because Rylee was a girl and only a year apart from him, he'd always felt protective of her.

Rylee rose to her feet, brushed off the hay from her jeans and rushed over to Caleb. He enveloped her in his arms. "Missed you, sis." He kissed her forehead.

"Missed you too," she said, then gave him a light punch. "That's for keeping me waiting."

"Ouch." He feigned being hurt.

"Please, that didn't even register. So, I'm waiting."

"I told you I was with Uncle Duke."

"And that you met someone. So where is she?" Rylee glanced behind him.

"At the main house with Chynna getting the grand tour."

"So she's really here," Rylee said, grabbing her medical bag.

"What's that supposed to mean? Did you think she was a figment of my imagination?"

Rylee laughed. "Of course not." She pushed him out the stall and closed it behind her. "It's just that you've never brought a woman home before."

"God, why is everyone making such a big deal out of this?" Caleb's voice rose. "She's my wedding date, that's it."

"Whoa! Whoa!" Rylee held up her hands in defense. "No need to get all riled up, but haven't you always been the one to give it to me straight? I believe you called me out about Amar on a number of occasions. Turnabout is fair play."

Caleb instantly softened. "Yeah, I had to give him hell, but he deserved it. He'd left you without a word at the Derby."

"Because his father was dying. Those were the last days he got to spend with him before he passed away last year."

"I still can't believe you're marrying royalty." Caleb shook his head in amazement.

"He's not royalty."

Caleb scoffed. "He would have been *King of Nasir*." He made light of the small kingdom on the outskirts of Dubai where Amar's father had once reigned.

"Yes, but he turned it over to his brother Khalid."

"Who I heard is coming to the wedding."

Rylee nodded. "I know. I was surprised when Amar told me, but he's made some progress with him.

I know Amar would like to have a stronger bond with Khalid like he has with his younger brother, Tariq. He wants what we have." She smiled.

"Oh, yeah, what's that?"

Rylee walked over to him and linked her arm with his. "Unconditional love."

ADDISON WAS nervous as she zipped up the blue sequined cocktail dress. She and Caleb were getting ready in his bedroom suite. Soon she would meet Caleb's entire family, and she wanted to make a good impression. Her sleeveless dress was simple, with a scalloped hemline, but fancy enough for a rehearsal dinner. Meeting Duke, Jada and Bree was one thing, but she was about to be introduced to Mr. and Mrs. Hart; Kenya, who was Chynna's twin; Kenya's fiancé, Lucas, and his family; and Rylee, Amar and Amar's family from Nasir who were royalty. It was a daunting task and butterflies were swarming in her belly.

"Let me help you with that," Caleb said, coming over to Addison as she admired herself in the mirror.

But instead of zipping up the dress, Addison could feel Caleb unzipping it. Then she felt Caleb's warm hands circling her waist and bringing her backside closer to him. "Caleb—don't start ..." But her voice faltered as he began nibbling her neck.

"What was that?" he asked.

"We'll be late," Addison said, "and I can't be late when I meet your parents for the first time."

Caleb spun her around and grasped her face as he peered into her eyes. "You really are nervous, aren't you?"

She nodded.

"Babe, don't be. My family is going to love you."

Addison took a deep breath. "I appreciate you saying that, but it's still nerve-racking. Now help me with this." She turned back around and this time, he zipped her dress.

"You look stunning. Good enough to eat, and I can't wait to do just that later."

Addison colored. Sometimes she wasn't used to Caleb's bold manner and forthright statements. "Let's go." She headed toward the door.

They ran into Jada, Bree and Duke in the foyer, along with another woman Addison had yet to meet. Duke greeted her with a hug while Jada said, "Addison, you look lovely."

"Yeah, I wish I could rock that dress," the other woman said. She was full-figured and tall, nearly five foot ten, with dark-brown, smooth skin; but it was her hair Addison loved. It was long and hung in dark curls down her back.

"I'm sorry, I don't believe we've met."

"Addison," Caleb said, stepping forward, "this is my cousin London. She's Duke's oldest."

"Great to meet you." Addison offered a smile.

"You too," London replied.

"Looks like the limos are here," Duke said just as Chynna and Noah descended the stairs.

"Are we late?" Chynna asked as she slowly made her way down.

"No, so take your time," Caleb replied. "That's my little nephew in there."

Several minutes later, they were all heading out the front door. Two limousines were lined up outside waiting for them. Caleb, Addison, Noah and Chynna got in one while Duke and his daughters got into the other.

"Where's your other half?" Caleb asked Chynna.

"Kenya, Lucas, Rylee and Amar went ahead," said Chynna, "so they could greet any early arrivals."

"I can't believe Rylee is getting married," said Caleb. "It seems like just the other day we were racing to the mountains to see who was the better horseman, or horsewoman in her case."

"Yeah," Noah concurred. "Our sis is all grown up."

The rest of the drive was sprinkled with other anecdotes about Caleb's family, and Addison soaked it all in. She was enjoying their time together even though she knew it wouldn't last, but it was nice to dream that just for a moment she too was part of this dynamic family.

About twenty minutes later, the limousine stopped in front of a large church. As Caleb helped Addison out of the backseat, she looked up to admire the house of worship's stylish architecture. Then hand in hand, they walked up the church's steps through the doors to meet the remaining members of the Hart clan.

As soon as she entered, the curly-haired woman from the picture came rushing toward her with open arms, and Addison realized she had nothing to worry about. "You must be Addison." Rylee Hart gave her a warm welcoming hug.

"Yes, I am," Addison said as they parted. "Congratulations, Rylee."

Rylee glanced over at Caleb. "You did good, baby brother." She curled her arm around Addison's. "C'-mon, let me introduce you to everyone." She headed down the aisle toward the altar. "You can come too," she said over her shoulder to Caleb.

~

CALEB WATCHED Addison as Rylee introduced her to his parents. Addison was the first woman he'd ever brought home to meet them, and he could see his parents were smitten by her. She was a total class act.

His mother greeted her in a similar fashion as Rylee had, and his father grasped her hand and shook it gently.

"Where have you been hiding her?" Madelyn Hart asked, turning to Caleb several feet away.

Caleb walked toward his parents. "I haven't been hiding her. We met a couple of weeks ago and then reconnected again in Dallas."

Amar and Lucas gave Caleb knowing glances. It was clear that they remembered meeting her in the Vegas nightclub, but his parents didn't need to know every detail. He walked next to Addison and slid his arm around her. "Must have been in the cards, right?" He tipped Addison's chin up to look at him.

When she did, he got lost in the innocence of her eyes. He wondered if he would ever tire of looking at her.

"Ahem!" His father coughed across from him, reminding him they'd been in the middle of a conversation.

Addison had that effect on him. Whenever she was around, he got caught up. Perhaps Noah was right. He'd thought he'd sprung Addison, but maybe the shoe was on the other foot?

"So, when are we getting started?" Caleb asked.

"That's a good question," Lucas said from their huddle. He was standing next to his mother and several other women, who, in Caleb's opinion, were inappropriately attired for a wedding rehearsal dinner. Two of them had on dresses too snug for their large bodies while the other female, who was slim, had on a dress so short, it was damn near indecent.

"They're Lucas's sisters from South Central LA," Rylee whispered in his ear. She had a way of reading Caleb's mind. It had always been like that between them. You would think they were twins, like Chynna and Kenya, the way they could be so in tune with each other.

"Figures," he replied.

"Forgive me," Amar said. "We're waiting on my brothers. They arrived late this afternoon and are coming from the Ritz- Carlton. Tariq texted me that they left the hotel thirty minutes ago, so they should be here—" He cut off his sentence. "They're here now."

All eyes glanced down the aisle to see two men and a woman strolling toward them. There was an air about the threesome that said, "We're important." One of the men, who was tall, olive-skinned and had straight jet-black hair, smiled broadly. He had the same facial features as Amar: square jaw, dark eyes and the same broad shoulders, which were prominent in the expensive dark suit he wore. He had to be Tariq, Amar's younger brother, Caleb thought.

The other man with the woman ... well, he wore a stone-cold expression and had eyes as chilly as ice. He wasn't as tall as his brother, but he had the same dark hair and olive skin. This had to be Khalid, the new King of Nasir, and the woman–his wife, Freya. She was petite, maybe five foot four, and she wore a simple, yet colorful hijab.

"Brother," Amar said, rushing toward Tariq, "I'm so glad you could make it."

"I wouldn't miss this for anything in the world," Tariq said. "I'm sorry I missed the bachelor party, but with the unrest in our neighboring country, I was needed at home."

Amar turned to his other brother. "Khalid, Freya, thank you for coming."

Khalid nodded. "It would be rude if we didn't."

Caleb couldn't resist laughing, to which his mother returned a chastising look.

"We are glad you both could come," his mother said, walking along with her husband toward both men. "I'm Madelyn and this is my husband, Isaac. Welcome to Tucson."

It didn't take long for Madelyn Hart to wrap both men around her little finger. Caleb was impressed by how she had a way with men that made them mush. She warmed up stuffy Khalid in no time. Soon the rehearsal was going along as scheduled.

AFTER HE GOT Addison settled in a pew, Caleb took his place as did everyone else in the double-wedding party, and they walked through the paces of the wedding.

When the rehearsal ended, they all took limousines back to Golden Oaks, where the rehearsal dinner was being held. Madelyn Hart had gone to great lengths to ensure the evening would go off without a hitch by hiring additional staff to oversee the evening. The house was full with wait staff, family, the wedding party and the family of the brides and grooms.

And the meal, well, Madelyn had outdone herself. The selection was gourmet and straight off something Caleb may have seen on the Food Network. While everyone busied themselves with getting settled after four delicious courses, Caleb took a moment and pulled Addison to the side and onto the terrace outside the great dining room. He knew it had to be overwhelming for her to meet all these new people in one night.

"How are you doing?" he asked, pulling off his suit jacket.

He hated wearing the damn thing, and the fact that the night air had a slight chill gave him a reason to wrap it around Addison's bare shoulders.

"I'm fine." She smiled at him.

He peered at her. "Are you sure about that? I know it has to be exhausting meeting that clan." He pointed in the direction of the French doors.

"It is," she answered. "I mean, there's nearly thirty people in there."

He laughed. "Yeah, I guess we Harts don't know how to do anything small."

Addison stared through the window at the guests milling around the room. "True, but I love it. I grew up the exact opposite. After my mom died, it's always been just me and my father. I would have loved to have been part of such a big family."

Caleb pulled Addison into his arms and stared at her. "Well, you can borrow mine anytime you want." He smiled, then he lowered his head and kissed her deeply.

The kiss took on an intensity he hadn't been angling for, but once they began, Caleb couldn't stop himself. Before he knew it, he was pushing Addison backward against the façade of the house. He grasped the sides of her face and plunged his tongue deep inside her mouth. She responded with a deep, throaty moan that made his manhood immediately come alive. He loved hearing her moan and that she enjoyed their kiss.

"Caleb," Addison said as she pulled away, "we can't. Your family is in the other room."

"Then we should get out of here and go upstairs to my room."

"That would be rude."

"The evening is over," Caleb responded, "and I've done my part. Now it's time for what I want." He pulled her closer so she could feel his swelling manhood. "And I want you, right now. So, it's out here or upstairs. What's it going to be?"

Addison chose upstairs. It didn't take long for him to remove their clothing, lay her down on his king-size bed and sheath himself with a condom before joining her. He grabbed one of her legs and wrapped it around him while he teased her womanly folds. She was already wet for him just as he knew she would be. Oh, God, he couldn't get enough of this woman, he thought, just as he sank deep inside her.

"Oh, yes," she cried out.

He sank deeper and deeper, joining them as one, and Addison took him all in and then began undulating underneath him. "Yes, babe," he murmured.

She moved her hips in a rhythm that he soon picked up. They made love ...

12

———

Addison was embarrassed as she entered the dining room the next morning. The entire Hart family was present, including Duke and his daughters. They had to have wondered what happened to her and Caleb last night after they'd disappeared. They must think her a hussy. Caleb had a way of making her behave inappropriately and do things she would never do.

"Good morning," she said brightly as Caleb pulled out her chair and she sat beside Rylee.

Noah grinned as if he knew something, while Rylee said "Good morning" back.

"How did you sleep?" Caleb's mother asked.

Noah chuckled and Addison thought he might choke on his coffee because Chynna had to pat his back. "You okay, honey?"

He nodded, but Addison felt like everyone knew the truth. Several times throughout the night, she'd covered Caleb's mouth to prevent him from hollering when he orgasmed. She hadn't wanted anyone to hear them. Thankfully Amar, Lucas and both their families had gone back to the Ritz-Carlton because the men couldn't see their brides before the big day.

"My siblings and I have our own wings," Caleb had told her.

"Aren't your uncle and the girls staying in this wing?" Addison had asked. Afterward, he'd been much quieter.

Addison attempted to wipe the embarrassed expression off her face and finally answered Madelyn Hart's question. "I slept well. Thank you."

"Good," Madelyn replied, then turned to her daughter. "So, my dear," she said as she reached for Rylee's hand, "today's the day. Are you ready?"

Rylee smiled. "I can't wait to become Amar's wife."

"And you, Kenya?" Madelyn leaned over to reach for her. "How are you feeling today? I know I'm not your mama, but I'm here for you too."

Kenya beamed. "Thank you, Madelyn. And like my fellow bride," she said, glancing at Rylee, "I can't wait to marry the man I love. It was a long road with my work schedule and the Oscar, but I'm thrilled for this day."

"Alright, well let's get this party started," said Madelyn.

~

THE REST of the day went in slow motion for Addison. It was like she was watching the life she'd always wanted play out in front of her. A hairdresser came to do all of the ladies' hair while Rylee and Kenya both had facials. Addison was tickled to be included with Chynna, Jada, Bree and London. They made her feel at home, like one of the Hart clan. After hair, it was time for makeup.

It took several hours to complete them all, but eventually everyone was done and headed to get dressed before traveling to the church. Addison only caught sight of Caleb once when he stopped in to tell her that he was going to the hotel. He and Noah were going to help Amar and Lucas get ready. Tariq was standing up as Amar's best man while Noah would stand in for Lucas. Unfortunately, Lucas's former best friend and business partner, Eli Ross, had embezzled funds and nearly gotten Kenya raped when she was impersonating Chynna. Eli was now in the LA County Jail, so Noah was standing up as Lucas's best man.

"I'll see you soon, baby," Caleb said when he kissed her in the foyer.

"Promise?" Addison was already starting to miss him.

"Promise," he whispered and lightly nipped her nose before leaving.

~

"You were looking an awful lot like a couple right then," Noah commented when Caleb entered the limousine several minutes later.

"Don't start, Noah," Caleb said as he pointed his finger at him.

Noah shrugged. "I'm just saying, last night and just then you looked really happy."

Caleb turned to look at Noah. "Really?"

"Yeah, I think it's the happiest I've ever seen you."

"Well, I am," Caleb said and stared out the window, effectively ending the conversation. He didn't want to talk about Addison. He was having a good time and that's all that mattered. He couldn't stop thinking about the softness of her skin or how good she'd tasted when he'd made her sit on his face last night and come. She'd been so shy and nervous, but once his tongue had invaded her, she'd been shy no longer.

Caleb was the first to jump out of the limo and head to the grooms' suite. The party had already started because when he and Noah arrived, the men were already sipping champagne.

~

SEVERAL HOURS LATER, Caleb grinned when he saw Rylee come down the aisle. His sister was stunning in the one-of-a-kind designer dress that Amar insisted she have, but as much as Caleb loved her, she wasn't anywhere near as beautiful as a certain woman sitting several pews behind the bridal family in the cathedral.

He'd only seen her briefly when he'd stopped by the bridal suite earlier. She'd donned the pale pink, strapless tulle gown and looked like a goddess. Chynna had tried to shoo him away, but he had reminded her he wasn't the groom and wanted to see his lady.

"Caleb." Addison had grinned. "You're supposed to be in position."

"I know," he had said, "but I had to see you, make sure you're okay."

"I'm a big girl. You need to stop worrying about me. Your family is amazing, and they've all treated me wonderfully. So you can stop worrying and go back and fulfill your groomsmen's duties, okay?"

"But ..." He had pouted. "What about a kiss?"

"You'll mess up my makeup. Now shoo." Addison had pushed him toward the door.

He made another pouty face before taking his leave. When he had returned to his position, the guys made fun of him and told him he was whipped, but

Caleb had brushed it off. He'd seen Addison, and now all was right with the world.

He brought himself back to the present. Minutes later, Rylee and Amar were about to recite their vows, and then Kenya and Lucas would follow suit. Caleb listened as Amar spoke first.

"From the moment I laid eyes on you, Rylee," Amar began, "there has never been another woman for me. You've seen me at my best and worst. You've gotten me through grief and all my emotional baggage. And yet you still love me. I'm a better person, a better man who is capable of loving and being loved because of you. You're my soulmate, Rylee Hart, and I look forward to sharing our life together as a married couple."

Rylee looked up into her soon-to-be husband's teary eyes. She thanked him for never giving up on their love, which she acknowledged had had a rocky start, and for not letting his fear of commitment get in the way of their happy ending. "Your strength, confidence and loyalty have shown me that you're the man I want to spend the rest of my life with," she said, her voice shaking with joy. "You're the man I want to father my children. You're the man I want to grow old with. And I can't wait to be your wife."

Kenya and Lucas's relationship had also not had an easy trip to the altar. The sentiments they expressed to one another were similar to Rylee's and Amar's.

"You learned my true identity in the worst way possible," Kenya said as she held Lucas's hand, alluding to the fact she'd been impersonating Chynna at the start of their relationship. "Many wouldn't have blamed you if you'd walked away, but you forgave me the lies and saw deep down inside to the real me that I rarely let anyone see. You helped me grow into the strong, confident woman who can stand here today and say that I love you more than life itself."

Tears fell from Lucas's dark eyes. "We know what we have because we've fought hard to keep it," he said, losing his battle to fight back more tears. "I know you're not perfect, and I accept you with all your flaws because I love you. And that's why I know that we will thrive in the sanctity of marriage—because we know how to endure the hard times. Why? Because love is patient, love is kind. It does not envy, it does not boast, it is not proud. It is not rude, it is not self-seeking, it is not easily angered. It keeps no record of wrongs. Love does not delight in evil but rejoices with the truth. It always protects, always trusts, always hopes, always perseveres. That's the kind of love we have, Kenya. And I promise to be patient, kind and loving and to always protect you and our family, to always preserve us and never give up, because you're the woman of my dreams, Kenya James."

At those words, family and friends burst out in clapping, tears and smiles.

Caleb was so stunned by what he'd heard that he failed to clap. He had been struck by how each couple had endured heartache to get to the point where they could commit to each other in front of God, their family and friends. He wasn't sure he could ever do it. He glanced over at his parents. He had an example of what enduring love looked like, yet it scared him to death. Would he ever be able to let go? And was Addison the woman to make him want to?

~

Addison was enjoying the wedding reception at the Ritz- Carlton about thirty minutes outside of Tucson. The mountain setting was picturesque. The double wedding was nothing short of spectacular. She couldn't believe she was amongst royalty and then there was the press all eager to get an exclusive of Oscar- winning actress Kenya James's wedding dress. Because they'd had a double to fool the paparazzi, they hadn't caught sight of Kenya. The press had also been shut out of the reception even though helicopters were flying overhead. In the bridal suite, she'd heard Kenya and Lucas would release wedding photos in their own time, the way they wanted to.

Addison was happy she didn't have those kinds of problems, but she also knew that her weekend was almost over. She would be heading back to Dallas the day after tomorrow and her time with Caleb would come to its inevitable end. During the day, she'd imagined that they were as happy and in love as the other couples in his family.

She'd pictured them dancing the night away and announcing their engagement to everyone. His mother would be over the moon, and his father would be tickled pink to add another member to the ever-expanding Hart clan. She thought about all of Caleb's cousins congratulating them and talking over wedding plans. But none of that happened except the dancing.

She'd been sitting at one of the round tables with Duke and Caleb's cousins London, Jada and Bree when Caleb suddenly appeared, having left the main wedding party table on the stage. He'd removed his overcoat and tie and loosened the first few buttons on his tuxedo shirt. "May I have this dance?" He offered her his hand.

"Yes, you may." Addison accepted the proffered

arm and allowed him to lead her onto the floor, where the newlyweds were having their first dance. When Caleb's large masculine hand joined with hers, Addison's breath hitched. She was amazed at how giddy she became at his touch even after they'd shared a bed for nearly a week.

One hand moved down to rest on her waist while the other led her around the dancefloor. Caleb was smooth on his feet, and Addison easily followed along. "Did I tell you how beautiful you looked today?" he asked, peering at her.

"A few times." Addison smiled. "But I wouldn't mind hearing it again."

He looked deep into her eyes and said, "You're beautiful, Addison."

She could see that he meant it. He wasn't bullshitting her or telling her what she wanted to hear. "Thank you," she whispered. "Have I told you how much I've enjoyed the wedding, your family? It's been wonderful. Th-thank you for-for including me." She hadn't meant to get choked up, but the words came out in a rush.

"There was no one else I wanted to bring."

That warmed her but wasn't exactly what she needed to hear. She would take it though because it was all Caleb was willing to give.

They continued to sway to the music and even danced a few fast songs until it was time for the bouquet toss.

"Okay, we need all the single ladies over here," Rylee and Kenya yelled. "There are two opportunities to catch a bouquet."

Addison tried to stay in the background and allow Caleb's cousins to be front and center, but Rylee came forward and pulled her to the front next to her best friend, Camryn. "Don't you dare," Rylee teased. "One of you or both," she said, pointing to Camryn and Addison, "have to catch these."

Kenya threw her bouquet first, and Bree caught it. "You're next, you're next," several women teased Bree, including her sister Jada.

"No, I'm not. Marriage is not on the table for me yet," Bree replied stiffly.

"You're up next." Kenya looked over at Rylee as she lifted her wedding dress and left the dancefloor.

Addison glanced across the room, and if she wasn't mistaken there was a bead of sweat on Caleb's forehead. He probably didn't want her to catch the bouquet, but fate had something else in mind because Rylee's flowers came right toward her and she had no choice but to grab them.

Rylee was beaming and clapping her hands. Addison held up the bouquet and smiled. She glanced around for Caleb, but he seemed to have disappeared. Was he afraid that now that she'd caught it, she might be looking for something more? She didn't know how right she was.

CALEB FELT ill on the other side of the dancefloor. Addison had caught Rylee's bouquet. Damn! Visions of wedding dresses were probably already dancing around in her head. He must have looked petrified because Noah came over to see him.

"Hey, man, don't sweat so much. Otherwise it goes right through your shirt," Noah said, laughing.

"Does it show?" Caleb asked.

"The absolute look of terror on your face? It's just a bouquet, so lighten up, okay?"

Caleb inhaled deeply. He supposed Noah was right. He was probably making a bigger deal of it than it was. He was just catching his breath when Lucas and Amar yelled, "Where are our bachelors?" Then Amar added, hollering across the floor, "C'mon, Tariq, you know you're one."

"So are you, Caleb." Lucas eyed him standing in the back of the room with Noah. "Get your butt up here."

"Go take your medicine," Noah said, pushing Caleb toward the dancefloor.

Caleb stood next to Uncle Duke, Tariq, Sharif, Chynna's manager Deacon and several other single men quaking in their dress shoes. *God, please don't let me catch this garter*, Caleb prayed. His prayers were not answered. It was like the gods were against him because he caught Amar's garter; Tariq caught Lucas's.

"Put it on, put it on," the crowd chanted, urging both men to slide the garter on each of the women who'd caught a bouquet. As annoyed as he was that he'd caught the garter, Caleb wasn't about to let Tariq slide his hands up Addison's thigh.

He sauntered toward Addison, who was standing along the sidelines. "You ready to do this?"

She didn't say anything and merely walked toward one of two chairs that had been placed in the center room, as did Bree.

The DJ turned on some music to pump up the crowd. Tariq was very formal as he kneeled in front of Bree and asked if he could lift her skirt before sliding the garter up her leg.

Not to be outdone, Caleb danced around Addison before finally making his way to kneel in front of her. Addison's eyes were so focused on his that once again he became lost in those depths, but his conscience kicked in. He knew he had to stop this before it got out of hand.

"You know this is just for show?" he whispered, sliding the garter up her silky leg and thigh. When he was nearly to the promised land, he stopped and said, "To be continued." He rose to his feet and everyone clapped.

Addison was not happy, however, and quickly exited the dancefloor.

"Shit!" Caleb said underneath his breath. He was about to go after her when Rylee came toward him and put a hand on his chest.

"Don't!" she said. "I'll get her."

ADDISON PACED the terrace as she thought about what had just happened. In her daydream, she'd caught the bouquet and then Caleb had stated his undying love for her. But reality was far from that. Once Caleb had slid the garter on, he'd made it clear it was all for show and that it meant nothing to him, other than a means to an end later in the bedroom.

Why did she have to be so foolish? Why did she want something she would never have? Caleb was never going to be her prince charming and sweep her into his arms and declare his undying love for her. She needed to get her head out of the movies and romance novels.

She heard footsteps behind her and turned to see Rylee standing there in all her wedding glory. She broke down and started crying as she made her way to a nearby stone bench.

"Addison," Rylee said as she rushed toward where

Addison was sitting, "don't cry." Rylee sat next to her on the bench. "Please don't cry."

Addison shook her head. She didn't want to talk, especially to Rylee, who had everything that Addison one day hoped to have.

Rylee reached for her hand. "Addison, look at me."

"I can't." Addison lowered her head.

"Why not?"

"Because." Addison turned her head away. "Because I've been a fool."

"For falling in love with my brother?"

Addison turned around and stared at Rylee in bewilderment.

"If you're wondering how I know," Rylee responded, "it's because it's written all over your face. And all over his."

"It's not, Rylee. I don't know what you're seeing but Caleb is not in love with me."

"Not like you are with him?" Rylee said. "You can admit it to me, Addison. I won't betray your confidence."

"But Caleb's your brother."

"And you're the first woman to ever make my brother *feel*. And I want that for him. He's been more real with you than he ever has been. He's finally blossoming into the man I know he can be, not just some playboy with wanderlust and a love of riding bulls. There's more to my brother than that, if he'll only allow it."

Addison smiled through her tears. "I know that. He's amazing and I am falling for him, but he doesn't want me, correction, he only wants me physically. And I thought that would be enough, but, but it's not."

"Don't give up on him, Addison."

"I don't know, Rylee. I can't promise that. Not if he won't let me in."

Rylee nodded. "I know it's hard. Amar was that way too, but in time, I wore him down." Addison couldn't help but smile. "You just have to be patient, Addison, because I believe you're the woman for my brother, but you're going to have to fight for him, 'cause trust me, he won't make it easy for you."

"He sure as hell hasn't."

"Listen, I have to go." Rylee rose to her feet and gathered her skirt. "I'm headed for my honeymoon, but I hope to see you again real soon."

"Thank you, Rylee." Addison certainly hoped that was the case and that one day she too might be part of the Hart family.

13

***

The following morning, Caleb woke up ornery. He hadn't slept well the night before. It was the first time he and Addison had gone straight to bed without making love. Since they'd reconnected in Texas, every time they were together, they'd spent the night and much of the following morning being intimate, but last night he'd gone to bed horny, all because he'd opened his big mouth.

He knew why Addison was upset. It was because of what he'd said when he'd slid the garter up her thigh. He'd told her that it meant nothing, that if she had any ideas that the symbol might mean marriage, she was wrong. Dead wrong. And now he had the blue balls to prove it. Damn! Why had he been so harsh?

When he opened his eyes this morning, he'd found the bed and his room empty. No Addison. He showered and eventually went downstairs to find she was having breakfast in the morning room with his parents and the rest of the Harts.

"Good morning." He inclined his head to his father and kissed his mother's cheek before joining Addison, who was sitting next to his mother.

"Good morning," everyone echoed at the table.

Caleb kissed Addison's head as he sat beside her. "How are you?" he whispered so that only she could hear.

"I'm fine."

Fine? That didn't bode well for him. It meant he was definitely in the doghouse. He glanced up and saw Noah shaking his head. Caleb rolled his eyes. He knew he was in the wrong. Although he'd been honest with Addison from the start, he didn't have to be so crass and throw it in her face at such a sensitive moment. He'd regretted it as soon as he said it, but it had been too late. The hurt look on her face before she'd run away had spoken volumes.

It was no surprise that she'd steered clear of him for the remainder of the evening. When she'd returned to the ballroom, she hadn't spoken a word to him nor in in the limo ride with Noah and Chynna. As soon as they'd made it back to the ranch, Addison had gone upstairs with barely a whisper of goodnight.

Noah had felt the chill and asked Caleb about it, but Caleb had shrugged him off.

"Can we talk?" Caleb asked in a low tone.

Addison didn't even look up. She merely answered, "I'm having breakfast."

Caleb took that as his cue that she wasn't interested in talking about it now or at least not with an audience, so he leaned over to Bree at his side. "Can you pass the bacon?"

The rest of the breakfast was a typical Hart affair, with lots of laughing and talking. As expected, they rehashed parts of the wedding and reception.

"I can't believe you caught the bouquet, Bree," Jada teased. "Of all of us," she said, glancing around the table at the other single women, "you're the least likely to want to get married, considering you're tied to your Crackberry, I mean BlackBerry."

Everyone laughed.

Bree glared at her from across the table. "Some of us have other priorities. And it's not like I don't want to get married, there's just a few things I want to accomplish first before settling down with a husband and kids."

"It's possible to have it all," Chynna commented from the other end of the table. "Look at me."

Bree chuckled. "You're the exception, Chynna. I mean you're rich and famous and can hire a slew of nannies."

"Oh, there won't be any nannies raising my son," Noah replied as he sipped his coffee.

"I plan on being a full-time mom," Chynna said. "My son will know who his mommy is."

"Well, Bree wasn't the only woman to catch a bouquet," Madelyn Hart said. "I believe Addison caught one as well."

Caleb felt Addison instantly stiffen at his side. This was exactly the topic of conversation they didn't need.

"You needn't worry, Mrs. Hart," Addison said, wiping her mouth and rising to her feet. "Caleb is very content with his bachelorhood, so there's no chance it will ever be put to use. If you'll excuse me." She inclined her head to everyone sitting at the table and fled from the room.

All eyes turned to Caleb, and he wished the floor would open up and swallow him. Addison had put him in a tough position, and now the spotlight was shining on him.

His mother was the first to speak. "Caleb, what was that about? What did you do?"

"You mean, what did he say?" Noah smirked.

"Noah!" Chynna chastised him.

"Mom, not now." Caleb glanced at the door Addison had just left from.

"Well, aren't you going to go after her?" Isaac Hart asked.

"Your father's right," his mother added. "Addison is clearly upset; you need to go after her."

"I don't think she wants to hear anything I have to say."

"You won't know until you go talk to her," Uncle Duke chimed in. "Go make it right."

Caleb rose from the table and without a word left the room. He had to find Addison. Tell her that he hadn't meant to hurt her. Tell her that he enjoyed spending time with her and cared a great deal about her. Tell her she was the first woman he'd ever felt completely himself with and that he wanted them to end on a positive note.

AFTER ADDISON LEFT the dining room, she went on a walk around the grounds. Eventually, she walked past a Zen garden with a wheelbarrow and hammock, past a guesthouse and then headed toward the stables.

"Good morning," a stable hand said as she approached.

"Good morning," Addison replied.

"Would you like to go for a ride?"

A ride sounded wonderful. It would be a great way for her to clear her head and see the rest of the ranch. She wouldn't have a tour guide, but she could figure it out herself. "Yes, would love to."

"What horse would you like?" The man motioned to several stalls.

"I'd like the chestnut beauty," Addison said, walking over to the stall the chestnut mare had poked her head from.

"I'll saddle her up for you."

Several minutes later, the stable hand brought the horse outside. It was already saddled and ready for Addison to ride. "I put a cantina of water in the saddle and some trail mix in, in case you get hungry."

"Thank you."

He gave Addison a lift. She gave the mare a little kick, and it took off.

The wind blowing through her hair felt good. Addison enjoyed the ride and the beauty of the scenery, which helped put her troubles on the backburner. She passed by a hay storage facility, a dozen smaller guest cabins and another row of mini-houses she assumed housed the onsite staff. She didn't know where she was going, so she let the horse guide her.

She passed by the petting zoo and skeet shooting areas before reaching open land. It was so beautiful that she kept riding. After she'd ridden for what seemed like miles and miles, she took a break. She allowed the horse to graze while she sat on the dry earth and looked out over the horizon.

How had she gotten here? She was supposed to meet a random sexy stranger, have sex to end her virginal status and move on with her life. Instead, she'd gotten caught up in the moment. She'd gotten caught up in being with Caleb. Not only had the sex been amazing and exciting, but she'd fallen for the man when she'd sworn she wouldn't. She didn't think it would happen so fast. She'd known him for only a week, but it didn't matter. She was in love with him, and he didn't want her.

You know this is just for show? Those words echoed

in her mind. Caleb put on a show for everyone at the reception, like he was an actor in *The Best Man* movie. And just like the Quentin character, he only wanted her in bed, nothing more. As much as she might hope for another outcome, there wouldn't be a happy ending of him getting on his knee and proposing to her.

And so it was time to end this; it was time to move on. It would hurt like hell because Caleb was her first true love. She had to do it for her own preservation. But would she ever find a love or passion like this again?

Eventually, she started back toward the stables. She was surprised she could remember how to get back, but she supposed she was on autopilot. When she returned to the house, she would pack her bags, call a car service and take a flight back to Dallas. It would be costly at the last minute, but better she cut the cord quickly rather than drag it out another day. Plus, Addison wasn't sure she could sleep another night beside Caleb without succumbing not just to his charms, but to her own body's traitorous desire to be with him. It would be too easy to fall back into a pattern and allow him to make love to her until their bodies were spent.

She was nearly at the stables when she noticed a figure standing outside watching her as she approached. Addison didn't have to guess who it was. Caleb.

She slowed the chestnut's pace before coming to a stop a few inches away from him.

"Get down!" he ordered sharply, grabbing the mare's bridle.

"I don't appreciate—"

"I said, get down, now!"

Caleb's tone told her he wasn't to be trifled with and that she had better do as she was told. So she swung her leg over to disembark and felt his hands on her hips as he lowered her to the ground.

She glanced up to look at him, and she couldn't read his expression, so she remained silent. He took the reins from her and began walking the chestnut back into the stall. Addison watched from the doorway as he filled the horse's trough with water and fed her a few treats. "Good girl," she heard him whisper as he brushed her down.

Addison felt stupid just standing there watching him be gentle with the horse. She needed to start packing so she could get to the airport. She turned to head for the door when she heard, "What the hell were you thinking?"

～

CALEB WAS furious as he helped the mare cool down. He couldn't believe how reckless Addison had been. She'd just taken off on the horse with no thought for where she was or how to get back. She wasn't used to the tough desert conditions. What if she'd gotten lost? Golden Oaks was on hundreds of acres of land. Who knows how long it would have taken for them to find her. He'd read the stable hand the riot act, and the man had gone off in a huff.

Caleb wasn't mad at him, he was mad at himself for letting the situation get out of control. Addison wasn't thinking clearly, which could put her at risk if she wasn't used to her surroundings.

He'd ridden around the immediate tourist areas of the ranch as soon as he'd learned she'd taken off. When he hadn't found her, he stomped back to the house and huffed and puffed until his mother had reminded him that she was a grown woman and capable of looking after herself. "There's no need to worry just yet," Madelyn Hart had said.

"It's been four hours," Caleb had responded.

"Relax. There's probably no need to worry," his father had added.

So Caleb had gone back outside to the stables and paced. Then he'd heard the horse's hoofs and had immediately rushed outside to see Addison riding up as pretty as she pleased. She looked so sexy sitting astride that horse that he'd instantly wanted to pull her off and make her *ride him*.

"I was thinking," Addison said, turning to face him and answering his earlier question, "that I needed some time alone, or did I need to ask your permission?" Her eyes rained fire on him.

Caleb stopped brushing the mare and glared back at her. "No, but it was dangerous for you to go out on your own without an escort. Golden Oaks is extensive, and you could have gotten lost."

"I didn't think you cared."

Caleb threw down the brush and stalked toward her, grabbing her arms. "Dammit, I care, Addison," he said seconds before he lowered his mouth and kissed her hard. She tried to push at his chest, but he didn't let up. He kissed her with all the frustration he'd had over the last few hours worrying about her safety. He'd intended the kiss to be more of a punishment, but it didn't take long for it to change from anger to passion.

Soon Addison was moaning and wrapping her arms around him. He pushed her against the stall door across from the mare and slid his hands down her curves. God, he'd missed this last night. He hadn't known just how much until this very moment. Addison was his drug of choice, and he had to have a hit, now.

As he kissed her, he fiddled with the latch on the stall door. The stall was empty, as he knew it would be. He broke the kiss long enough to pull her inside and shut the door behind him. He deepened the kiss by sliding his tongue inside her mouth and exploring every crease and crevice. Addison returned his passion.

He didn't know which of them reached for the other's clothes, but his shirt was off before he knew what happened and she was caressing his chest with her warm hands. Soon he was unbuttoning the denim shirt she wore and pulling it loose from her jeans. He threw it on a stack of hay in the stall. He left her mouth long enough to plant kisses over her bare shoulder, nipping it lightly with his teeth while his hands came around to her back. He unclasped her bra, and she stepped backward, allowing it to fall to the floor.

When Addison's brown eyes fixed on his, Caleb forgot that they were in the horse stables and that anyone could walk in and find them making love. He lowered his head so he could feast on her bare breasts. He flicked his tongue over the already-swollen buds. He laved them with his tongue and then began sucking gently, one then the other, while she held his head in place.

"Oh, God!" Addison's head flew backward.

Caleb pulled her closer so he could fully taste each breast. While his tongue paid homage to them, his hands began exploring her stomach and waist until they came to the waistband of her jeans. He unzipped them, began easing them down her hips, and then lowered himself to his knees and helped her out of them and her bikini panties until she was completely naked to his admiring eyes. The jeans joined her shirt on the haystack.

"Don't ever do that to me again," Caleb stated just before he spread her legs, grasped her behind and lowered his head to her womanly center.

"Jesus!" Addison cried out when he inserted his tongue inside her.

There was no preamble. He just wanted to taste her and he did. Over and over. He slid his tongue in and out until her juices began to flow. When he was sure she was ready for him, he got to his feet and began unbuckling his jeans.

"Condom?"

Damn, it had been hard for him to think because she was teasing his earlobe with her tongue, driving him crazy. He let out a long sigh.

"P-pocket," he urged, and he felt her fiddling to get the protection out as he sprang free from his jeans. He kissed her neck, suckling her favorite spot. She moaned deeply, but didn't stop until she'd sheathed him.

He grasped her thigh in one hand, pushed her back against the stall door and thrust inside her. He grasped her behind and surged deeper. She accommodated him easily and began undulating against him. He grasped her other thigh and lifted her off her feet.

Addison began bouncing up and down on his shaft. "Oh, yes, baby," Caleb murmured. "That's it. Ride me."

With her upper back against the wall and Caleb holding her lower half, Addison wrapped her legs around his hips and alternately rode and bounced on him until his breathing became more and more labored.

"Jesus, Addison!" he groaned, but he didn't want her to stop.

And she didn't. He didn't how long they were at it before her entire body tensed and contractions began to overtake her. He grasped her shoulders, pulling her to him and kissing her long, hard and deep as his own climax hit with full force.

Caleb held on to her until the tremors began to subside. When her breathing began to return to normal, he lowered her to her feet.

She moved away from him and went to the haystack to collect her discarded clothes. Caleb didn't know why he felt so bereft afterward; maybe it was because deep down he knew that something had changed between them. He didn't want to let her go. When they were making love they were so in touch, he didn't want to lose her even though he knew it was inevitable.

He reached for his jeans and pulled another condom free and put it on his already-hardened penis. Just thinking about being with her one last time had caused him to get erect in minutes. He was behind Addison in one long stride. Her back was to him, and he grabbed ahold of her and began kissing her neck.

"Caleb, don't," she said, but when his hands came around and grasped her breasts and began tweaking them between his fingers, he felt her resolve weaken. To ensure she was his once more, he slid his hands down her flat stomach to the curls between her thighs. He parted her lips and slid his finger inside. She was still moist, and his penis got harder.

"I need you, Addy. Please don't deny me." Using his knees to spread her legs, he bent her forward against the haystack and entered her.

"Oh ...," Addison moaned as she clutched hay.

Caleb thrust inside her while his fingers played with her clitoris. Addison moaned louder and louder. He knew he was overstimulating her, but he wanted her to break for him. He knew their relationship was coming to an end, and he wanted her to remember him as the only man that could please her. His penis pumped deeper inside while his hands played with her sensitive flesh.

He smacked her behind with his free hand and she groaned, "Oh, God, yes ... Caleb."

Caleb was lost in being inside Addison and lay over her as he began thrusting feverishly. Perspiration dampened his forehead and chest, but he didn't stop. He fondled her breasts until they were peaks, his peaks. Then he pulled out and spun her around to face him. He wanted to look in her eyes as he made her come.

He saw her tears, but she didn't stop him when he lifted her onto the haystack, grasped her face and kissed her before entering her again. He lifted his head so he could see her eyes as he thrust inside her repeatedly. Her eyes became dilated, and he knew she was reaching her climax. He wanted to reach it with her and began pumping furiously. Just as her body trembled, his body began to contract and they climaxed together.

14

Addison dressed quietly in the stall. She couldn't look behind her at Caleb. How could she? He'd just proven that, yet again, she had no control when it came to him. For Christ's sake, he'd just made love to her in a stable at his family's ranch where anyone could have walked in and found her butt-ass naked having sex.

It was clear to her that Caleb was immensely attracted to her and enjoyed making love to her no matter the time or place. But what was also very clear was that she was fooling herself if she thought great sex would lead to something more. And they both knew it. Just now when they'd made love, there had been a finality to it. They knew they'd come to the end of the road, and it was time for her to go home.

When she turned, Caleb was already dressed. He'd been leaning against the stall watching her, for how long she didn't know. Was he waiting for her to say something? Was he waiting for her to beg him? Well, she wouldn't do that. She wasn't going to beg him to reconsider a future with her. If he didn't see it, didn't feel it, she wasn't about to throw out her pride and lay her heart bare.

"I'm leaving today," she said.

Caleb nodded. "I figured as much," he mumbled.

And you're not going to try to stop me? Her heart pleaded with him to say something.

"I'm going to go pack." She headed for the stall door. Caleb must have sensed her distress because he met her there and leaned his head against the back of hers.

"I'm sorry, Addy."

Heartache bubbled inside her and Addison thought she might lose it, but she merely nodded, opened the latch and fled the stable. She was running toward the main house when she saw Noah.

"Is everything okay?" Noah inquired, but Addison couldn't answer him. She just kept running until she made it to the safety of Caleb's suite. She closed the door and locked it. She didn't want to talk to or see anyone until it was time to go.

She went through the motions of calling the airline, a car service and Collette, who promised to meet her at the airport. Thank God for Collette, otherwise she'd be a wreck.

She was packed in record time, but stayed until the driver called to tell her he was near. That's when she made her way downstairs. She went to say her goodbyes and found that the family was out and about. Addison was happy for that. She could walk out of Caleb's life with a clean slate and never look back.

~

CLUTCHING HIS HEAD, Caleb was still sitting in the empty stall that he'd just shared with Addison. When he glanced up, he saw Noah in the doorway. "Don't start," Caleb said, rising to his feet. He brushed the hay off his jeans and started toward the door, but Noah blocked him.

"Get out of my way, Noah."

"No." Noah shoved him in the chest, and Caleb nearly fell backward, but righted himself.

"I'm not in the mood." Caleb's eyes were dark as black ice.

"What the hell is wrong with you?" Noah asked. "How could you break that girl's heart?"

Caleb paced the stall. "Listen, Noah, I told you I'm not going to talk about this with you right now."

"Then who with?" Noah glanced around him. "You don't have many friends 'cause you're always on the go. What are you running from? When are you going to stop long enough to see what's right in front of your face?"

Caleb lifted his chin defiantly. "And what's that?"

"That your ideal woman was right here. I saw it, hell, we all saw it. She's crazy about you and you feel the same way, but your dumb ass let her walk away."

Caleb rushed toward Noah and pushed him against the stall door. "Don't talk like you know everything, Noah." He pointed his index finger in his brother's face. "Not everyone can find two great loves in one lifetime like you."

"How would you know?" Noah countered. "You've never allowed yourself to be vulnerable and go there."

"I don't have to listen to this." This time Caleb was able to push past him and head to the stable exit.

"You'll regret this, Caleb. I promise you. You'll regret ever letting a good woman like Addison slip through your fingers."

As Caleb left the stables, he wondered if Noah was right. Would he regret letting Addison get away?

～

"ANOTHER TISSUE?" Collette asked as she rubbed Addison's back.

Addison had returned the day before, and she'd immediately gone to her room. She hadn't emerged from it in twenty-four hours. When her father had tried to see her, she'd refused to see him and told him to go away. She didn't want to hear him say "I told you." It would be like pouring salt in her wound, so she remained in bed. She'd been stone-faced when Collette had picked her up yesterday and hadn't wanted to talk, but eventually the façade she'd put on to get her through the day had crumbled and she was now crying in front of her best friend.

"Yes, thank you." Addison accepted the tissue.

"I know it's hard, Addy," Collette said. "Whenever you're as connected physically to a man, it connects you to them emotionally. We're just wired that way. But this too shall pass."

"I should have stuck to my original plan of a one-night stand," Addison said, scooting to sit up. "That's where I made my mistake."

"It wasn't a mistake to fall in love. And I don't want you thinking that way."

"Why not? It's the truth. My love was thrown back in my face."

"Because a one-night stand wasn't in the cards for you; you're just not made that way. It was meant for you to meet Caleb and fall in love. Isn't it better that you did and you know what it feels like?"

"If you're going to tell me it was better to have loved and lost than never to have loved at all, I'm going to hit you with this pillow," Addison threatened and held the pillow up.

"Threat by pillow," Collette laughed and shuddered. "I'm so scared."

Addison swung the pillow at Collette's head. The next thing she knew, Collette had grabbed one too and they were in a true pillow fight, just like when they were in middle school. Eventually, they yelled ceasefire and fell back onto the bed in a fit of laughter.

"We haven't done that in years." Addison turned to her side and peered at her friend.

"I know. It felt good, right?" Collette said.

Addison smiled. It did. It had taken her mind off Caleb, if only for a few moments. Collette was right. She couldn't regret the time she'd spent with Caleb— it had been the most incredible experience of her life. She would always remember him fondly as her first love.

CALEB SIGHED as he packed his suitcase at the hotel and prepared to hit the road for a rodeo event in Waco, Texas. It had been several weeks since Rylee's wedding, and he wasn't ready to go back home, so he'd signed up for a few more events. He hadn't been able to stay at Golden Oaks after Addison had left. It would've been too hard to sleep in his bed that they'd shared and remember how good it had been between them. Remember how good she'd felt in his arms. Remember her soft moans as he'd thrust inside her welcoming body.

God, just thinking about it now made him hard as granite. He had to focus on something else, like his next event and how he could win in bull riding. Another rider had been beating him left and right in the last few events, probably because his heart wasn't it.

He was still managing to do well with steer roping and tie-down roping, but he had to get his whole self back in the game because losing in bull riding was costing him money.

The next event in Waco had a pot of fifty thousand dollars attached and would go well with the nest egg he'd been setting aside. Caleb was sure everyone in the family thought he was spending his money on booze and women, but that was far from true. He was saving his earnings. He just had to figure out what to do with it all. Investing in Uncle Duke's next business venture might be a sound way to go.

After he won these next events, Caleb planned to hang up his rodeo hat and start getting down to business, namely the oil business. Duke was ready to hand over operations of Hart Enterprises to him, and it was time he took over the reins. He knew that didn't sit well with Bree, who thought because she was the most business-minded of Duke's daughters that she should take over. Or his son, Trent, who thought Caleb was taking his place. If Duke truly wanted to leave Hart Enterprises to Trent, Caleb would step aside and work underneath him, but that's not what Duke wanted. And Caleb wasn't about to pass over this opportunity to show his family that he was more than just a bull rider. Yes indeed, he was a businessman.

~

"Where are we going?" Addison asked Skylar. Their friend was being particularly cagey about where they were headed for ladies' night. Addison, Collette, Emma, Violet and Skylar had already left Dallas nearly an hour ago and were still on the road in a limo.

"You'll see," Skylar replied with a mischievous grin. "It's right up your alley."

They laughed and talked another hour or so before the limousine finally came to a halt. When they exited the vehicle, Addison looked up at the arena. "What's this all about?" she asked.

Collette poked her with her index finger and pointed in the direction of the marquee. It read "Heart O' Texas Fair and Rodeo." Addison's stomach plummeted instantly, and she thought she might faint. She hadn't been near a rodeo, much less a horse, in nearly four weeks because she hadn't wanted to think about Caleb. She'd been doing a good job of it ... until now.

"I don't think so," Collette said. "We're leaving." She started to get back inside the limo.

"What's the problem?" Skylar asked. "I mean, I saw the pictures of Addison with a certain Caleb Hart at his sister's double wedding with Kenya James. Oops, I mean Kenya Kingston now."

Addison's eyes widened. "How do you know about that?"

Skylar laughed and turned to the other girls. "C'mon, Addison. The pictures of the wedding were everywhere. I mean, Kenya and Lucas released them to the press. Imagine my surprise when I saw you in them. I had to Google him and find out who he was."

"And when you found out he was a bull rider, you decided to bring her here?" Collette said. "That's just great. You're a real piece of work, Skylar. I knew I was right about you years ago and should have steered clear."

"What's the problem?" Skylar bunched her shoulders. "I mean, I thought you'd be excited to see your main squeeze, Addison. Or has he already tired of you?"

"Oh, you're a real bitch!" Collette lunged for Skylar, but Addison and the other girls held her back.

"Collette, please," Addison whispered in her ear. "Please don't make this worse than it already it is."

"Fine, fine." Collette tried to shake free of them. "Let me go."

"It's none of your business what has or hasn't happened between me and Caleb."

"You and *Caleb*?" Emma asked, raising a brow.

"So there *was* something going on between you?" Skylar said. "Since Vegas?" When Addison didn't respond, Skylar continued, "Aren't you the sly devil? You certainly know how to keep a secret. Well, if it's over between you, you should have no problem going to the rodeo. I mean, unless you're afraid to see him."

"I'm not afraid."

"No? Prove it."

Collette walked past Skylar and faced Addison. "You don't have to prove anything to her, Addy. We can leave now or just stay out here in the limo and drink up all this champagne until it's over."

Addison shook her head. "No, she's right. It's over between Caleb and me, so let's go." She started walking toward the entrance without looking back.

Collette caught up to her after she'd walked several paces. She looped her arm with Addison's. "You don't have to do this, you know."

Addison turned to Collette. "I know that, but did you ever think I'm doing it for myself? To prove that I'm over him? I'm not as fragile as you may think."

"Alright, then I'm with you."

∼

ONCE THEY'D PROCURED some drinks and found their seats, Addison sat to watch the show. She was doing well until she heard the announcer say Caleb's name. It seemed like she was holding her breath forever before he finally came out for the first event, Bareback Bronco Riding, and it went well. He scored high and was among the event's top riders.

"How you doing?" Collette asked from her side.

Addison sipped her beer. "Fine." She was far from it. Her stomach had curled in knots at just hearing Caleb's name, but she wasn't going to show weakness. Or at least she didn't plan to.

After one too many beers to relax her nerves, however, she went to the ladies' room to relieve herself and that's when she saw him.

Caleb was surrounded by nearly half-a-dozen women as he signed autographs. Most of them were dressed in tight jeans and even tighter tops, which, given the size of their bosoms, was completely inappropriate, but Caleb didn't seem to mind. He seemed to be eating up all the attention. And if Addison wasn't mistaken, he was flirting with them.

One of the women was so blatant, she was bending down to retrieve a program for Caleb to sign, giving him a view of her ample breasts. His eyes were certainly wandering to do just that when he saw Addison from across the hall.

Time stood still for a moment and they just looked at each other, drinking in their fill, but just as quickly Addison remembered he didn't want her. He wanted this, this bachelor life with a different woman each night. Well, he was welcome to it.

"Addison!" she heard Caleb call out, but she'd already begun walking back toward the bleachers.

"Dammit!" Caleb cursed. Why did Addison have to see him with those groupies? He was just being friendly but wasn't interested in any of them. He hadn't wanted to be with any woman since Addison, so when he'd seen her standing behind the crowd staring at him, his heart had stopped. *What is she doing here?* he had wondered. *Is she here to see me?* He had to know and yelled out her name, but she was already walking away, walking away from him because he'd hurt her and she didn't want another dose.

He caught up to her before she reached the bleachers. He grabbed her arm. "Addison, wait!"

She spun on her heel and glared at him. Her stare was so icy cold that he immediately removed his hand. "Can we talk?"

When she didn't answer, he continued, "It's so good to see you." And it was. She looked damn good in snug skinny jeans, a sparkly top and leather boots.

"What do you want?" she asked impatiently.

"What are you doing here?"

"I'm here for the show."

He took a deep breath. She wasn't going to make this easy. "I know that, but—"

"You want to know if I'm here for you?" she asked. "Well I'm not. My bitch of a girlfriend sprung this on me when we arrived, so no, I'm not here for you."

Caleb nodded. "I deserve that. But that doesn't mean I'm not happy you're here."

Addison chuckled bitterly. "Why? So I can get you off?" She came closer until she was inches away from his face. "Do you need to take me in another utility closet?" She glanced behind him. "Or how about we go out there," she said, pointing in the direction of the arena, "and just put on a show for the crowd? Would that help your enormous ego?"

Caleb was shocked, not by her words, but that it showed him she still had feelings for him. There was a fine line between love and hate. And the hate she was spewing was out of character for her, which told him there was still hope.

Just then the lights blinked, reminding him that he had to get backstage and get ready for the next event: bull riding.

Caleb began walking backward. "I know you're mad at me, Addison, but we need to talk. There's unfinished business between us. Promise you'll stay after."

Addison shook her head. "No."

He stopped and stared at her. "Addison. We *need* to talk. You know we do. Promise me." The lights blinked again. "Promise me, Addison."

Several seconds ticked by before she eventually said, "I'll stay." Her words were heaven sent. He went backstage, and he felt like he was walking on air.

15

Addison didn't know why she'd agreed to stay at the rodeo. In her head, she knew she should leave, but her heart, her heart wouldn't allow her to do that. She wanted to stay and hear what he had to say. He was right when he said they had unfinished business, but was he ready to pick up where they left off or did he just want more of the same?

"Is everything okay?" Collette asked when Addison came back to sit on the bleachers. The rest of the girls were deep in conversation and hadn't seen her return.

"I just ran into Caleb."

"And?"

"He said he wanted to talk, that we had unfinished business."

"I don't know, Addison. I think you should steer clear of him," Collette replied.

"How can I, when he's here?"

"Because you're wearing your heart on your sleeve right now, and I fear that if Caleb puts the moves on you, like the player he is, you'll crumble and fall back into his bed and then where will you be?"

"Thanks for the vote of confidence, Colette."

"I'm just being honest and so should you. You

know I'm right. Can you really be objective about this?"

Deep down, Addison knew Collette was right. She should go, but her feet remained rooted in place. Maybe if she just saw him on the bull one last time, she could free herself?

The announcer called out the first rider, who proceeded to last on the ferocious bull for all of about ten seconds. The second rider didn't fare much better. And so it continued for nearly a half-hour before Caleb's name was called.

Addison wanted to turn away, but this might be the very last time she would see him and she needed to have one final look.

The announcer said, "And Caleb Hart is going to take a shot." His arm came down and the gates opened.

Seeing Caleb on the bull was frightening, especially because he was determinedly hanging on as the bull tried to flail him about. Addison's hand flew to her mouth as she watched Caleb thrash around on the bull's back. There was a moment when she thought the bull was going to throw him, but he doggedly held on.

Addison held her breath. It looked like he was going to make it without incident. The buzzer rang, signaling he'd won the round. As he was about to disembark, the bull made a run for it, flinging Caleb off its back like he was nothing more than a ragdoll. Addison watched in horror as Caleb hit the back of the arena enclosure, and before they could get help, the bull came charging at him and stomped him in the back.

"Omigod!" Addison turned away into Collette's

shoulder. She couldn't watch him be pummeled to death.

"It's okay, it's okay." Collette hugged her tightly to her bosom. "They've got him now."

Addison turned back around and saw the entire rodeo community was on its feet as emergency medical technicians took Caleb out on a stretcher. "I've got to go to him," Addison said and began pushing past several people in the bleachers.

"Okay, I'm behind you," said Collette, apologizing as she pushed her way through the throng of people eager to see what had happened.

Addison made it out of the bleachers and through the crowd by bulldozing anyone in her way. Her focus was singular: Caleb. She knew he was injured, but she didn't know how severe. Maybe it wasn't as bad as it appeared from the bleachers?

By the sheer tenacity of her will, she made it backstage, even past the guards who were trying to keep the onlookers at bay. That's when she saw the ambulance; she made a run for it as the EMTs put Caleb's lifeless body inside the vehicle and immobilized him for transport. He was on a long spinal board, and his neck was in a cervical collar.

"Let me through," she said to one guard who tried to hold her back. "I know him."

"Sure, lady. Everyone does."

"But I do," she pleaded. "He's my boyfriend. You have to let me pass. I have to get on that ambulance."

"Let her pass," ordered a deep masculine voice.

When Addison glanced up, she was thankful to see Josh, Caleb's friend whom she had met before. "Josh, thank God," she cried. "Please, I have to go with him."

"C'mon." Josh grasped her hand and pulled her past the guard and through the crowd.

Addison glanced back at Collette, who was being swallowed up in the masses. "I'll call you from the hospital," she yelled and rushed toward the ambulance just as they were closing the doors.

"Are you family?" the EMT asked.

"Yes," she lied. "I'm his fiancée." She knew it was a lie and more like wishful thinking, but she wasn't leaving Caleb's side, not now. Perhaps not ever.

THE NEXT FEW hours were excruciating for Addison. More because of the not knowing than anything else. During the short ambulance ride, Caleb had briefly opened his eyes and smiled when he saw her.

"This is some way to get my attention, cowboy," Addison tried to joke.

Caleb merely squeezed her hand before passing out again.

"Is he okay?" Addison asked, looking worriedly at the EMT.

"He's stable for now," he replied, "but we won't know how extensive the damages are until they run some tests. He definitely has a concussion and probably some internal injuries, but the doctors will tell you more."

Once they made it to the hospital, everything happened quickly. The doctor examined him and told her he was going to need tests before he could make a diagnosis. In the meanwhile, Addison had time on her hands, so she called Collette, who was already en route, and then she called Caleb's family.

Initially Madelyn Hart had been happy to hear

from her, but as soon as she heard the reason for the call, she dropped the phone. Isaac Hart was more stalwart than his wife and told Addison he would make arrangements to be there in a few hours. In the interim, he was sending Duke on their behalf if any major decisions came up between now and then.

Addison needn't have worried because before Collette could even arrive, Duke was already barging through the ER. "Where's my nephew?" he asked, raising his voice to anyone who would listen.

When Addison saw him, she rushed over. "Duke!"

He glanced up when he heard her voice and enveloped her in a big bear hug when he saw the absolute fear in her eyes. When they finally pulled away, he asked, "How's Caleb?"

Addison shook her head. "I don't know. They're still running tests, plus I'm not sure they bought that I was his fiancée since I wasn't wearing a ring." She held up her empty left hand.

"Don't you worry, girl," he said, pulling her toward him with a one-armed hug, "I'll get some answers."

Addison didn't know how long they waited in the ER before the doctor came out to speak with them. He was a tall, thin man with a receding hairline and wire-rimmed glasses. "Mr. Hart is awake."

"Oh, thank God!" Addison said, clutching Collette, who'd arrived several minutes after Duke.

"So, we'll have to limit visitors to one at a time."

"That's all fine and good, doc," Duke responded. "But how's my nephew? What's the prognosis?"

"It's still too early to tell," the doctor replied. "Caleb suffered a concussion and some broken bones, but—"

"But what?" Duke urged. "What are you saying?"

"The initial tests show some swelling and bruising

on his spine. We've given him a high dose of methyl-prednisolone for the swelling."

"And?"

"We'd like to take Caleb in for surgery to stabilize his spine."

"What about a less invasive approach—to allow the bones to heal naturally with the help of halo traction?" Addison asked. She'd looked it up online on her phone to find out as much as she could about spinal injuries.

"We could do that and try the wait and see approach," the doctor said.

"But you're obviously hedging your bets," Duke replied. "There's more, isn't there? What aren't you saying?"

The doctor sighed, clearly uneasy at being pushed into a corner, but Addison was with Duke and the doctor wasn't saying something. "If I had to speculate and present a worst-case scenario, Caleb could be paralyzed and you'll need to prepare him for his new reality."

"Omigod!" a woman screamed from behind Addison, and they all spun around.

It was Madelyn Hart. She'd arrived at just that moment with Caleb's father, Isaac, and Noah in tow and was falling to the floor.

"Sis." Duke rushed toward her, but Isaac shooed him away.

"I've got her," Isaac said, helping her toward a seat.

"Listen," the doctor said, "it's too early to make these pronouncements. Let's see how he reacts to the steroids and complete another round of tests in a day or so. In the meantime, who would like to go in first, one at a time?"

Several pairs of eyes landed on Addison. She

wanted to go and rush into Caleb's arms, but his mother was here. "Mrs. Hart, you should go see your son."

Isaac shook his head as she held his arm, sobbing softly. "You go on ahead. It's best she calm down before she goes in. Otherwise, Caleb will know something's wrong."

Addison glanced at Collette and then at Duke. "Go on," he agreed. "I'll be after you."

Addison nodded and slowly walked with the doctor down the long corridor toward Caleb's room.

When she arrived, the room was quiet save for the beeping of the machines. Caleb was lying still on the hospital bed, but as if he sensed her presence as she approached, his eyes popped open. "Hey, beautiful," he murmured groggily.

She tried for a half-smile when she reached him, but instead her emotions took over. She broke down and started crying and laid her head on his chest.

"It's okay," he said, caressing her head softly. "I'm okay. It was nothing more than a scratch."

At his attempt at a joke, Addison raised her head and looked into his eyes. There were several covered cuts and lacerations across his face from where the bull had attacked him, but there was a nasty one above his left eye that would leave a scar. "It was definitely more than a scratch."

He smiled wanly. "I'm glad you're here," he said, caressing her cheek. "When I woke up in the ambulance and saw you there, I thought I was dreaming, but now I can see I wasn't."

Addison's eyes filled with tears. There was no place she would have been but in that ambulance.

"And you're here now."

She nodded.

"I wa-wanna know what that means," Caleb said, "but these drugs they just gave me are amazing."

"It's okay." Addison nodded. "Sleep. Just so you know, your parents and Duke are here." But Caleb was already out like a light.

16

The next morning, Caleb knew something was wrong the moment he woke up and saw his mother's somber face. It wasn't that he was surprised she and his father had come. He was injured and he'd listed them and Duke as next of kin, but usually his mother was always happy and hopeful. This morning, however, she looked far from having either of those emotions.

"Mom?" Caleb attempted to rise and scoot himself backward, but when he pushed his arms down to lift himself up, he couldn't move. He immediately glanced at Noah, who was standing near the door, and for the first time in his life, his older brother didn't look him in the eye. Instead, Noah looked downward.

Frustrated, Caleb tried again to right himself into the seated position, but couldn't. "Dammit! Will someone tell me what's going on?"

"Son." His father came toward the bed.

"Don't son, me," Caleb spat. "I know that tone." He pointed his finger at his father. "That tone is never good news. So what is it? What the hell is wrong with me?"

"Please don't get agitated," his mother replied softly. "It won't help in your recovery." She walked to his bedside and began pouring him a cup of water from the container the nurse had left on his bedside tray.

"Don't tell me what to do!" Caleb yelled.

"Don't speak to your mama that way," Isaac said.

"I'm sorry, Ma," Caleb apologized, "but for Christ's sake, will you all stop looking at me with these sad faces and shoot straight from the hip. Noah?" He looked at his big brother. He trusted him more than any man.

Noah glanced up, and Caleb's heart sank. "It's your spine, Caleb. It's been badly damaged from the fall when the bull threw you and kicked you. He may have br-broken your b-back." His voice cracked. "Right now the doctor says your paralyzation could be temporary, but we won't know for sure until the swelling goes down."

"D-did, did you just say P-A-R-A-L-Y-Z-E-D?" Caleb yelled, his eyes widening with fear as the truth began to sink in.

Noah nodded and began walking toward the hospital bed, but Caleb stopped him. "Don't come any closer! I wouldn't want you to catch what I have."

"Caleb," his mother sighed aloud.

Caleb scratched his head. "Paralyzed?" He tried to move his body again, to wiggle his toes, but he couldn't and tears began to streak down his cheek. He didn't even know he was capable of crying until now. "Paralyzed." He balled his hands into fists and slammed them down hard on his legs, but still he felt nothing. "I can't be. I can't. I won't accept this."

"I'm sorry, son, but it's true," his father said. "We

don't know how long it's going to last, so you're going to need to go into occupational therapy to show you how to cope with everyday life. It'll help you with daily tasks such as dressing, bathing, and food preparation, going to the toilet, and learning to maneuver in a wheelchair."

Caleb's eyes followed his father's, and he saw the wheelchair sitting in the corner of the room. Was that device really his new reality? Was this some horrific nightmare that he would wake up from? He blinked several times wishing himself awake, but when he opened his eyes, his family was still staring at him with sadness.

"Get that thing out of my room," Caleb said, pointing to the chair.

"Caleb, you're going to need it to get around," his mother said.

"I don't care, Mama. I want it out. Now!"

Sensing his distress, Noah walked over to the chair and wheeled it out of the room.

Caleb leaned back in the bed and stared at the ceiling. "I would like you to all leave."

"Caleb ...," his mother murmured.

"C'mon, Maddie." Isaac used the nickname he called his wife when he was cross with her. "Let the boy breathe. It's a lot for him to take in right now."

Out of the corner of his eye, Caleb saw Noah return to the room, but Isaac Hart shook his head and said, "He wants to be alone."

When they were gone, Caleb threw the water pitcher at the door and watched water splash everywhere. He didn't give a shit. He was crippled, and his life was over.

ADDISON HAD HARDLY SLEPT the last couple of days. She'd spent most of them at the hospital waiting for news on Caleb until Collette had finally pulled her away to come home, get a few hours of sleep, shower and change.

Sleep had eluded her, so after tossing and turning on her bed, she finally gave up on sleep and showered. The hot pulsating water had done her good, and she felt rejuvenated and ready to deal with whatever life had in store. She was not, however, prepared for an encounter with her father.

"Addison, wait!" Benjamin Walker caught up with her in the hallway as she was on her way out the door.

"Yes, Daddy?"

He was dressed as he always was most weekends—in trousers and a button-down shirt—but instead of the smile he usually greeted her with, he wore a frown. He came toward her and assessed her frankly. "You look exhausted. Have you gotten any sleep?"

She shook her head. "Can't."

"Because that young man injured himself?"

"Why do you make it sound like that, Daddy? You act like *he* hurt himself, and that isn't what happened."

"But that's the life he chooses, is it not?"

She shook her head. "I don't want to hear this right now." She didn't want to hear it was Caleb's fault that he was lying in that hospital bed, possibly paralyzed. She'd done her research online after she'd showered. She knew the odds were not in his favor, but she was hoping for the best.

"Because it's the truth?" her father asked. When she sighed loudly, he continued, "Listen, baby girl. I'm sorry the man was critically injured, but that doesn't change the fact that your relationship with him was over before this accident. If you recall, you were the one who told me it was over between you two when you returned to Dallas after going to that wedding."

Addison rolled her eyes. "You're right. I did say it was over, but the other night changed everything."

"How so? Do you think that young man will marry you now when his entire future is on the line? I think not. You need to cut the cord." At her horrific expression he added, "No pun intended."

"It's not that easy, Daddy." Tears filled Addison's eyes.

"Because you love him, don't you?"

Addison nodded. "And I can't let him go."

"Then I'm sorry, because I think you're in for a world of hurt."

HER FATHER'S words echoed through Addison's mind as her heels clicked on the tile floor in the hospital corridor on the way to Caleb's room. Was she in for a world of hurt? Would Caleb hurt her again? She knew he had a rough road ahead of him and would need help in his recovery. She was prepared to stand by his side until he was the old Caleb again ... and *even* if he wasn't.

She found Noah leaning against the windowsill outside of Caleb's room. "How's the patient?" she asked.

"In a foul mood."

Fear shot through her. "Why? What happened, Noah?"

"Nothing happened. All the test results came in this morning."

"Dammit! I should have been here!" Addison berated herself. She should have never allowed Collette to talk her into going home. She should have been here when Caleb learned of his condition.

Noah touched her arm softly. "It wouldn't have mattered, Addison, and quite honestly, I don't think you would have wanted to be here."

"What did the doctors say?" Addison asked, even though she suspected the answer.

"That he has a lot of swelling on his spinal cord and that he's injured several areas of his thoracic and lumbar regions. They're giving him steroids to reduce the swelling in the hopes it'll give them a better idea if he'll recover. But the prognosis isn't good based on the initial tests."

Addison nodded. "So the doctor's worst-case scenario is true? Caleb could be paralyzed?"

Noah looked at her with the same dark-brown eyes that Caleb had. "Yeah, how did you know?"

"I did a little research online when I went home. I had to know more. How did he take the news?"

"He went out of his mind. Yelled at Mama and threw us all out of the room. He said he wanted to be alone. That was nearly four hours ago." He glanced at Caleb's door. "I want to go in there and help my brother, but what can I do? I can't help him, Addison." Noah's voice broke, and Addison pulled him into a hug.

She didn't know how she could be strong at this moment, but she knew she needed to be. She would be there for Caleb's family because they might be hers one day. They were both so wrapped up in emotion that hearing Noah's name coming from a female voice caused them both to pull away.

When Addison glanced up she saw Rylee nearly running down the hall toward them with Amar not far behind. Rylee reached them in seconds and grasped Noah's hands. "When Sharif got through to us on the island and told us about Caleb's accident, we chartered a plane and got back as fast as we could. How is he, Noah?"

Noah shook his head. "Not good." He pulled Rylee aside several feet while Amar walked toward Addison.

"How are you?" Amar asked, searching her face intently.

Addison glanced up at him. With his six-foot-four stature, Amar had such a regal bearing that before, when they'd met in Tucson, she'd been too intimidated, but not today. Addison felt like she'd aged in the span of a couple of days. "I'm hanging in there," she finally responded.

"Are you sure?" he asked. "I hate to be indelicate, but you look like you could use some rest."

Addison looked at Caleb's closed door. "It's been hard to sleep when Caleb's hurt and in pain."

Amar nodded. "I understand. I would feel the same way if anything happened to my Rylee. You will let me know if there's ever anything I can do for you?"

"I will." Addison was just about to head to Caleb's room when Rylee pushed past them.

"I'm going in there, Noah," Rylee huffed, looking at the door and then at her brother. "He can't keep us out here. We're his family. And for Christ's sake, I need to lay eyes on him for myself and know he's okay."

"Perhaps now is not—," Amar began, but Rylee was already barreling through the door.

And if Rylee was going in, thought Addison, so was she.

"GET OUT!" Caleb roared with his head facing the window. He didn't appreciate the interruption of his pity party.

"Caleb, it's me," Rylee said.

Hearing his sister's voice gave him pause, and he twisted as best he could to see her. Tears were streaming down her cheeks, which were rosy from her extended honeymoon.

"Rylee, you shouldn't have come. You should be on your honeymoon enjoying life, 'cause trust me, life can change on a dime." He was about to turn his head again, but Rylee tapped his arm and he glared at her.

"I'm sorry," she said. "Did I hurt you?"

He rolled his eyes. "You didn't hurt me. That's about the only thing I can feel right now."

"I know," Rylee said, wiping away her tears with the back of her hand, "but I couldn't stay away, Caleb, not when I heard you'd been hurt. You're my baby brother. I love you."

"Well, your love isn't going to do anything for me right now."

"Wow!" Rylee covered her mouth. "I've never known you to be this cruel."

Caleb snorted. "And I've never been paralyzed before and confined to a damn wheelchair, Rylee. Dammit! Why are you making be mean to you? You should leave."

"You want me to leave too?" Addison asked softly from behind them.

Caleb moved his head and saw her standing in the back of the room behind Rylee, Amar and Noah. Hadn't he told his brother to go? Shouldn't he be with his pregnant wife, who was ready to deliver at any moment?

Caleb thought about Addison's question for several moments. Did he want her to leave? Hell no, he didn't! But what did he have to offer Addison now? Before the accident, he'd been ready to tell her that he'd made a mistake and that he hadn't been able to get her out of his mind. She was the first woman he'd truly cared about. After the rodeo, he'd planned on telling her that he was willing to try commitment, but that had all changed the moment that bull flung him off and slammed its feet into his back.

He was a broken man now. In every way. After he'd kicked his family out of his room, he'd called the doctor back because he wanted to know how severe the paralysis was. He might not ever walk again, and they wouldn't know for a while if it was permanent. Okay, he'd gotten that. But Caleb had wanted to know if that also meant he would no longer be able to make love to a woman.

"I'm sorry, Caleb," the doctor had replied, "but incomplete paralysis does lead to a loss of sensory and sexual function." Absolute horror had overtaken him, and it must have shown on his face because the doctor had been quick to say, "Again, it's too early to know for sure, but yes, for now you're impotent."

And that's why he had to talk to Addison right away. She was too young to spend her time with a broken man unable to make love to her. As expressive and passionate as she was, Addison deserved a man who could not only give her the world, but make her toes curl. He wasn't that man anymore, and he would rather tell her now than let her waste her time hoping for a happy ending that might not ever come.

"No, I would like you to stay," Caleb replied. "We

need to talk. Rylee, Amar, Noah, can you please give us some privacy?"

Rylee stared back at him resolutely.

"Please," he stated more emphatically.

"Alright, but I'm not going far," Rylee said.

He knew she meant it, but that was different. Rylee was family. She was obligated to love him no matter what. Addison he needed to set free.

Several seconds later, the three of them departed, leaving Caleb and Addison alone.

As he patted a spot beside him on the hospital bed, he saw her perk up. She quietly walked over to him and sat on the edge. Her hand reached out and softly caressed his face. That tiny action broke his heart because he would never again feel her touch after today. He would never feel her wrapped in his arms.

"Addison, don't." Caleb pulled away.

"Why not? Why can't I touch you?"

Her question was innocent and naïve enough, but fraught with uneasiness.

"I'm so glad you're awake," she continued, not waiting for his answer. "Each time I've visited, you've been asleep."

"Yeah, well, I'm in pain and the medications they're pumping into me are no joke, puts me out like a light."

"I don't want to make your pain any worse," Addison said, rising from the bed.

"Things can't get much worse."

"Caleb, I know—"

He cut her off before she could finish. "Listen, Addison, we need to talk."

"There's nothing to talk about. There's no need to rehash the past few weeks. Let's just focus on your recovery, Caleb. I'm here for you, and I'll help you get through this however long it takes."

"However long it takes?" Caleb snorted. "Do you hear yourself? Do you even know what that means, Addison?"

"Don't patronize me, Caleb."

"Someone has to. You're living in a fantasy world. Do you think I'm just magically going to wake up and walk? I won't!" His voice began to rise. "I may not ever walk again. Do you realize what that means?"

"I—"

"It means I might be in that godforsaken wheelchair for the rest of my life. And do you think I want you by my side out of pity or worse, obligation? All because we shared a great week in bed. Well, I don't, Addison."

"Why are you being so hateful?" Addison turned away from him. "You're not the man I've come to care for."

He hated to hurt her this way, but he had to get through to her. There was no way he was going to be able to stand the next few weeks, let alone the next few months with her by his side if there was a chance he wouldn't recover. And according to the doctors, the odds were not in his favor. It was highly unlikely that he would make a full turnaround, and he had to accept and deal with that on his own terms. He couldn't afford the distraction of worrying about her feelings when his life and entire future were on the line.

"Because you're making me," Caleb responded. "If you would just go ..." He sighed and lowered his head. Using his upper body, he shifted himself away from Addison so he wouldn't have to look at her. *Why is she making this so hard?*

"And make it easy for you to cast me aside?" Addison walked around the bed to face him. "You would like that, wouldn't you? But I'm not going to make it easy for you, Caleb Hart. If you don't want me, you're going to have to tell me to my face."

Caleb lifted his head and stared in her eyes. "Alright, if you recall, you and I were supposed to be about good times, nothing more. We were never more than fuck buddies and now that those good times are over, you need to leave, but for some reason you can't get that through that naïve head of yours. You have visions of roses and sunshine. Well, that's not real life, Addison. This is." He slammed his fists on the bed. "Real life is ugly and nasty and not at all pretty. So here're the facts: I'm a cripple! A cripple who can't make love to you. So since you quite enjoyed my acrobatics in the bedroom, you should know that I won't be able to accommodate you anymore."

Almost instantly, Caleb felt the sting of the slap from Addison's palm. It was like he could feel her pain through her anger. She was red with it, but it was her eyes that said it all. He'd not only offended her, but he'd humiliated her too.

"You're a real bastard, Caleb," Addison cried. "You really know how to cut a girl deep."

"I aim to please."

Addison glared. "You must really feel less than a man to strike out at me this way."

"You need to leave, Addison, and not come back. There's nothing for you here."

Addison nodded in agreement. "You're right. There's nothing here, probably never was. Goodbye, Caleb." She turned around and walked out the door.

~

HOURS LATER, after the sun had long since set, Caleb sat in his hospital bed staring out the window. He'd been in pretty much the same position since Addison had left. Sending her away had cut deep, but he'd had to do it. It was simply what was right. He couldn't let her keep holding on, especially when he didn't have anything to offer and could make no promises.

A knock sounded on his door. "Come in."

Uncle Duke walked in, removing his cowboy hat as he approached Caleb. "How you doing, son?"

Caleb shook his head. He wasn't much in the mood for talking. After Addison had left, Rylee and Amar had tried to visit with him, but after an hour of his sullen mood even Rylee became fed up and told him she'd come back later in the evening.

"I spoke with Noah a short while ago," Duke said.

"Is that right?"

"Yeah, it is, Caleb." Duke walked over to stand in front of the window. "And you're not going to ignore me like you're doing everyone else or push me away like you just did poor Addison. Rylee told me the girl left your room crying."

"Don't, Duke."

"Don't what? Pussyfoot around you because you're in a hospital bed? 'Cause I won't. I know you've just been handed a tough break. But sometimes those are the hands we're dealt with in life."

"Are you honestly going to preach to me about life's unfairness, Uncle Duke? Hell, I'm living proof of it!"

"Yes, you are, but rather than face it head-on with the people in your life, family and friends and a woman who loves you, you're pushing them all away."

"I love you, Uncle Duke," Caleb said, "but I'm

warning you ... you're on dangerous ground here, and you need to mind your damn business."

Caleb didn't want or need another person reminding him of what he'd lost. He knew what he'd lost. He'd just lost the woman he loved.

17

*F*our Years Later—Present Day

"Win me back?" Addison laughed aloud even though her entire body had responded to his words. She must have heard wrong. She looked deep into Caleb Hart's penetrating stare and knew, however, that in fact she'd heard it right. And wow, he looked even better now than he had all those years ago. He was extraordinarily sexy, so much so that heat suffused her body, zinging her with its potency. The man had enough sex appeal that he could bottle it up and sell it.

"Do you see me laughing?" Caleb asked.

"No," Addison responded, expelling a breath, "but you should be. Clearly you must have lost your marbles when you fell off that bull four years ago if you even *think* you have half a chance of getting me back." She reminded herself that she could handle Caleb.

"Ah." Caleb smiled knowingly and nodded.

"Don't you smile at me," Addison returned. "Don't you dare mock me!"

"I'm not mocking you, Addison. I'm just enjoying the mature, worldly woman you've become. You're not the same sweet ingénue I met all those years ago."

"Did you expect me to stay the same?"

"No, but this, this isn't you, either."

"How would you know? You haven't seen me in four years."

"Touché."

Caleb was staring at her, and it made her uneasy. She felt like his very essence was enveloping her, filling her lungs and sparking a fire within her.

"You're right. I don't know the woman you've become, and the way I treated you was one of the single greatest regrets of my life. My behavior was deplorable."

"Caleb, don't go there." His apology shocked her. She hadn't been expecting it and certainly didn't want it. She'd wanted to show him her new smooth composure, but instead of being in charge, he was throwing her off-kilter.

"Why not? It's the truth."

"Because I don't want to hear it. I've moved on from you, Caleb. I've met someone else. I'm with Raphael now."

"And who's Raphael? How did you two meet?"

"I won't be twenty-questioned by my old boyfriend about my new one."

"Was I your boyfriend? I think not."

"What were we then?"

"We were lovers."

Addison blushed, and as if sensing a kink in her new armor, Caleb asked, "Since you won't tell me about this Rafael, can I ask if you're happy with him?"

"I am." And she was. Raphael was wonderful. He was kind, caring and compassionate.

"Are you sure about that?" Caleb circled around her like a panther stalking his prey.

"Of course. I'm over you, Caleb."

"Even though I was your first?"

His boldness shocked her. *Does he have no boundaries?* She'd just told him she had a man, and he was openly asking her about their sexual encounters. "How uncouth of you to remind me. But I've changed, Caleb. I'm not that naïve girl that you can lead around by the nose."

"Then let's see how skilled you've become."

She knew his intention and stated, "Stay away from me." Those were the only words Addison managed to get out before he reached over, pulling her into his arms. Addison struggled in his embrace, but that only seemed to bring her closer to him, closer to the solid expanse of chest she remembered so well. He slid his hands behind her neck and brought her face closer to his.

"Don't!" she warned, and at first she thought he might listen because his mouth hovered near her lips for what seemed like an eternity, but then he brought his mouth down on hers. His lips were soft and tender as they brushed across, but his kiss became more insistent as his tongue teased at the seam of her lips, demanding entry. She tried to keep them closed, but Caleb was an expert kisser, and when he squeezed her behind and she felt his erection, an involuntary purr escaped her lips—and that's when he slid his tongue inside.

She didn't want to lose control, but the attraction between them was so potent that she could only feel Caleb's tongue stroking hers and the fire he stirred within her—just as he had so long ago.

"Hmmm ..." Caleb licked his lips when he finally pulled away from her trembling body. "You've become very skilled indeed."

Addison colored and took several steps backward

away from him. She wiped her lips with her hand. "You had no right to do that."

"No, I didn't, but I've never played fair before and I don't intend on starting now. Not when it comes to what's mine."

"And you think I'm yours?" The sheer audacity of his statement made Addison want to strangle him. She hadn't been his in a very long time and never would be again. He'd made sure of that when he'd sent her away from that hospital.

"Yes. You've been mine, Addison, from the moment I first made love to you. You may be with someone else now, but I doubt he moves you the way I do."

"You're arrogant, Caleb Hart, and that hasn't changed. You may be a good kisser and my body may have responded, but I'm not interested in what you're selling. You broke my heart, and I will not let you hurt me again."

"Addison—"

"Stay away from me, Caleb. This time for good." She turned and strode toward the patio doors.

~

CALEB WATCHED ADDISON WALK AWAY. He inhaled deeply, breathing in her scent, still wafting through the air. Kissing her just now had played havoc with him, and he throbbed. He hadn't intended on kissing her, hadn't intended on acting so brazenly on his secret desires, but he was glad he had. Her lips were the sweetest he'd ever sampled, and he wanted more, much more. And despite Addison's protestations, she was just as affected by the kiss as he'd been. Her body had melted into his during their embrace, and if he hadn't been mistaken, she actually moaned when he'd deepened it.

Whoever this Raphael person was, he may have Addison for now, but it was clear to Caleb that there was a crack in Addison's armor, and he intended to widen it enough to squeeze back in, possibly into her heart.

"EVERYTHING ALRIGHT, BABE?" Raphael Toussaint asked when Addison returned from the patio and eased back into the crowd at the Dallas Country Club's charity event. She slid into his arms as he stood next to her father and a congressman's aide, and was about to answer him when she caught her father's gaze. Instantly she stiffened. She didn't need to turn to know Caleb had just entered the room. The frown on her father's face said it all. "I'm fine," she finally got out.

She smiled up at Raphael. He was incredibly handsome. He wasn't quite as tall as Caleb, but he was just as good-looking if not more so. Raphael had classic features, unlike Caleb's sexy rugged ones. Raphael's creamy brown skin was smooth, and his sculpted cheekbones and permanent five o'clock shadow made him a pure dream.

Addison had to remind herself just how great she and Raphael were. They were perfectly suited to each other. She didn't have to try to understand or figure him out. He didn't play any games. What you saw was what you got, and Addison appreciated that he was for real with her.

She leaned on her tiptoes and kissed his jaw.

"What was that for?" he asked.

"Just wanted to." She smiled up at him. She ignored her father's obvious stare. She knew he wanted to know if she'd seen Caleb, but that was none of his business.

After her relationship with Caleb had ended, Benjamin Walker had expected his daughter to come home with her tail between her legs and cry on his shoulder, but she hadn't. She'd also refused to hear him say "I told you so," especially after he'd warned her about Caleb. So she'd left the States and gone to Paris to visit some old college mates. He hadn't been happy about it, and she'd thought he was going to cut her off, but after she'd explained he'd understood and had actually championed it.

She hadn't been looking for love when she'd met Raphael, but it had slowly snuck up on her and she was grateful for a man like him, a man who appreciated all she had to offer and who wasn't just using her for sex.

THE CHARITY EVENT ended a couple of hours later and Addison, Raphael and her father prepared to head home. As they did so, Addison couldn't help but notice that Caleb was nowhere to be found. Perhaps he'd taken what she'd said out on the patio to heart and was going to steer clear.

Once they made it back to the mansion, Addison exhaled and began removing her three-inch heels. She and Raphael were staying at the Walker mansion temporarily until they could find a place of their own.

"Ready to head up?" Raphael asked in the foyer.

"Sure thing, babe."

They were both headed to the stairs when her father snuck up on them and said, "Addison, may I have a word?"

Addison stopped in midstep. It was amazing that her father had no problem with Raphael sharing a room with her. He hadn't said a thing about it, but he wasn't going to be able to let her seeing Caleb rest. He was determined to speak his mind.

Addison turned around. "Of course."

Raphael stared at her for several long moments before heading up while she descended the few steps she'd taken and followed her father into the living room adjacent to the foyer.

"Yes?" She folded her arms across her chest.

Her father wasted no time laying into her. "Do you really think it was appropriate spending time with your former lover while your current one is in the next room?"

"Daddy—"

"Don't 'Daddy' me." He strolled toward her and grasped her shoulders. "I warned you, Addy, that man was dangerous before and that edict still stands. Just because he's dressed himself up in some fancy clothes doesn't mean he still isn't trouble. In fact, it makes him more so."

Addison snatched her shoulders away. She was tired of being manhandled today. "I don't need you of all people to tell me that. Do you think I've got amnesia? I didn't forget what he did to me, Daddy."

"Then act like it!"

Addison glared at him, and her eyes became narrow slits. She didn't appreciate being scolded like a child. "Thank you for your concern, but I'm capable of taking care of myself. I didn't fall apart before, and I won't now."

"No, you just had to move thousands of miles away.

Away from everyone who loved you, who could help you."

"You couldn't help me, Daddy. Don't you see that? You couldn't have protected me from heartbreak. It was bound to happen sometime. It's just a part of becoming an adult, and when I look back, it made me a stronger person."

"I can see that."

"Then respect me enough to allow me to handle this, handle him in my own way."

Her father nodded. "Alright, honey. I'm sorry if I overreacted, but seeing that man again ..."

Addison patted his arm. "It's okay. I've got this."

When she finally made it to the suite she shared with Raphael, he was already in bed, bare-chested and wearing silk pajama bottoms. "Everything okay? Your father seemed a little uneasy. Are you sure he doesn't have a problem with us sharing a suite?"

"All is well," she answered as she bent down by the bed so he could unzip her dress. When he'd lowered it to her waist, she rose and stepped out of it. "You don't have to worry about us sharing a room. My dad thinks the world of you."

She draped the dress over the chair and walked over to her vanity set to sit and remove her jewelry. She was placing it in her jewelry box when Raphael asked, "Did he think the world of Caleb Hart?"

Hearing Caleb's name roll off Raphael's lips sent fear through Addison. She turned around in her chair to face him.

"Did you think I wouldn't notice? We've been together awhile, Addy, and even before then, when we were just friends, I could sense when you were in distress. And I sensed it tonight, and then imagine my surprise when Duke Hart mentioned that his nephew was here."

Addison couldn't speak. What could she say? He'd caught her red-handed. Not in a lie per se, but a lie of omission.

"And then when I searched for you, I couldn't find you." Raphael rose from the bed and walked toward her. "My mind began to wonder where you could be, or should I say, who you could be with. So were you with him?"

Addison inhaled deeply and rose from her seat, never breaking eye contact with Raphael.

"He was why your father wanted to talk to you, wasn't he?" Raphael searched Addison's face. "Why? Does your father think he has that much power over you?"

Addison blinked rapidly. He was throwing so many questions at her, she didn't know where to start.

"Well? I'm waiting, Addison."

"Yes, I was with Caleb."

"Dammit, I knew it." Raphael turned away from her. "I thought I smelled another man's cologne on you when you kissed me earlier."

"Raphael, please ..." She touched his arm, but he moved it away. "It wasn't like that."

He walked over and sat on the edge of the bed. "How was it then? Explain it to me."

"I didn't go looking for him."

"So he came looking for you?" He said it as more of a statement than a question.

Addison nodded. "He found me on the patio, and we talked."

"Talked?"

Raphael sounded like he didn't believe her.

"Yes, talked."

His eyes searched hers, and she could see he was trying to reconcile her answer with his thoughts. When he glared at her again, she knew he didn't believe her. "Is that all? What did he want?"

"To apologize," Addison said, "for how he treated me all those years ago."

"And?" he pressed. "Don't make me pull it out of you, Addison, just tell me for Christ's sake. We've always had honesty going for us. Don't change that now because of him. Don't keep something this big from me."

A tear trickled down her cheek. She wouldn't have said anything. She would have taken it to her grave, but he was pushing her for the truth, and she couldn't deny him. He deserved better. "He said he wants me back and then, then he kissed me."

"He did what?" Raphael rose and so did his voice.

"I'm sorry. I had no idea he would do something so brazen, Raphael. I swear. I haven't seen him in four years."

"Yet he still thought he could put his hands on you, kiss you, even though you're with another man?" Raphael's disgust was evident. "You did tell him, didn't you? That you're with me?"

"Of course I did."

"That's why your father's worried. He thinks that you could be persuaded."

"I won't be. I love you, Raphael."

"God, I can't believe this." Raphael grasped his head in frustration. "I thought that man was finally out of your life and that we were free to be together, but he's not, is he?"

"He is. I don't want Caleb back."

"But he's not going to give up trying to get you back, Addison. And I don't want to believe he has a chance, but I was there. I saw how devastated you were after your breakup."

Addison shrugged. "What do you want me to say, Raphael?"

"I want you to make me believe that he doesn't have a chance," Raphael replied, coming toward her. When he reached her, he pulled her into his arms. "I want you to make me believe that I won't lose you to him."

Addison wrapped her arms around Raphael's neck and brushed her lips across his. "He doesn't have a chance." But even as she said those words, she was worried that Raphael should be worried. Caleb was her first love, and she'd fallen hard for him, but when he'd sent her packing she'd made her peace and accepted his decision. But she'd done so with the assumption she'd never see him again. Caleb had changed the script, and now Addison wasn't so sure how the second act would end.

18

"Last night was pretty interesting," Duke said the next morning to Caleb as they ate lunch in Duke's office at Hart Enterprises.

"Yes, it was," Caleb replied, never glancing up from the papers he was reading.

"C'mon, Caleb, are we not going to talk about the elephant in the room? That you didn't see Addison again?"

Caleb put down the papers and looked up. "No, we can talk about it."

"So? I assume you spoke."

"We did, and it went much better than I thought it would."

"Really? How so?"

"I expected Addison to be angry with me ... and she was. She reamed me out pretty good, which is what I deserved, but—"

"But what?"

"There's still a chance for us, Uncle Duke."

"You think so? After all this time? After how you ended things?"

Caleb nodded. "Yes." He'd stayed up nearly half the night thinking about it all. If he'd read the signals correctly, Addison was happy with her new beau, Raphael whatever his name was, but she wasn't over Caleb either. Anger and hate were the opposite coin of love, which meant she still had feelings for him. They might be buried, but he'd unearth them. And that kiss last night had been the first shovel.

"But she's dating someone. And if the rumors are true, they are close to engagement."

"Not if I have anything to say about it." Caleb's voice had a fire to it. "I'm not going to lose her again."

"So you're going to try to steal her away from this fellow? That's not right, Caleb."

"I'm not stealing her. She's not a prize to be won," Caleb said, "plus she was never his to begin with. And I'll prove it."

"I doubt it's going to be as easy as you think. Do you honestly think this man is just going to step aside without a fight?"

Caleb thought about what Duke had just said. "No, I don't suppose he will. But I have a plan." He'd thought about a way to get close to Addison. Hart Enterprises had a new public relations campaign coming up, and Addison's firm would be dying to scoop up a contract to do the work. Caleb intended to use that to his advantage.

Later that afternoon, Caleb put his plan into action and arranged for a meeting with the principal of Addison's firm for the following day to discuss the particulars of what they would need. Soon, he would reconnect with Addison, and hopefully, with time, he would be able to show her he was a changed man.

ADDISON STARED at the computer screen. With her personal life in turmoil, she was unable to concentrate on the campaign in front of her. On the one hand, she had Raphael, her ideal man who was handsome, smart, funny and kind with a giving heart. On the other, there was devilishly sexy Caleb, the former bull rider who'd once had her heart and whom she'd never truly forgotten. Perhaps it was because of the "what if." The accident had abruptly ended their short courtship, and she'd never truly known if they would have survived of their own free will. She'd always wondered.

But she'd never known the option was still on the table, so she'd had to move forward with her life and Raphael was a part of that. *Was I supposed to have waited indefinitely to see if Caleb would ever walk again?* At the time, he'd made it very clear that he didn't want to be with her. Of course, his sister, Rylee, had disagreed, and after that horrible day at the hospital when he'd told her to go, Rylee had called Addison and begged her to give him some time. But Addison had refused to be his punching bag and had left town instead. *Did I make a mistake? Should I have waited for him?*

Her intercom buzzed. "Addison, can I see you please, in my office?" her boss, Stella Hayes, asked from the other end of the line.

"Sure thing. I'll be right there." Addison rose from her high-backed chair and walked in her three-inch pumps down the hall.

She couldn't believe how lucky she'd been in landing this gig after returning from Paris. It was a coup, and she knew every PR agent in Dallas had been vying for it, but once Stella knew she'd worked for a large firm in Paris, it had sealed the deal for her, not to mention her grasp of several languages: French, Italian and Spanish, which she'd acquired while abroad.

As she walked toward Stella's all-glass corner office, she could see a man sitting inside it. His back, however, was facing the glass pane in front of her, so she couldn't see his face. She opened the door and before she even set foot inside, the man turned around. Addison's heart nearly stopped. Caleb. *What the hell is he doing here?*

"Addison." Stella got up off her sofa. "Why didn't you tell me you had this campaign in the works?"

"Pardon?" Addison was dumbfounded by Stella's question, and, of course, Caleb.

He was sitting on a white leather sofa with one long leg crossed over the other. He looked quite dapper in the designer suit he wore. Addison was charmed, seeing him so smartly dressed again as he was the other night. And there was the signature smile. He was giving her a sexy smirk, clearly pleased with himself that he'd caught her off-guard yet again.

"I was just telling Stella," Caleb said, putting his arm across the back of the sofa, "that we were discussing bringing Hart Enterprises next campaign to Hayes & Hayes."

"Were we now?" Addison asked with a touch of sarcasm.

Only Caleb seemed to catch it and he cocked his brow, daring her to say otherwise to her boss.

He smiled broadly. "Yes, and I'm eager to share with the oil community the new refining process that we've incorporated. The oil business gets such a bad rap that I'd like to improve on it."

"Sounds great," Stella said, "doesn't it, Addison?"

"Of course."

"We would be more than happy to put together a proposal on handling Hart Enterprises' business," Stella added.

"Excellent!" Caleb rose from the sofa and extended his hand toward Stella. "I look forward to hearing from Addison." At Addison's surprised look, he said, "I explained to Stella that with our long friendship, I wouldn't dream of anyone else handing HE's account but you."

Addison plastered a fake smile on her face even though inwardly she was fuming that Caleb had placed her in such a precarious position. She could envision the smoke coming out of Raphael's ears once she told him of this latest development involving Caleb.

"Good day, ladies." Caleb nodded at them before leaving the office.

As he walked out, Stella turned to her. "Addison, how could you have left out your connection to Caleb Hart and Hart Enterprises? This would be a great campaign for us."

"It's a recent development," Addison said as she continued to watch Caleb head for the elevators. She needed to speak with him before he left. "If you'll excuse me." She rushed out and took a shortcut to the elevators to head him off.

She caught up with him at the elevator bank. "Caleb."

He smiled when he saw her with her arms folded across her A-line sheath dress. "Addison."

"My office. Now." She headed toward it and didn't look back to see if he was following her because she knew he was. When she made it to her office, she held open the glass door and once he was inside, she closed it. She wished she hadn't because Caleb's large presence overwhelmed the tiny room.

Caleb strolled over to the chair across from her modern, sleek desk, and Addison walked behind it. She wanted distance between them.

"What can I do for you?" Caleb asked.

"Don't play coy, Caleb. It doesn't suit you. You know why you're here."

"If it's that's obvious, why don't you tell me?"

"You're trying to come between me and Raphael by inserting yourself into my life. And clearly you figured the best way was through work by creating a scenario that would force us to do business together. You knew that the idea of us leading your campaign would be too good for the company to pass up."

He smiled, revealing a brilliant pair of white teeth. "Okay, I admit it."

"So you're not even going to try to deny it?" Addison laughed derisively. "You're really too much."

Caleb leaned forward, and his deep-set brown eyes focused on her. "I told you the other night that I wanted you back, and I intend to do everything in my power to ensure that happens. If it means I have to play a little unfair," he said, shrugging, "then that's what I'll do, Addison."

Addison was flabbergasted. Words escaped her.

"I made a mistake four years ago when I asked you to leave me," Caleb continued, "and it's a mistake I intend to rectify. We can be good together again, Addison, if you'll only allow yourself to entertain the idea. I'm not the same man I was. How can I be when I was forced to face my own mortality? I had to figure out if I was going to let that accident define me or if I was going to move on from it. I chose the latter."

"And you walked again," Addison added.

Caleb nodded. "I had to learn how all over again like I was a toddler. I can't tell you what a humbling experience that was. And all I can say is that I'm sorry that I wasn't able to do it with you by my side, but I wasn't sure what was in store for me and if the rehabilitation would even work. What if I would have been disabled all my life? Unable to make love to you? I couldn't take that chance, not with your life."

"It wasn't your decision to make," Addison replied. She could feel her eyes becoming misty, but she refused to allow him to see that he was affecting her. He would take that as a sign in his favor, and she couldn't afford that. "It was mine, and you took that choice away from me."

"I know and I've regretted it, but I used it to fuel me."

Again, Caleb was surprising her with his forthrightness. She'd been prepared to read him the riot act once she had him alone in her office, but he was being upfront and honest. "And you recovered."

"It was a long, hard road, Addison. Don't doubt that for a moment it was easy, especially knowing that I'd lost you."

"You didn't lose me, Caleb. You let me go."

"Agreed." He lowered his head.

"We can't keep rehashing this," Addison said. "What's done is done, and we have to move on."

Caleb shook his head. "I can't do that. Not until I know that I've tried my best to get you back."

"Dammit, Caleb!" Addison rose from her chair, stormed to the window and glared out of it. "You can't come back here and do this."

Caleb must have eased out of his chair stealthily because suddenly Addison felt his presence behind her. Then she felt his hands on her shoulder, felt him spinning her around to face him. "Addison—"

"Hey, girl, I'm here for lunch," Collette said as she swept into Addison's office breezily. She stopped short when she saw Addison and Caleb standing close together with his hands still on her shoulders. "Oh, I'm sorry. Am I interrupting something?" She stared daggers at Addison.

Addison stepped away from Caleb. "Of course not. Caleb was just leaving. Weren't you?" She looked at her former lover. He seemed to understand without her having to ask.

"For now," he answered. "Colette," he said, nodding to the redhead as he made his way to the door, "it's good to see you again."

"I wish I could say the same," Collette responded curtly and then turned to Addison once he'd left. "What the hell are you doing? What if I'd been Raphael? Can you imagine how that would have looked to him?"

"Nothing was going on."

"Do I look stupid to you?" Collette asked, placing a hand on her hip. "I know what I saw. I don't know what you were talking about, but I do know I caught you both in an intimate moment."

"It wasn't like that."

"Girl, you're in danger of losing your man if you continue down this path."

"Can we just go to lunch?" Addison asked. "I don't want to talk about this."

"Fine, you're living on the edge, Addison, and if you don't watch yourself, this could end badly for you." Collette grabbed her bag. She held open the glass door, and Addison preceded her out.

CALEB SLAMMED his fists on the steering wheel of his Aston Martin Vanquish. He'd been so close to getting through to Addison if only Collette hadn't interrupted them. They were getting real with one another, and if he'd had more time he was sure he would have made some progress in breaking through the wall Addison had erected up around her heart. A wall he was responsible for. When he'd first met her, she'd been open, giving and ready to let love in, but now she was closed off, and it wasn't going to be easy convincing her to give them another try. It was why he'd taken the unconventional approach and used her working environment as a way to get close to her. He knew it was sneaky, but he was desperate.

He wouldn't be able to reach her personally or at home, with Raphael, her father and now even Collette against him. He needed a way for them to spend some time together so she could see that there was more to him now than the arrogant bull rider she fell for four years ago. Like her, he'd matured. He'd had to.

If he hadn't, he would never have been able to push himself day after day with the grueling rehabilitation that had been required after his first surgery. It had taken him nearly two years, but he'd done it and he was a better, stronger man and not just physically. His ordeal had taught him humility and patience, but it also had given him a dogged determination, which is exactly what he would need to win Addison back despite opposition from all around her.

19

"Caleb, oh my goodness," Madelyn Hart exclaimed when her son walked into the Hart family living room two days later. On the spur of the moment, he'd decided to go home. He rarely visited the ranch much these days, except for a holiday or odd birthday here and there for his nephew, Zane. Noah and Chynna had produced a beautiful little boy.

"Hey, Mama." Caleb bent down and kissed his mother's cheek.

"Daddy." He walked over and gave his father a one-armed hug.

"Good to see you, boy," Isaac Hart said. "It's been too long."

Caleb smiled. "Good to see you too." He walked over and gave his brother some dap before heading toward Chynna and his nephew sitting next to his mother on the sofa. "Come here, little man."

His chubby-cheeked nephew walked over to him. "Uncle Caleb." It still amazed Caleb that Zane was walking and talking. He'd missed so much of his early life because of all those months in rehabilitation. Caleb bent down, picked him up and swung him in his arms. Zane laughed uncontrollably.

"Easy now," Noah said.

"I've got 'im." Caleb playfully sat his nephew on his shoulder.

"What brings you to Golden Oaks?" asked Noah.

Caleb frowned and stopped playing with Zane. "I didn't realize I needed an invitation."

Their mother looked at both her sons. "Of course you don't need an invitation. It's just been awhile, and we've all missed you." She glanced at Noah. After Caleb's accident, Caleb's relationship with Noah had never been the same. Caleb had pushed them all away during his recovery. The only person he seemed to want around was her brother, Duke. She'd been happy for that much—at least he would have someone.

"I'm sorry." Caleb glanced first at Noah and then his mother. "I know I haven't been around much the last few years. I had a lot to work through, but I'm here now." He picked Zane up and kissed him on the cheek. "And I'd like to change that."

"Well, it's about time," Noah said with a smile.

A smile which Caleb happily returned. He'd missed his brother and couldn't wait to talk to him later. He could use some advice on what he should do next with Addison.

THE NEXT MORNING, Caleb got his chance. He'd specifically woken up early because he knew Noah's habits. As general manager, his brother was up at the crack of dawn and after a quick shower, followed by some piping hot coffee that Noah had brewed and left warming in the kitchen, Caleb found him in the stables.

Noah's shocked face told Caleb that he was the least likely person he'd expected to see.

"Good morning."

"Good morning," Noah said as he saddled up a horse. "What are you doing up this early?"

"Well, I was hoping we could talk. That is, if you could spare a few minutes."

"For you? Of course." Noah stopped what he was doing and faced Caleb. "What's on your mind?"

"I need some female advice."

"From me?" Noah laughed. "I have to admit I'm surprised because you've never needed that before."

"There's a first time for everything." Caleb laughed too, leaning against the nearby column. "Seriously, though, I'm in a bit of a sticky situation."

"Please tell me you're not messing around with a married woman."

"No." Caleb rubbed his goatee. "Not exactly." At Noah's frown, he continued, "She's with someone. Dating that is."

"I see."

"Yeah, I know. It's not cool in your book, but it's not just anyone, Noah. It's Addison."

Noah's eyes widened. "Addison? The Addison you sent packing four years ago?"

Caleb nodded.

"Damn! That's a flash from the past."

"I know," Caleb said, "and I never thought I'd ever have another chance with her. I thought I'd blown it, so imagine my surprise when I'm with Uncle Duke, Rylee and Amar at some party and she shows up with her father and beau. Jesus, Noah! It was like time ceased to exist and I was brought back to that club in Vegas when I first saw her across the room and knew I *had* to have her."

"But she's with someone else now."

"Yes, but—"

"But what? Would you want someone messing with *your* lady?"

"Of course not! But here's the thing: I think she still loves me."

"You think? Or you know?"

Caleb shrugged. "I don't know, but I have to find out. I'll never forgive myself if I don't try. I already messed up once when I let her go. If I did the same thing when I could have had a chance with her, I'll always wonder."

"I don't know, Caleb. This is pretty messed up."

"So you think I should steer clear?"

Noah chuckled. "When have you ever done as I said? Even when you were a little boy, if I said left, you went right, so what's the difference now?" When Caleb didn't answer, Noah continued, "All I can tell you is that you shouldn't play around with Addison again if you're not going to go the distance."

"What do you mean?"

"If you're not going to marry her, Caleb."

"Marriage." Caleb hadn't thought quite that far out, but now that Noah mentioned it, he should be. He'd been thinking commitment for sure, but marriage? Then again, why should Addison leave Raphael for him when he wasn't offering her anything other than a good time? She and Raphael were headed to the altar, according to the gossip in Dallas. If he didn't strike soon, he would lose her ... and he didn't want that.

"You're right," he agreed with his brother.

Noah was stunned by his response. "I am?"

Caleb nodded. "If anyone knows how short life is,

it's me. I won't make the same mistake twice. Raphael isn't the only marrying kind."

"Wow! I have to say, little brother, you've come a long way from the wandering and arrogant and at times selfish man you once were."

Caleb frowned. "Tell me how you really feel, Noah."

"If anyone can speak honestly with you, it should be family, and you had a lot of growing up to do. And I can see that that's happened."

"Losing the ability to walk and having to learn all over again can do that to a person," Caleb returned.

"I'm sorry I wasn't there for you."

"I'm sorry I wouldn't let you be," Caleb responded. "I let my stubborn pride get in the way. But not anymore. I've missed you, Noah."

"And I've missed you, Caleb." Noah pulled him into an embrace.

ADDISON WAS NOT LOOKING FORWARD to the meeting ahead of her. Her morning had gotten off to a bad start thanks to another row she'd had with Raphael. It had been several days since Caleb had come to her office, and it hadn't taken long for Stella to ensure he had a proposal, which it so happened, Hart Enterprises then proceeded to sign almost immediately upon receipt. Raphael hadn't been pleased to learn over the breakfast table that she was going to meet with Caleb later that morning to tour the HE refinery facilities. It didn't matter that she wouldn't be alone with him and would be with Stella too. Raphael was pissed that she'd agreed to take on the campaign, but what was she supposed to do? Tell her boss she couldn't take on a big client? Then she would be forced to explain her personal life, which she wasn't prepared to do. So she would do what was necessary and in so doing make it clear to Caleb that their relationship had ended a long time ago.

Stella was waiting for her when she arrived, leaning up against her Mercedes Benz as she talked on her iPhone. Addison nodded to her as she exited her own vehicle.

Right on time, Caleb pulled up and hopped out of his Vanquish. "Good morning," he said to Addison and then noticed Stella standing not far off by her Benz. "I see you brought re-enforcements."

"This is a business meeting, is it not?"

"Yes, it is," Caleb replied. "You're looking good." His eyes traveled down her face and the entire length of her body, from her designer boots, past her skinny boyfriend jeans and up her leather Moto jacket.

"Are you done?" Addison asked.

He continued eyeing her. "Not quite." He walked behind her and openly stared at her bottom as he walked toward Stella, who'd just finished her call. "Stella, so glad you could make it out. I think it's important you understand the process before you present to the public."

"I couldn't agree more, Mr. Hart," Stella said, walking toward Addison.

"Please call me Caleb." He smiled at her and then at Addison as he led them inside.

An hour later, Addison had to admit she was impressed by all that Caleb and his uncle had accomplished. Her mind was racing with ideas of how to put the best possible spin on this so they could get the biggest bang for their buck.

"How about some lunch?" Caleb asked.

"Oh, no." Stella shook her head. "I have to get back to the office, but Addison can stay. Can't you, Addison?" She gave her a look that indicated her answer had better be affirmative.

Addison smiled warmly. "Of course. Anything for a client."

"Good, I'll leave you both to enjoy lunch. Addison, I'll see you back at the office this afternoon."

After she'd gone, Addison glanced at Caleb and could see he was grinning like a Cheshire cat. Clearly he was pleased with the outcome of events that had put them alone together. Just like he'd wanted, no doubt.

"Alright, let's get this over with. Where would you like to go?"

"Follow me," Caleb said. They walked through the facility corridors and toward a metal ladder. He pulled it down and began climbing. When he noticed she wasn't following, he looked at her. "You coming?"

"Do I have a choice?" She grabbed a rung. "I'm glad I wore jeans," she said as she climbed. When she reached the top, she swung her leg over the metal enclosure and realized they were on the roof. Addison glanced around. "What are we doing up here? You did say we were having lunch."

Caleb grabbed her hand and a spark shot through her, but she ignored it. "We are." He pulled her forward, and they walked a short distance until they came to an area that looked like grass ... and on top of it was a blanket with a picnic spread.

Addison glanced at Caleb. "This looks awfully romantic, Caleb."

"I meant it to be."

"And what if Stella could have attended?"

"Well, I had no idea she was going to show up with

you. But after I saw her, I figured that as a principal of a PR firm she would leave you to attend to lunch with the client ... so I still asked you to lunch, and my gamble paid off." He walked on the grass toward the blanket, bent down on his knee and held out his hand. "Care to join me?"

Addison knew she shouldn't, knew she should leave before the situation got out of control, but instead of listening to her head, she followed her heart and accepted his hand.

~

CALEB WAS RELIEVED. He'd thought when Addison saw the romantic spread she'd bolt, but instead she'd stayed; that told him that all was not lost. There was still a part of her that felt a pull toward him, and he intended on taking full advantage of that. He pulled her down, and she knelt on the blanket beside him. Touching her reminded Caleb how classy Addison carried herself. She'd never been flashy and wore a simple French manicure on her nails while her fingers were graceful and elegant, yet soft. He could remember those same elegant hands caressing him.

"Champagne?" he asked, reaching for the bottle that was chilling in an ice bucket on the blanket.

"In the middle of the afternoon?"

"Why not?"

Addison shrugged, so he went ahead and pulled out two flutes from the wooden basket. "Hold these." He handed her the flutes as he took care of uncorking the champagne. When he popped the cork, she quickly placed the flutes underneath before the bubbly spilled out. He poured them each a flute. "To the future."

Addison paused several seconds before clicking her flute with his.

He watched her sip the champagne and wished he was the flute so he could taste her lips. He knew she would taste sweet just like he remembered. He blinked and reminded himself that he needed to take things slow. He'd already pissed her off by creating this working relationship; he didn't want to push her away by trying too hard.

"So how did you get involved working in PR? If I recall, you were working for your father."

"Are we really going to make small talk?" Addison's tone was snarky.

"Would you rather we talk about us?"

Addison thought better of her previous response, and she answered, "Yes, I was working for my father because that's what he expected of me, but it was never what I wanted to do. My degree was in Marketing and Finance. When I graduated, my father pressured me into joining his company when I really wanted to stretch my creative muscle. So when I decided to leave the States, I chose to go back to my first love."

"You left because of me?"

Addison stared at him long and hard, and Caleb was wondering if she wasn't going to answer him, but she did. "Yes and no. I wanted to get away and make a clean break from my father, and our breakup was just the excuse I needed. He seemed to understand and was glad that I was getting away from you. And while I was in Paris, I started working for a large PR firm and slowly began building a reputation for good work. So when I was ready to return to the States and heard Stella had an opening, it seemed like the right fit."

"And Raphael followed you?"

She seemed surprised by his interest, but answered, "Yes, he'd wanted to leave Paris and try something new, and our relationship was solid, so yes, he followed me here. Does that satisfy your curiosity about your competition?"

"A little. It tells me he's a smart man and knew a good thing when he found it and wasn't about to let you go."

Her expressive face became somber. "Yes, he did."

They stared at each other for what seemed like an eternity before he said, "How about some lunch? Salmon or beef?" He reached inside the picnic basket and pulled out containers of lightly smoked salmon, dill caper aioli and chilled petit fillet of beef with caramelized onions and horseradish cream.

"I'll have the salmon." He handed her a container.

"How about some antipasti to start?" He pulled out a small platter of steamed artichokes, aioli, imported olives, Tuscan salami, slow roasted tomatoes, baby heirloom tomatoes and double cream brie with a freshly baked baguette. They ate some of the antipasti along with apples and grapes before venturing to their entrees.

"Thanks." She opened the container. "Looks good, and I'm starved."

They ate in relative silence, making the odd comment or two about the lunch. The conversation perked up when Addison asked about the roof, and he explained it was a green roof.

"What's that?"

"A roof with a waterproofing membrane that's covered with vegetation."

"Why would you have one?"

"I know oil companies have a bad rep, so Hart Enterprises wanted to show we could preserve the environment by absorbing rainwater and providing insulation by helping to lower urban air temperatures and mitigate the heat island effect."

"How does it do that?"

"Since we have a white roof, it reflects more sunlight and absorbs less heat."

"Very interesting. Is there any dessert?"

"Sure is." Caleb reached inside the basket. "Lemon pound cake or salted caramel chocolate brownie pop?"

"Brownie pop."

He handed her the brownie pop and watched Addison eat the gooey dessert. The way her mouth bit into the chocolate had Caleb thinking all kind of lascivious things. He blinked. He couldn't go there, but he could talk about what hung between them.

"Listen, Addy, I know I've made mistakes in the past—," Caleb began, but Addison cut him off.

"Can't we just eat in peace?"

"No, I have to say this because I want you to know how serious I am."

"And how serious are you?"

"As I said, I know I've made mistakes, but I'm hoping in time that you'll forgive me and give me another chance."

"Why? Why should I leave Raphael?

"Because I'm in it for the long haul, Addy," he responded. "I see a future with us. I guess I probably did all those years ago, and it scared me, but I'm not scared now. I see you as my future wife."

Addison stopped sipping her bubbly and stared blankly at him. "What did you just say?"

"I said, I see you as my wife ... and the mother of my children." He said this with deep feeling.

Addison sat upright. "Oh, now you really are

laying it on thick, Caleb. When have you ever wanted a wife and kids? Never! And now? When I'm with another man, you want a wife and babies? Ha!" She rose on her shins to get up, but Caleb couldn't let her. If she left now, he might not ever get through to her again.

He grasped her by the arm and hauled her against him, but in so doing, he fell backward onto the blanket, bringing Addison square on top of him. Their gazes locked, and he immediately felt the blood rush from his head to his groin. Addison wasn't just beautiful, she was what fantasies were made of. His fantasy. He'd dreamed of this moment, and his mouth suddenly became dry and parched. Caleb knew of only one thing that would quench his thirst.

With one hand, he pulled Addison's head toward him and guided her mouth toward his. The moment her lips touched his, passion erupted inside him so thick, Caleb thought it might consume him. He inserted his tongue inside her mouth, and immediately, she kissed him back, caressing her tongue against his. The sexual chemistry between them was so strong that the kiss was not gentle at all. Instead, there was a desperation behind it.

Addison's hands grasped the sides of his face as the kiss deepened. Thanks to some delicious tongue action, Caleb got to enjoy taste of her and the champagne they'd shared earlier. She pressed intimately against him, and he knew she had to feel his hardness. He moved his hips underneath her, wanting her to get used to it, to remember it, to remember how good it was between them.

Caleb couldn't resist pulling her blouse free from her jeans and sliding his hands underneath her shirt. They roamed over her slender back, reaching higher for her breasts. He wanted to feel them in his hands, to squeeze and mold them. When he finally reached her breasts and pushed aside her bra to ardently caress the tips of her hardened buds, it must have been like he'd poured cold water on her because she instantly pushed away from him and pulled her shirt down.

"Omigod! Omigod!" She was holding her hand over her mouth. "What have I done?" She jumped to her feet almost immediately, and before Caleb could recover and get to his feet, she was rushing across the roof to the ladder. Seconds later, he saw her curls as she quickly descended it.

"Damn!" Caleb fell back against the blanket. He'd pushed her too far. Now what?

20

Addison was ashamed by what she'd just done with Caleb. She'd all but made love to him on the roof in the middle of the afternoon. Dear God! What was wrong with her? How could she have allowed things to get this far? The kiss the first night on the patio had caught her off-guard, yet she could explain it away.

But today was different.

Today, she'd kissed him back with an intensity she hadn't thought she still possessed. It was like they'd wanted to devour each other. She'd forgotten where she was and who she was with and allowed him to have his way with her, and to her shame, she'd enjoyed it. She'd even angled herself over him for more, and her panties were wet now from craving him.

She loved Raphael or at least she thought she did, but Caleb's return was screwing with her head, and she didn't know which way to turn. Instead of going home, she drove to Collette's. She didn't know who else to see to talk about her topsy-turvy emotions.

Addison parked in the garage and took the elevator up to Collette's flat. She didn't press the buzzer. Instead, she pounded on the door until Collette opened it wearing a paint- stained smock and jeans. "Addison?" When Collette saw her friend's tear-streaked face, she rushed her inside. "Come in, girlfriend. What's wrong?"

"Everything," Addison wailed.

"Alright, come into the living room, and I'll make you a cup of tea."

Thirty minutes later, after she'd calmed down and drank a cup of the steaming hot herbal tea, Addison filled Collette in on everything that had happened with Caleb. When she was done, Collette eked out, "Oh, my—"

"It's bad, isn't it?" Addison looked over at her friend on the opposite side of the couch.

"Addison, I warned you that working with Caleb was opening a can of worms, and now, well, they've been let out."

"What am I supposed to do?"

"Honey, you clearly aren't as over Caleb as you thought. Otherwise you wouldn't be making out with him on a roof-deck."

Addison lowered her head in shame. She knew Collette was right, but it was painful to hear. She thought she'd dealt with the past and left it in Paris. How wrong she'd been. Once she was put to the test, she'd failed miserably and succumbed to Caleb's charms. But she couldn't blame him entirely. She'd participated.

"Addison, have you ever asked yourself why you can't commit to Raphael even though it's clear he wants to marry you?"

Addison frowned. "He's never asked."

"Perhaps because deep down he's felt you holding back."

"And you think he's right?" Addison said, but she

knew the answer and didn't wait for a response. "What do you suggest I do?"

"You've got to figure out what's between you and Caleb before you enter into a life with Raphael. Otherwise it won't be fair to either man. You can't ride the fence any longer. You're going to have to make a choice."

Addison was prepared to talk to Raphael when she got home later that evening, but he'd left a message on her phone that he would be working late. So instead, she would have to live with her guilt and her scandalous behavior for another night.

In his office at Hart Enterprises, Caleb was reading through papers when he saw a shadow out of the corner of his eye. When he looked up, he found Raphael standing in front of him. He knew who he was because although he hadn't met him at the charity event, he'd made a point of finding out everything he could about the man who'd stolen Addison's heart. He wasn't surprised Raphael had come here. In fact, he'd been expecting it.

"You don't seem surprised to see me," Raphael said as he stormed toward Caleb's desk.

"No, I'm not." Caleb put down the papers he'd been poring over.

"Then you know why I'm here."

Caleb nodded as he rose. "To warn me to stay away from Addison?"

"That's right."

"Well, I can't do that." Caleb came from around the desk.

The two men stared each other down. "Can't or won't?"

"Is there a difference?"

Raphael cocked a brow. "I guess not. I thought I would come here and ask you to do the honorable thing to step aside for Addison's own happiness, but I can see that I was wrong. You don't know how to be selfless."

Anger suffused Caleb, and he took a dangerous step toward Raphael. "Don't presume to think you know the first thing about me."

"Oh, no?" Raphael said. "I think I know my fair share, Caleb Hart. You're that guy that every father warns their daughter about. You're the love 'em and leave 'em type, and that's exactly what you did to Addison. The accident was just an excuse to do what you'd always planned on doing."

Caleb lunged at Raphael, grabbed him by the collar and threw him up against the wall, raising his fists as if he were going to strike him. "How dare you say anything about my accident? You don't have a clue of what it's like to wake up and realize you can't move your legs or your feet. You don't know the hell I endured."

Raphael pushed back at Caleb and straightened his suit jacket. "No, I don't, but I know the hell Addison endured getting over you after you cast her aside as if she meant nothing."

"You're wrong," Caleb snorted. "I let her go because I was being selfless. I let her go because I didn't want her to have to live her life with a paralyzed man."

"No! You let her go because you couldn't be the almighty bull rider you'd always been. You let her go because of you," Raphael said, pointing to Caleb, "not her! Because you were afraid to let her love you with all your imperfections. And trust me, Hart, she would have loved you no matter what, paralyzed or walking, and that's what burns you up, doesn't it? Because you let her get away. And now, because you can walk, you want her back? Well, you don't get to do a do-over because you don't deserve her. She deserves better than you."

"And that's you?" Caleb spat.

"Damn right, so let her go. You had your chance, and you blew it!" With that, Raphael stormed out of Caleb's office.

Caleb reached for a nearby vase on the cocktail table and threw it against the wall. Damn him! Raphael was right. He'd lost Addison because he was afraid he couldn't be the man she'd fallen in love with, but now he was that guy. Would he lose her all over again?

~

Addison knew what she had to do, but she wasn't looking forward to it. After last night, however, she realized she couldn't go on this way.

Raphael had returned in the worst mood she'd ever seen him in. He'd been so curt with her that even her father had noticed and told him to settle down. He'd eventually said he wasn't hungry and had gone upstairs to their suite.

When she finally made it there herself, Raphael had been sitting on the bed waiting for her, but it was not to talk as she'd expected. Instead, he'd wanted to make love. He'd kissed her deeply and tried to rouse her passion. He'd done all the right things, nipping at the tender spot on her nape, massaging her breasts through her shirt and French kissing her to within an inch of her life. But try as she might, Addison couldn't respond. She tried to block out images of Caleb's hand and mouth on her that very afternoon, but she couldn't. Eventually, she'd pushed Raphael away and rushed into the bathroom to shower. When she was finished and opened the bathroom door, she'd found their suite empty and no Raphael.

She didn't have a clue where he was, and deep down she was kind of glad. She needed the time alone to sort through her emotions. The afternoon with Caleb had struck a chord and reminded her of how attracted she was to him. She'd thought after four years she'd be immune, but when those sinewy thighs and lean legs had pressed her into the blanket, her entire body had remembered what is was like to be with him. She'd enjoyed it.

It was wrong that she felt this way when she was with Raphael. How could she continue to stay with him when it was clear that her feelings for Caleb were unresolved? Didn't she deserve to find out where they might lead? On the other hand, she had Raphael. He didn't deserve her wishy-washiness, and she wouldn't make him sit around while she figured it out. There was only one decision to make. It was just that Addison had never fathomed that she'd be the one hurting him, not after all they'd meant to each other.

God, she felt terrible, and she wished there was some other way to get out of this mess, but there wasn't. She couldn't have predicted that Caleb would pop back into her life four years later. She truly thought she'd put him behind her, but clearly she hadn't.

She didn't bother with dressing up for breakfast because before coming downstairs she'd called in sick to work. She needed to figure her life out once and for all.

When she arrived to the morning room, Raphael was sitting at the table eating grapefruit and toast. "Good morning," Addison said, but she didn't hazard a glance in his direction and walked instead to the settee where their cook had laid out the coffee service. She poured herself a cup from one of the mugs and joined Raphael at the table.

"I missed you last night," she began. "Where did you go?"

Raphael didn't look up as he continued eating his food. "I thought you might need some time to yourself since my presence didn't interest you."

"Raphael—"

"Don't, Addison." He shook his head.

"Don't what?"

"Just say what you have to say," he responded, glancing up at her.

Addison's eyes watered. Not a sound passed her lips.

Raphael slammed his fork down. "Just say it!"

"I'm conflicted," Addison shot out, "and I need some time to sort through my feelings."

"Bullshit!"

Startled, Addison looked at Raphael. A violent storm swirled in his eyes. "Why don't you try again?"

"What do you want me to say, Raphael?" she cried.

"I want you to be honest. I want you to say what you truly mean, that you need time to sort through your feelings for the cowboy. I'm not blind, Addison. Before we were lovers, we were friends a long time, and in a few short days I've seen a change in you.

You're cold and distant with me. You were never that way until Caleb reappeared. And last night?"

Addison hung her head.

"Last night, you wouldn't even make love with me. Heck, you couldn't even fake a response to my love-making attempts. All because of him! Dammit, Addison!" His voice cracked, and he thumped the table with his fist. "He's the one who broke your heart. How can you consider letting him back into your life again?"

"I'm not. I-I mean I don't know." Her thoughts were jumbled.

"Don't chicken out now. You know. You're just afraid to say it."

She blinked back tears. "I am afraid of hurting you, Raphael. I'm afraid of committing to you until I deal with the unfinished business I have with Caleb."

"You're hurting me now, Addison, because you're not being honest with me or yourself. You already know what you want. You just have to be woman enough to go for it. You should know that I won't settle for being second best," Raphael said, rising from his chair and throwing down his napkin, "not when I've been there for you the last few years."

"Raphael." Addison grabbed his arm when he attempted to leave the room. "Please don't leave this way."

"I have to." He bent down and kissed her head. "Like you, I deserve someone who only wants me."

Slowly, Addison removed her hand. "That's fair." She nodded her understanding. "I'm sorry that I can't say beyond a shadow of a doubt you're the one I want to be with. I'm so sorry."

"I know, my love," Raphael said, caressing her

cheek. "That's why this hurts so bad. I'll be gone within the hour." Seconds later, he left the room.

Addison didn't know how long she sat there at the table crying. Raphael was a good man, and she couldn't be disingenuous with him. She'd done the right thing and let him go so he could find someone who loved only him. She'd had no choice—she had to figure out her feelings for Caleb.

Her father found her with her head on the table, sobbing. "Addison, what is it?" He lifted her head so he could look at her. "What's happened?" But all she could do was let out another sob. "No, sweetheart." He shook his head. "Please tell me you're not going back to that bastard who broke your heart."

"Daddy, please," Addison said, lifting her chin, "I can't do this now."

He stared at her for a long moment. "You still love him, don't you?"

Addison squeezed her eyes shut for a moment. Why was everyone putting words into her mouth? She opened her eyes and looked up at her father. "I don't know, maybe, but until I do, I couldn't lead Raphael on."

He nodded. "That wouldn't be fair to him. He's a good man, so now what?"

"Let me figure it out in my own time and my own way. I promise you that I can handle it, whatever the outcome may be, but I need you to back up and allow me to make my own mistakes. If you don't, you could lose me again."

"I don't want that," her father rushed out. "When you left four years ago, it broke my heart. If I was honest, I know it was partly Caleb, but partly because of me. You wanted to spread your wings and used your breakup as an excuse."

Addison's eyes widened. She'd never known he knew.

"Yeah, you think your old man is pretty slow, huh? But I'm not. Having you back in the States has been such a joy, and I wouldn't want you to go, so ... I'll keep my opinions to myself."

Addison smiled. "I appreciate that. I do."

21

"It's so good to see you, sis," Caleb said when Rylee dropped by in a surprise visit to Uncle Duke's mansion.

"If I don't come to you, I'd never see ya," Rylee replied. "So here I am."

"Don't act like I'm the only reason. I bet you're here because old man Brewster is looking for a good vet to take care of his prize horse, Hercules."

Rylee smiled. "How'd you know?"

Caleb laughed. "Because I'm the one who recommended you. I mean, I know that you're over Amar's prized Arabians, but c'mon, you're the hottest vet in the States."

"Oh, stop." Rylee smiled. When he did, she hit his arm. "Do, and go on."

Caleb pulled her into a hug and gave her a friendly tickle.

"Hey, hey, easy, easy." Rylee tried pulling away. "You wouldn't want to injure a pregnant woman."

Caleb paused midtickle and righted Rylee onto her feet. "What did you just say?"

Rylee beamed with pride. "You heard me, right."

"Oh, Rylee." He pulled her into a hug and spun

her around. "Omigod, that's great news." Then realizing he could hurt her, he put her down on her feet. "How far along?"

"I'm a few weeks into my second trimester," Rylee said, patting her small baby bump.

"And everything's okay?"

Rylee's eyes misted slightly, and he knew she must have been thinking about the miscarriage she'd suffered last year. "Yes. Thankfully, this time, yes."

"Are you sure?"

She nodded. "Amar took the miscarriage pretty hard, and it's why we waited before trying again, but I'm nearly five months so we thought it was safe to start telling the family."

Caleb squeezed his sister's hand. "That's wonderful, Rylee. I'm truly happy for you both."

"Thanks, baby brother. So what's new with you?"

He could hear the expectancy in her voice, and he wished he had more news to share, but he didn't. He'd just found Addison again, but he couldn't expect her to fall into his arms. Not to mention, he had Raphael to deal with. The man clearly loved Addison and planned on fighting for her, which wasn't going to make it easy convincing her that they were meant to be, but Caleb was determined to try. He wasn't going to let fear rule him this time.

"Not much," he finally answered Rylee's question.

Rylee frowned. "No progress with Addison?"

"Some." That's when Caleb filled his sister in on last night's conversation with Raphael. "Wow!" Rylee said, taking a seat on the couch. "Sounds intense."

"It was."

"Did you guys come to blows?"

"We almost did, but what good would it have

done? It's Addison's decision who she wants to be with."

"I couldn't agree more," a feminine voice said from the doorway.

Rylee and Caleb glanced up. It was Addison. She was wearing a white cardigan and tank top over leggings and pumps.

Rylee was the first to make a move and rose from the couch to greet Addison with a warm, friendly hug. "It's good to see you."

Addison returned the hug while Caleb was rooted to the couch. He couldn't believe Addison had come to him, not after she'd run off the other day from the roof. He'd phoned her, but she hadn't returned any of his calls. And when he'd called the office, he'd learned she hadn't returned yesterday afternoon or this morning. He hadn't known what to make of it.

They stared at one another. An awkward silence filled the room. Rylee coughed. "Well, I'm just going to go make myself scarce. I'll see you soon." Seconds later, she was gone.

Now, Caleb watched Addison remove her jacket and place it over a nearby chair as she approached him.

"I'm surprised to see you here."

Addison chuckled derisively. "Really? I highly doubt it. You should be happy now because you succeeded in running Raphael away."

Caleb sat straight up. "Excuse me?"

"You heard me."

"Did I? Or did you give him his walking papers, because you know deep down that you and I aren't over yet?" He peered into her eyes.

She didn't look at him when she answered, "Does it matter?"

Caleb scooted toward her and lifted her chin, forcing her to look at him. "Yes, it does, because I'm not walking away this time, Addison, and I need you to know that. I'm here to show you that I'm worthy of you. And not just by being a stud in the bedroom, even though I'm good at that too."

His response brought a curve of a smile to her lips.

"Ah, there's the smile I love. But I mean what I said. I'm in it for the long haul, Addison. Marriage, babies, the whole bit."

Addison's smile broadened. "You don't have to sell me, Caleb."

"I don't?"

"I'm here, aren't I?"

"Does that mean Raphael is out of the picture?"

Addison nodded.

"Thank God." Caleb's long arm reached behind her head and brought her mouth closer to his. He was about to kiss her, but Addison placed her finger on his lips.

"What?"

"There's rules, here, Caleb," Addison began.

"Like what?"

"I'm not about to jump back into the relationship with you. We have to date and find out who we are, because I'm not the same woman you met four years ago. I've changed, and I'm sure your paralysis and recovery have changed you. We have to be sure we like the people we've become now, and that will take time. So, in the meantime, there's a moratorium on sex."

"Excuse me?"

"You heard me. In order for this relationship to work, there will be no sex. It confuses things, emotions. You need to woo me."

Caleb was surprised but intrigued. Clearly she'd

given this a great deal of thought during her twenty-four-hour hiatus. "Why on earth would I agree to that? You know as well as I do that the chemistry we share is off the charts." *How am I supposed to be able to keep my hands off her?*

"Because in our previous incarnation, the relationship was primarily about sex."

"And what's wrong that?" He smiled.

She couldn't help but laugh. "Because there's more to a relationship than sex. So those are my terms. Take it or leave it."

"As disappointed as I am by your sex moratorium," Caleb responded, "I agree." He held out his hand for a handshake. "But let it be known that I'll do things your way—that is until you ask me to make love to you."

"I'm not going to do that."

"You wanna bet?"

Addison and Caleb were still talking when Rylee peeked her head into the room. "Is it safe to enter?" She held up a small American flag and waved it back and forth.

Caleb and Addison laughed. "Yes, it is, sis," Caleb said, and Rylee entered.

"So ...," Rylee's voice trailed off as she looked at Caleb and then at Addison.

Addison glanced at Caleb and smiled. "So what?"

"Are you guys back together again or what?"

Caleb nodded. "We're going to give it another shot, yes."

"Oh, my goodness." Rylee rushed toward Addison. "I'm so happy. I always knew you were meant to be a part of our family."

"Hold up, big sis, no one's mentioned marriage

yet," Caleb replied, "though I foresee it in the horizon for us."

"That remains to be seen," Addison stated.

"I'm just happy you're back in the fold." Rylee squeezed Addison into a big hug.

When Addison pulled away, she said, "It looks like we're not the only ones with news."

Rylee blushed and rubbed her stomach. "Yes, Amar and I are expecting."

"Congratulations, Rylee. That's wonderful!"

"Thank you." Rylee beamed. "So now that you two are back together, I mean, giving it another try, that means you can come to Chynna's concert with Amar and I."

"I dunno, Rylee. That depends on Addison's schedule. When is it?" Caleb asked.

"This weekend. You guys can hitch a ride with us on the jet, and then we'll drop you back."

Caleb turned to Addison. "Sounds like fun. What do you say?"

"I say let's do it!"

~

"I CAN'T BELIEVE you're going away with Caleb this weekend," Collette said as she watched Addison pack for her getaway. She was sitting Indian style on Addison's bed and eating popcorn.

"Neither can I." One minute she was with Raphael considering a future with him, and the next minute, she was hopping a jet with Caleb and his family and going to a concert.

"You're the one who agreed to this date."

"Thank you for the reminder," said Addison. "And I did. It's just happening so fast."

"Well, I for one am not surprised."

Addison paused from packing her bag to look at Collette. "What do you mean by that?"

Collette put aside the bowl on the bed and uncrossed her legs. "How long have I known you?"

"Fourteen years."

"Then you know that I know you. And once Caleb reappeared there was no contest as to who you would ultimately choose, it was just a matter of when."

"You make it sound so inevitable."

Collette shrugged. "It was."

"How can you say that with such authority when I'm struggling to understand all of this myself?"

"Because Caleb was and is the love of your life, your first love, and you've never truly gotten over him. I don't think you would have ever fallen for Raphael if you'd known Caleb was free."

"I'm not that much of a hopeless romantic, am I?" Addison sure hoped not, because she was going to be a lot more careful with her heart this time around. She wasn't just going to give Caleb all of herself like she'd done before and have that love cast aside.

"It's your nature, Addison. Don't fight it!"

"Is that your advice for this weekend?"

"Sorta." Collette gave her a cocky smile before reaching into her pocket and tossing Addison something.

When Addison opened her hands, she saw a three-pack of flavored condoms.

"And always be safe."

Addison laughed as she shook her head. "Only you, Collette. Only you. But you don't need to worry because I have no intention of needing these."

Colleen snorted. "We are talking about Caleb with

whom you burned up the sheets or should I say a utility closet with?"

Addison blushed several shades of red at Collette's reminder of how brazenly she'd behaved with Caleb years ago and how he'd had the power to make her do just about anything. "I'm older now, and there will be no utility closets in my future."

Collette frowned. "Now you're ruining all my fun." She reached for the bowl of popcorn and tossed a few kernels into her mouth. "I always did enjoy your sexcapades."

CALEB WAS SO excited he couldn't think straight as he drove to pick up Addison from her home. A few weeks ago, he had no idea that his life would suddenly change for the better. He hadn't known that a life with Addison was still a possibility, but now it was.

Since his recovery, he had resisted serious relationships with other women. Perhaps he hadn't dared because no other woman had ever made him feel the way Addison had. She was simply unforgettable.

When he arrived at the Walker estate, he was greeted by the butler, who escorted him into the living room. He hadn't been in this room in years, yet he could still remember his first visit here and how he'd felt uncomfortable because he didn't fit in. He'd been trying to find himself back then, but not anymore. He was comfortable in his own skin and didn't have to prove to Addison's father or anyone else that he was worthy of her.

Her father's ears must have been burning because he walked into the living room right at the moment Caleb was thinking about him.

"Good afternoon."

"Good afternoon, Mr. Walker." Caleb was surprised at how cordial he was being. He knew Addison's father didn't think he was worthy of his baby girl and only daughter. But Caleb was going to try his best to get along with him for Addison's sake. He was determined that *this time* things would be different.

"Addison tells me you're going away for the weekend."

Caleb nodded. He couldn't believe her old man was going to make small talk with him. "Yes, we're going to my sister-in-law Chynna James's concert in Miami."

"Ah, yes, Chynna James is a beautiful woman," Benjamin Walker acknowledged.

"Yes, in more ways than one. My brother is a lucky man."

"He is. As are you." Mr. Walker's tone suddenly changed. He became more serious.

Oh, great. Here we go, thought Caleb. *Let the tongue-lashing begin.* "I know that, sir," Caleb replied. "I'm thankful that Addison is willing to give me a second chance."

"Over a great man like Raphael."

Caleb snorted. He wasn't about to sing the other man's praises, not when he felt *he* was the man for Addison. "I can only hope that one day I'm worthy of her, but until I am, I'll keep trying to be the best man I can be."

"Noble words," Mr. Walker replied. "You be sure and stick to them." He started toward the door just as Addison and Collette entered the room.

Fear and apprehension registered on Addison's face at seeing Caleb and her father together.

"Have fun, sweetheart." Mr. Walker bent down and kissed Addison's cheek before leaving the room.

Collette stepped backward. "Did I just see that right? Did your father just tell you to have fun even though he knows you're spending the weekend with Caleb? Times have changed."

"We had a long talk," Addison said, "and we've come to a meeting of the minds."

"I'm glad to hear it," Caleb said, coming toward Addison and bending down to sweep his lips across hers in a tender kiss. "Ready?"

Addison nodded. Caleb picked up her luggage, and they walked out of the mansion together hand in hand.

22

Fans were screaming and yelling for Chynna backstage as Addison and Caleb entered the American Airlines Arena in Miami. Several of them had received VIP passes and couldn't wait for their chance to meet the illustrious Lady of Soul who'd just released her fifth album.

Addison, Caleb, Rylee and Amar were ushered by several beefy bodyguards to Chynna's dressing room, where they found her getting made up for the night's event. Noah was seated on a sofa bouncing their son, Zane, on his lap.

Chynna was seated in a director's chair facing a well-lit mirror, but when she saw Addison walk into the room, she jumped up, scaring her makeup artist to death. "Omigod!" She stomped her feet. "Addison!" She rushed toward her. "Is it really you?"

Addison smiled and bunched her shoulders. "Yes, it's me."

"Come here, girl." Chynna opened up her arms.

Addison couldn't believe how receptive Caleb's entire family was toward her. It was intoxicating. She slowly walked into Chynna's outstretched arms and when she did, Chynna whispered, "Welcome home."

CHYNNA PUT on an amazing two-and-a-half hour concert, which included a surprise appearance by her twin, Kenya, who joined her onstage so they could belt out their latest duet off Chynna's new album.

"This is amazing," Addison said from their front row seats.

Caleb smiled at her. "Yeah, it's the perk of having a family member who's a celebrity, huh?"

"Absolutely!"

He squeezed her to his side, and she didn't mind because a heated sizzle had gone right up her spine. She hadn't minded the other times he'd touched her throughout the night either. Some of it had been accidental, but she knew some of it hadn't. He'd wanted her to know that she was here with *him*. Not that she could have forgotten. Her stomach clenched whenever she heard the throaty sound of his deep masculine voice. There were times she couldn't help but sneak a glance at him and appreciate everything she saw.

Tonight was definitely one of those nights. He'd returned to his style of days past, wearing jeans that hugged his firm behind, but instead of a plaid shirt, he wore a burgundy dress shirt. It fit him like a glove, accentuating his expansive shoulders. And he smelled equally delicious. The cologne he wore was warm, yet spicy.

AFTER THE CONCERT was over and Chynna had changed, the entire Hart clan decided to go out and celebrate at a nightclub. Addison didn't know what they were celebrating until they were toasting much later in the VIP section.

"I can't believe I'm actually out," Chynna said as she sat on Noah's lap.

"It has been awhile since you guys have done this," Chynna's manager, Deacon, replied. "You usually go straight to the hotel."

"Thank God for nannies," Chynna and Kenya said almost at the same time and gave each other a high-five. As twins, they still were able to read each other's minds.

"You have children?" Addison asked, looking in Kenya's direction. She hadn't seen Kenya since her double wedding with Rylee and felt like she was out of touch.

Kenya nodded. "Would you believe it—we have a set of twin girls." She smiled, glancing over at her husband, Lucas, who'd arrived late to the concert but was able to join them later that evening.

"Congratulations," Addison said. It seemed like every woman related to the Harts was having babies.

"Don't worry, you're next." Rylee laughed.

"Me?" Addison touched her cheek and gave Caleb a worried glance. He only shrugged as if he didn't seem to mind that the women in his family had claimed her and couldn't wait for him to impregnate her.

"Oh, yes," Chynna said with a mischievous smile. "The Hart men are very potent. We should toast to that ... Deacon." She looked to her manager, who also could predict her needs, and soon the waitress was coming around with Cristal and handing them each a glass.

"None for me." Rylee shook her head.

"Sparkling apple cider for my wife," Amar said by her side.

The waitress returned several moments later with cider for Rylee, and once they all had a glass, Chynna raised hers. "To Caleb and Addison."

The entire Hart clan lifted their glasses. "To Caleb and Addison."

Addison stared in disbelief at all the smiling faces around her. She'd always wanted to be part of a large family, and now they were welcoming her in like she'd always dreamed of. A tear trickled down her cheek as they all clicked flutes.

CALEB HAD NEVER HAD SO much fun. Hanging out with his family like they used to do had been like old times. No, it was better than that because this time, he had Addison by his side. Unfortunately, his lady love had had one too many that evening and was a little bit tipsy as they walked back to her hotel room.

It was nearly three a.m., and they'd all but shut down the club, laughing and talking and dancing in VIP, but eventually they'd all departed back to the hotel. Caleb's plan had been to walk Addison back to her room and then begrudgingly return to his room and have a cold shower since Addison had made it clear that there would be no sex between them.

It was a hard stance, but he'd understood why she felt the need. Their relationship had always been about sex, and this time she wanted more. So he was surprised when, as he turned on his heel to leave after dropping her off at her room, she stopped him and invited him in.

He turned on the light at the entrance of the small

room. "I'm just going to put you to bed," Caleb said, "and head out."

She was stumbling as he walked her toward the king-size bed. She sat unceremoniously, and he bent down to remove the high-heeled sandals she'd been wearing.

"My legs are smooth, right?" Addison said, giggling.

"Yes, babe, they're smooth." In the metallic blouson top and pleather mini-skirt, it was hard for him not to notice. If he had his choice, Caleb would love to run his hands up and down her legs and other body parts if given the chance, but he'd promised himself he would be good. He removed one shoe and then the other and rose to his feet.

"Where are you going?" Addison asked.

"To my room. Let's get you under the covers," Caleb said and walked over to the other side of the bed to pull down the comforter. "Get inside."

"Don't you want to join me?" Addison said as she slid between the covers still fully dressed, placed her head on the pillows and looked up at him.

Damn, she looked so sexy. It reminded him of that night nearly four years ago in Vegas, when he wanted her something bad. So when Addison beckoned him with her index finger, despite his best judgment, he came toward her on the bed.

That's when her arms circled his neck, and she pulled him closer until he had no choice but to join her. His body slid over hers over the covers and the instant it did, heat swirled through him. They looked at each other for several moments before neither one of them could stop the inevitable.

They kissed.

As Caleb continued pressing his lips against hers,

Addison did the same, then she did something out of character. She licked his lips from corner to corner, letting him know that she wanted more. So he gave it to her. He took over her mouth, deepening the kiss as he eased his tongue inside. The kiss felt so good and so right as if he'd come home. So he dove his tongue even further between her lips, probing her mouth and reacquainting himself with every nook and cranny.

He had an overwhelming passion and primal need to taste her, to feel her. He plastered his body over hers and felt his erection begin to throb in his jeans. If he didn't stop himself, this would get out of hand soon.

But Addison was moaning and responding to his kisses, making it hard for Caleb to pull away and remember her edict of no sex.

"Touch me," she urged, pushing the covers away and placing his hands on her.

"Addison, no!"

"Please," she begged. "I want you."

He'd told her to say that she wanted him and when she did, he would oblige. How could he deny her now, especially when she was squirming underneath him? In short, he couldn't. His hands made their way up her mini-skirt to her panties and eased them down her legs, leaving her bare and open to his sight.

Caleb smiled. What would it hurt if he just sampled a bit? They weren't actually having sex, but he could give her the orgasm she craved. "Are you ready for me?" he asked, looking at her.

She grinned wickedly, so he obliged by hiking up her skirt and placing her legs over his shoulders. Her breath quickened when he lowered his head. She may be a bit tipsy, but she knew what was to come—his tongue.

He buried his face between her legs and slid his tongue between her womanly folds. She tasted just as good as he remembered, so he shoved his tongue deeper inside, greedily licking and lapping. Addison threw her head back and began undulating on the bed, desperate for more of what only Caleb could provide. He didn't let up and relentlessly licked, flicked and teased until she convulsed and released a loud, throaty moan. Contractions swept through her, but he wasn't done yet. Caleb didn't know how long it would be before they would get to this point again, and he wanted to give her something to remember. When he continued thrusting his tongue inside her, she tightened her legs around his head like a vise, but he didn't stop until the last spasm tore through her. Only then did he lift his head.

Addison's head fell backward against the pillows. He licked his lips one final time and said, "Goodnight, sweetheart." He pulled the covers over her half-naked body and quietly left the room.

When Addison awoke the next morning and stretched out over the bed, she was accompanied by a monster hangover. Why, oh why had she allowed herself to tie one on last night? Could it be because she'd felt like a part of the Hart family, where deep down she'd always felt she'd belonged? She'd felt that way since first meeting Duke and his daughters, and after the wedding weekend the feeling had only been reinforced. Last night, it had seemed predestined that she and Caleb would be together. And now they were.

Speaking of Caleb, where was he? She didn't remember much of last night, other than going to the club with his family and drinking bottles and bottles of Cristal. They must have come back to the hotel. How else to explain how she got here? But how had she gotten into bed?

Instantly, Addison popped up. Had she and Caleb made love? Damn, she was trying to be smart about easing into a relationship with him. She turned to look at the other part of the bed, but it was empty. She was alone.

Thank God! But her happiness was short-lived because when Addison threw the covers back, though she appeared fully dressed she realized she wasn't wearing any panties.

Sweet Jesus! Addison closed her eyes trying to recall the night before and how she'd made it to her room and ended up with no underpants. That's when a blurry image came to her: Caleb coming toward her on the bed and climbing on top of her. Then another flash—Caleb kissing her passionately. Then another —Caleb lowering his head between her thighs. Addison blinked rapidly, trying to think hard if it was last night or just a memory of years past. But it had to be last night, because her head wasn't the only body part throbbing. She was throbbing between her legs, aching for more of what Caleb must have obviously given her.

Another flash—Caleb feverishly tonguing her and making her come apart until she screamed. Addison placed her face in her hands. How could she have let this happen? She could blame it on the Cristal, but that wouldn't be fair. Subconsciously there was a part of her that had wanted to be with him again, and he clearly hadn't minded going there. But try as she might, there wasn't a memory of them having sex. So had he really just given her the best head of her life and gone to his room?

Her first instinct was to reach for her clutch lying on the nightstand and pull out her cellphone, but she needed to see him instead. Throwing back the covers, she headed for the shower.

Ten minutes later, she was knocking on the door to his hotel room. He answered half-dressed, wearing jeans and no shirt. "Good morning, Addy. How are you feeling?"

"Well, that depends on your answer," she said, pushing past him into his room.

"Excuse me?" Caleb closed the door.

She had to ignore his impressive pectorals and six-pack abs and focus on the task at hand. "Didn't we agree that we wouldn't have sex last night?" Addison folded her arms across her chest, facing him as she stood in the middle of the room.

Silence ensued, and Caleb lowered his head.

"Well?"

When he finally looked up, he said, "I wouldn't consider what we did last night sex, at least not in the usual sense."

"So you're denying that we made love?"

"Yes." He looked her directly in the eye, and Addison believed him. She sighed in relief. Her suspicions were confirmed, but she was livid that he hadn't just put her to bed.

"Alright," she said, "we didn't have intercourse, but we *had* sex."

"No, I gave you oral sex," Caleb replied with a smirk as he turned his back to reach inside the closet and remove a button- down shirt, "which you seemed to enjoy immensely. I, on the other hand, came back to my room and took a cold shower."

"Why did you?"

"Why did I what?" he asked, buttoning the shirt.

"Why didn't you make love to me last night? I know you could have, as it probably wouldn't have taken much coaxing." She had fuzzy images, but it was clear that she'd been the initiator.

"Because, we agreed to not have sex," Caleb responded. "And yes, I admit to being weak and not stopping at a kiss when you tried seducing me, but I'm a man. I'm only human." He tucked the fully buttoned shirt into his jeans.

Addison smiled as she stared at him. "Has anyone ever told you you're a flirt?"

He grinned broadly. "Many times."

"This can't happen again, Caleb. We have to stick to the rules until we get to know each other. No deviations."

"Aye, aye, captain." He saluted her. But he knew that it wasn't in his nature to play by the rules. Last night was just the preview. And it was just a matter of time before they would have the whole show.

23

Caleb stared out the window of Hart Enterprises and watched the five o'clock traffic begin in downtown Dallas. He thought about how his life had changed in the last couple of months. Having Addison choose to give their relationship another shot had been like the big man above giving him a second chance considering he'd already lucked out once by walking again.

He was so thankful, and so now he was determined to prove to Addison that he could be the man she needed, the man she wanted, the man she would be proud to have on her arm. He called and texted her several times each day to wish her a good morning or just to see how her day was going. His attentiveness surprised her at first, but as he continued his quest, she began to relax and enjoy it—even expect it. One day, he had to go out of town for business and hadn't had a chance to call. She'd given him hell when he returned, but then he realized it was because she'd been worried. So he'd promised to always try and call or at the minimum, text.

Their dates had been simple yet frequent, whether it was dinner and a movie or vegging out on the sofa and watching *Love Jones* or *The Notebook*. He and Addison were getting to know each other on a deeper level outside the bedroom. For example, they were learning each other's likes and dislikes. He learned that Addison liked fruit, but hated bananas because they were too mushy, while Addison learned he hated peas and most things green but could stomach the odd salad. He made sure he had lots of fruits and veggies stocked in his apartment. Her happiness meant everything to him.

Caleb realized that during their first relationship incarnation, he'd been more interested in discovering her body rather than learning more about her. He'd matured since they'd last been together and knew that life wasn't all about sex. In fact, he hadn't had much of it the last few years. Considering he'd been such a horndog, it would probably surprise Addison to learn that although he hadn't been celibate, he could count his sexual partners on one hand. That certainly wouldn't have been the case four years ago, but then everything had changed.

He'd had to learn the hard way that life is short and tomorrow isn't promised. Consequently, he'd had to dig deep within to find the strength to keep trying even though the odds were against him. His parents, Duke, even Amar had flown in dozens of specialists who'd all told him the same thing: The odds of him ever walking again were unlikely. The best they could offer was some movement in his lower region and the ability to go to the restroom on his own. Most had even said he'd never recover his sexual function, which had nearly had him hitting the bottle for comfort.

Thank God for Uncle Duke. He'd been a lifeline that Caleb had clung to and who, no matter how evil or foul-mouthed Caleb became, never gave up on him. Caleb could recall one instance in which Duke, fed up with Caleb's insolence and treatment of his therapist, had poured a bucket of ice water all over him. It had been a rude awakening, but one that grabbed his attention. After that, Caleb had promised to behave, and he'd gone a step further and pushed himself harder than he ever had in his life … and it had paid off.

"Penny for your thoughts," a feminine voice said from behind him.

Caleb spun around and saw Addison in his office doorway. She looked completely sexy standing there in a vivid psychedelic orange print form-fitting dress. "Hey, you." He walked toward her and pulled her into his office.

He lowered his head and swept his lips over hers. She immediately parted her lips and allowed him entry to deepen the kiss. When he finally broke it, he looked at her. "What brings you by?"

"Had a long day and was hoping we could grab a bite to eat."

"Sounds good to me. Let me grab my jacket."

They decided on a posh Japanese restaurant nearby that served some of the best sushi for Addison, but had a Hibachi grill for Caleb.

"Tell me about your day," Caleb said, laying a napkin across his lap once they were seated.

Addison filled him in on the big client presentation she'd had. They were laughing about it when Caleb noticed color drain from her face. When he turned around, he saw Raphael approaching with another gentleman.

Caleb wished Raphael would keep walking, but instead he came toward them.

"Raphael, what are you doing here? I thought

you'd gone back to Paris." Addison rapidly fired off statements to him, showing Caleb just how nervous and uncomfortable she was with the situation.

Raphael's face crinkled. "I guess that would have been easier for you, huh? Unfortunately, since I came here for you, I couldn't up and leave. I do have a contract."

Addison nodded. "Of course. My apologies."

Raphael glanced at Caleb and then back to Addison. "No need to apologize. Clearly you're happy with your choice."

Addison's eyes became misty, and Caleb could see she was holding back tears. He reached across the table and squeezed her hand.

"How touching," Raphael commented, rolling his eyes. "Guess he really is the better man."

"Not better," Addison said softly, "just the *only* man for me. And I'm sorry if that hurts you, Raphael, because I never meant to do that. I honestly never thought—"

Raphael held up his hand to prevent her from speaking further. "I don't need a repeat of our breakup. I hope he makes you happy, Addison. That's all I've ever wanted for you." He turned and walked away.

Addison glanced upward, blinking back the tears, but Caleb didn't let go of her hand. "I'm sorry," she said and rushed from the restaurant and onto the patio.

Caleb was hot on her heels. Thanks to the cool evening air, there weren't any patrons eating outside. "Why are you sorry?" he asked when he reached her and spun her around.

"Because—"

"Because you moved on with your life? I don't

blame you for falling for another man, Addison. How can I? *I pushed you away.*" Caleb stared at her.

"You're so quick not to blame me for putting us in this awkward situation with Raphael and just moving on with our lives, but we haven't really dealt with the past."

"I don't follow."

"You have to forgive yourself for your perceived weakness," Addison responded. "You were under tremendous physical and emotional duress. Your entire life had been turned on its head. You weren't thinking clearly when you asked me to leave. And if I hadn't been so young, I would have understood that and I would have stayed. I *should* have stayed." Tears began flowing down her cheeks, and Caleb reached out to catch them with his hand.

"Please don't cry, Addy." He wrapped her in his arms and then grasped her cheek so he could look into her eyes.

"We both made mistakes. I should have stayed. It's one of the things I've always regretted. If I'd stayed, would things have been different?"

"I don't know, Addison," Caleb replied. "I was so messed up back then. I was angry at God, the world, my family. I pushed everyone away. I may have turned your love into hate. Maybe it was meant for us to go our separate ways so that one day our paths would cross again and we'd find our way back to each other."

"That may be true, but I need you to forgive yourself and I need you to forgive *me*." Addison stared back up at him, and he pressed his lips hotly against hers and pulled her close.

He whispered in her ear, "I forgive you."

THAT NIGHT, they'd made a breakthrough in their relationship. Addison felt it, and she hoped Caleb did too. It was also why she felt that now was the time to take their relationship to the next level. She was amazed at how well-behaved Caleb had been over the last few months. They actually dated, unlike years ago when the only thing they'd known to do was to get horizontal. Even though there was an intense attraction between them simmering beneath the surface, they'd actually talked and he'd listened to what she had to say. She would even share with him her ideas about campaigns, and he would share with her news about the oil business.

It was refreshing to have such an open, honest and mature relationship. On the other hand, the ache at the juncture between her thighs every time Caleb was around was causing Addison extreme angst. At first, it had been subtle, but as they continued to spend more and more time together, it was becoming harder and harder to ignore her body's craving to be with Caleb again. Being near him as she'd been last night when, after dinner, they'd snuggled in his bed and fallen asleep fully clothed had her body remembering what it was like to have Caleb inside her ... all the way inside.

Whenever a kiss between them became too passionate, Caleb was the first to pull away. It was like he was trying to show her, rather than tell her, that he could be the man that she needed. And she was beyond grateful he had, but the time had come. Addison was ready to end the moratorium on sex and be reminded of just how good they could be together.

So she planned a weekend getaway to Galveston with him. She'd gotten permission to work a half-day, and she was about to scoop Caleb up at his office.

She called him on his cell. "Hey, handsome."

"A call during the middle of the day, I feel so privileged." Caleb laughed. "What's going on, babe?"

"You need to come outside and find out."

"Where are you?"

"Outside. Meet me in five. Tell Duke you've taken ill."

"Okay. See you in a minute."

He was downstairs and in front of her in less than five. A broad smile spread on his face at seeing her casually dressed in an oversized T-shirt and ripped jeans as she leaned against her Porsche Roadster.

He gave her a quick kiss. "You're looking hot."

"Thank you," she said, and then rose from the hood of the car. "Hop in. I'm kidnapping you for the weekend."

"Is that right?"

"It is," she said, opening the door.

"What about clothes?" Caleb asked as he came around to the passenger side.

"Already taken care of," Addison said as he slid in beside her. "Buckle up. It's going to be one helluva weekend."

It took less than two hours to get from Dallas to Galveston. She'd had to beg her father for the use of his jet and pilot to get her and Caleb there, but she was determined and he'd finally relented. When they arrived, a car was waiting to whisk them to the cottage on the bay that Addison had found while she was looking for the perfect romantic getaway. It hadn't been easy finding the right place. Caleb wasn't a man interested in the glitz and glamour of a resort. Addison knew he would appreciate something unpretentious that would just be about the two of them.

"This is it," she said when the car came to a stop.

In her excitement, she hopped out before Caleb could come around to open the car door for her. She glanced up at the cottage while Caleb took care of their luggage with the driver and tipped him.

Out of her purse she pulled the keys that had been Federal Expressed to her and opened the door. Caleb soon followed her and walked inside with their bags. The house was spacious and airy and had an authentic nautical décor with beautiful sailboat replicas. The living room had great big comfy chairs, from which they could relax, read or watch the flatscreen TV. She opened the French doors to the wooden deck and an infinity pool that overlooked Galveston Bay.

The outdoor area was extensive. There was a palapa-covered porch with a grilling area that housed a propane pit, cooktop, refrigerator and whatever utensils they would need to make them feel at home. There were two wooden piers that extended beyond the property into the water. One of them was sixty-five inches, which the owner had told her was good for fishing. The other held a hut on the edge with sitting areas for relaxing and unwinding with a firepit nearby. Not to mention they were a stone's throw from the beach. Everything they would need for a relaxing, romantic weekend was right at their fingertips.

"This is beautiful, Addison," Caleb said, wrapping his arms around her middle and staring out at the bay from the deck.

"I'm glad you like it." Addison glanced behind her.

Caleb brushed his lips across hers. "Let's look at the rest of the place."

There was a large eat-in kitchen fully equipped with all the latest appliances, including a Keurig coffeemaker. Addison walked over to the refrigerator and was happy to see the curator had indeed stocked it.

The cupboards were also filled with pans, dishes and utensils. "Looks like we won't be hungry."

Caleb bent his head and looked at the contents. "No, we won't."

Addison continued her tour down the small hallway to the bedroom, with Caleb following quietly behind her. It was a deep midnight blue and held a large king-size bed, flatscreen TV and wicker furniture and also had doors which led out to the patio. Did Caleb realize it was the only bedroom in the house? If so, he hadn't said a word.

Addison walked over to the adjoining private bathroom that had a walk-in shower and large Jacuzzi jetted tub.

"Looks like there's room enough for two," Caleb commented from behind. She spun around, and from a short distance he stared at her for a long time before finally asking, "So, what's all this about, Addy? I mean, if I'm reading you correctly, this is a pretty romantic spot."

Addison glanced over at Caleb and got lost in her admiration of him. She allowed her eyes to rove all over him, from his dark, luxurious ebony lashes to his hard cheekbones, strong jawline and nicely sculpted mouth. But it was his lips that she was most interested in and a zing of awareness shot through her. Tonight, she would make love to Caleb again after four years. She swallowed hard and finally said, "I know."

His eyes were dark and stormy and difficult for her to read. "Are you saying what I think you're saying?"

She nodded and in five seconds flat, Caleb had her pushed up against the shower door and was kissing her passionately. When he finally broke the kiss, she was breathless and panting, but he didn't let her go.

"I want you so much," Caleb said, caressing her backside.

"I want you too," she admitted.

He smiled. "My patience paid off."

"It did. It showed me you were ready for something more."

"I am, Addison. I'm ready."

She wasn't sure he meant that literally, but she would take it. "I know, and I can't wait to be with you, but not this second." She wrenched herself from his grasp. "I have a romantic evening planned."

24

Caleb appreciated Addison's thoughtfulness. She'd gone through a lot of trouble to show him that she was ready to take the next step in their relationship—from the romantic cottage on the bay to the exquisite seafood dinner that they'd just finished sharing at a quaint, yet romantic waterfront restaurant—but if he were honest, he was ready for the main event.

It had taken a great deal of restraint not to tear her clothes off in the bathroom earlier when she'd lifted the sex moratorium. Now all he could think about was when the dinner would be over and when he could once again experience the heaven between her legs. If he closed his eyes and thought back, he could almost, almost remember how she tasted. But he wouldn't have to recall anymore. Tonight, he would sample the real thing.

They continued walking hand in hand down the waterfront, listening to the waves beat against the shore until, eventually, Caleb couldn't stand it anymore and pulled Addison into a darkened corner between two nearby buildings and began devouring her mouth.

"I need you now," he groaned against her lips.

Mesmerized by the potent dark allure of his face, she said huskily, "Let's get out of here."

When they made it to the cottage bedroom, he turned on the bedside lamp. "I want to see all of you. Remember all of you."

It was just like the first time they'd made love and honestly, this was like their second first time because they were different people, yet oddly the same.

He let his eyes do the walking, studying her every feature as he soaked in this momentous occasion. The beaded bodycon dress she wore fit perfectly and hit right above her knee. And her hair was a mane of tumbling waves, just as he liked it. She looked striking. He could also see she'd expertly done her makeup, which encompassed a touch of mascara while her eyeshadow highlighted her doe-shaped eyes. And her glossy lipstick ... well, it made him want to taste her full lips. His groin tightened at the thought, and a heartbeat later, he reached for her.

He claimed her mouth with a passionate kiss. He toyed with her bottom lip, and then the top. When he finally released them, he and Addison were gasping for air. He wouldn't rush things. He had all night to make sweet love to his Addy.

Without a word, he began stripping off her dress. She didn't protest when he bent down and peeled her sandals from her feet before lifting her onto the bed in her lace-embroidered underwear, but not before punctuating each action by giving her a searing kiss. "You're so beautiful, Addy," he said, caressing the underside of her breasts.

"I want to see you too," she murmured with drowsy lashes as she sat on her haunches on the edge of the bed. She motioned him forward with her index finger.

He came willingly, and she helped relieve him of his jacket. Impatiently, her slender fingers attacked the buttons on his shirt until she reached gold. Slowly, she eased his shirt from his shoulders and then she lowered her head and licked one of his nipples.

He moaned. "Addy …"

She continued teasing his nipples with her tongue while her hands roamed down his chest and abdomen until she reached his trousers. He felt the zipper and pants being tugged down his hips, and he assisted her by stepping out of them until he was in black silk boxers.

Addison shot him a wicked smile as she reached behind to unhook her bra, sending those luscious breasts of hers tumbling from their confines. Then she hooked her fingers into the waistband of her panties and began sliding them down her thighs. Without taking her eyes off him, she leaned backward and eased them off until she was lying naked on the bed.

Caleb swallowed hard, and he knew his boxers were not concealing his extreme state of arousal. The old Addison would never have been so bold with her attraction for him. He liked this grown, mature version.

"Are you going to just stare or are you joining me?" she asked with a slight tilt of her head. "It's getting awfully cold over here." Wanton desire was evident in her brown depths.

"Oh, I'm about to turn the heat way up," Caleb said as he swiftly removed his boxers, letting his jutting erection spring free. He crawled toward her on the bed and lay over her body as he kissed her.

ADDISON SIGHED when Caleb's mouth moved from her lips to her breasts. He rubbed the crests with skillful thumbs and then laved them with the tantalizing warmth of his incredible mouth. Pleasure surged through her. She shut her eyes as he coaxed the points until he had her hips writhing on the mattress. "I'd forgotten how sensitive you could be," Caleb murmured.

Addison glanced up from the sexual spell Caleb was casting to see him smiling at her.

"And I love it." He turned his attention back to her nipples and made havoc of her senses while his expert fingers trailed a path past her flat abdomen to the silky brown curls covering her mound.

Addison's breath hitched as she remembered just how skilled Caleb was in this area. Fuzzy images of the nights in Vegas and Miami in which Caleb had given her this particular treatment dazzled her mind. But the memories were not nearly as good as the present. He toyed with the delicate pearl at her apex, and she whimpered breathlessly, arching her back against his skilled fingers.

"Yes, oh yes," she cried, even though she couldn't focus on anything but his fingers. They were going deeper, stroking at her very core, and she was drowning in pleasure of the most profound kind. When he withdrew his fingers and replaced them with his tongue, she arched off the bed.

Caleb lifted his head long enough to say, "I want you to come for me, baby." He placed her legs around his shoulders and buried his face between her legs. He slid his tongue inside her gently at first, teasing with light, precise flicks. Then he quickened the pace, and

Addison began to squirm as Caleb licked her to the edge of an orgasm, but then he would withdraw and ease in again. He tortured her with his tongue until she sobbed his name desperately for a release. "Caleb—please—"

He thrust farther inside her until she broke. Her thighs began to quiver. She was flying so high from his erotic skills that she didn't notice him slide a condom over his thick erection until he had shifted over her and slid between her thighs. She felt his iron-hard length push against her, and she spread her legs for him as he plunged inside. It was a sweet invasion that she welcomed.

Addison cried out, not in pain, but in the significance of the moment. They were about to make love. Her eyes connected with Caleb's as he withdrew and then slammed into her. Ripples of heat stirred through Addison as every nerve ending came alive. She wanted him, and he delivered.

Caleb thrust deeper yet again until he was at the hilt, and that's when he began to move and rotate his hips. A whimper of excitement escaped Addison's lips as their bodies joined as one. It felt amazing to be with Caleb again after all this time, and she clenched around him.

Fierce strain was etched across Caleb's strong face and a hunger lay deep in his eyes. He stroked her breasts until the tips became tight beads while the lower half of his body had her squirming and writhing underneath him. She was greedy with an elemental need that she couldn't describe, so when wild convulsions overtook her, she was shellshocked, but she welcomed them because she was finally with the man she loved.

CALEB AWOKE in the wee hours of the morning feeling hungry. Hungry for Addison. She was draped over him. Her soft breasts were cushioned against his chest, and her hair had fanned out. He inhaled deeply. He would never get tired of her smell. He flipped her over, tumbling her onto the pillows, and her eyes opened.

They were sleepy and languorous. "Caleb?"

"Yes, baby." He reached for a condom on the bed and protected them. Then he turned back around to find Addison watching him. Her eyes were wide with —dare he think it—lust.

He scooted beside her, and without leaving her eyes, slid a forefinger inside her. "Good morning." ·

Her eyelids fluttered closed, and she whimpered softly.

"Are you ready for me?" he asked, because every fiber of his body was leaping with eager excitement. He wanted to be inside her.

She nodded slightly, so he slid over her and began to drive himself in. As if she sensed what he needed, she angled her hips for his hard and fast entry. His heart hammered as sweet pleasure began to engulf him. He pounded into her as if he were penetrating her very essence.

Last night he'd felt the very same way. To be with her again after he'd thought he'd lost her forever ... oh! Once he'd started to recover from his bull riding accident and realized he was alone, despair had nearly overtaken him at the possibility of never seeing her again. But slowly, he'd come to accept it. And now, it was like he could breathe again. He withdrew and then with all his power, lunged into her again. She screamed his name as if she too were bent on consuming him as he was her.

Pleasure rose inside him as the fire and bitterness of those years of solitary existence began to die out. He rode her hard. She didn't seem to mind his frenzied nature because her responses were just as wild as his. She clung to him as her orgasm tore through her. Seconds later, he bellowed and hollered her name as he shuddered over her. His heart pressed into hers, and he could swear he heard her heart beating erratically too.

After all this time, their love was just as strong. LOVE. There it was. This time he could recognize it because it was beyond what he'd felt for her before, which was more akin to lust and possessiveness. The emotion he felt for her was ten times stronger. He was seconds away from saying it out loud and he would have meant it, but in the heat of the moment, he wasn't sure Addison would have believed him, so he said nothing. But soon, he would tell her that he had fallen madly, hopelessly in love with her all over again.

OVER THE NEXT FEW DAYS, Addison and Caleb enjoyed all that Galveston had to offer, from the fishing on the pier near the cottage to going out and feeding the dolphins in the bay. Their days had been perfect relaxation, and every day brought another fresh and wonderful moment. They'd eaten in tiny restaurants on the island that islanders loved and the tourists rarely frequented. Other times were just as idyllic because they'd barely made it out of the cottage. Like radar, Caleb picked up on her presence whenever she was near and would give her a smile or wink or one of his searing kisses that would send them back to the bedroom to make love for several more hours until they were both exhausted.

Addison was recognizing that Caleb was doing everything he could to please her and show her he had changed. During their walks through the shops, he'd bought her a single red rose and just last night, a simple diamond pendant necklace. He just hadn't said what she wanted to hear, which was that he loved her. She knew it was terribly unjust because she hadn't said it to him even though she was head over heels for him. She was just afraid to say it first.

Those old fears of having put herself out there four years ago and have him scorn her love were etched in her memory. Even though she'd forgiven him, she'd never truly forgotten, so it was much harder for her to put herself on a limb again and spill her guts without knowing how he felt about her.

She did, however, want him to overcome one of his fears—getting back on a horse. They'd talked at length over the last few months about Caleb's fear of riding. He hadn't been back on any animal since the accident, and Addison knew how much riding and his family's ranch had once meant to him. She wanted that back for him, so she'd arranged for a sunset ride on the beach.

"Where are we going?" Caleb asked the following afternoon as a driver took them around town.

"You'll see." Addison squeezed his hand. She hoped he wouldn't consider it presumptuous, but she knew he had to face his fears eventually. Why not on a docile horse used to riding on the beach?

Caleb came around to open Addison's door. He glanced at the setting. "A day at the beach? Why didn't you just say so?" He glanced down at the T-shirt and shorts he was wearing. "I didn't bring my swim trunks."

Addison grabbed his hand. "You won't need them." They were walking a short distance up the sand when Caleb must have seen the horses because suddenly, he couldn't take another step.

"Addison?" He was rooted to the spot in the sand.

She glanced sideways at him. "I know, you might think I'm ambushing you, but—"

She didn't get another word in. "Hell, yes, this is an ambush! You know how I feel about riding. Why would you do this?"

"Because, it's time for you to face your fears."

"And you're the judge of that?"

Her eyes began misting with tears. "Well, no, but I just thought—"

"That you would force me into doing the very thing that landed me in a wheelchair for two years? I never thought you were that insensitive."

"Caleb, I'm sorry."

But he pulled away from her and began walking down the beach.

"Please, please don't be upset with me," Addison said, running after him. "I know it was presumptuous of me to assume you'd want to ride again, but I know how much you love it."

"Loved it." He stopped long enough to correct her.

She nodded her head. "Loved it," she corrected herself. "And I just thought that with me by your side, I could help you face your fear. I'm so sorry. I never meant to offend you. I only want what's best for you. I would never do anything to harm you." Quietly, she turned away from him and began walking in the other direction.

CALEB COULDN'T BELIEVE Addison had ambushed him. He hadn't dared look at a horse yet alone any other animal that could buck him off in over four years. The thought of getting injured again had paralyzed him with fear. It's why he didn't visit the ranch or Rylee that much. Their life revolved around animals and horses and his didn't, not anymore.

But today, Addison was calling him out on his fears. He didn't appreciate it, but he could respect it.

Caleb sighed and then ran after her on the sand. He stopped her and whirled her around to face him. "You didn't offend me, and I know you would never do anything to hurt me, at least not intentionally, but, babe ... I can't do this."

"How do you know," she pressed, "if you never try?"

He shook his head. "I can't."

"Yes, you can." Her eyes pleaded with him to give it a chance. "You're just afraid to fall. And I know I can't say I will catch you, but I will be here for you if anything happens."

It wasn't the admission of love Caleb was waiting to hear, but it definitely meant Addison was in their relationship for the long haul. But should he really be surprised by that? Four years ago, she'd offered him the same thing, but he'd been too afraid to take her up on it. Could he now?

She held out her hand. Her eyes burned with confidence in him.

Caleb swallowed his fear. "Okay."

Thirty minutes later, after signing the appropriate waivers and saddling up, Addison and Caleb stood in front of two saddle horses. They had to be two of the most docile creatures Caleb had ever seen. The odds of them getting spooked and throwing him off were highly unlikely, but it could happen just the same. Images of being thrown from the bull in the arena and the subsequent kick flashed in Caleb's mind. He began pacing in the sand.

Addison must have seen him getting skittish because she slid her delicate hand in his and looked up at him. "You can do this."

He inhaled deeply.

"Ready to go?" the ride coordinator asked, looking at Caleb and then Addison.

"Caleb?" Addison's calling of his name was more like a question. Could he do this? Could he conquer his fears?

Caleb recalled how hard it had been learning to navigate life in a wheelchair. But he'd done it. Until eventually, thank God, he hadn't needed it.

Instead of answering, he held his hands out to give Addison a lift before hopping astride an American Saddlebred as he'd done four years ago before the accident. He looked at the coordinator. "Whatcha waiting for?"

Addison beamed across from Caleb on her spotted saddle horse. He could see how proud she was of him, but he was even prouder of himself for doing something his entire family couldn't even get him to do. But there was a difference. He would be riding with the woman he loved.

~

LATER THAT NIGHT IN BED, when they were wrapped in each other's arms after making love, Caleb thanked her.

"For what?"

"For forcing me to face my demons," Caleb replied, brushing damp hair from her brow. He'd just given her quite a workout.

"I just knew how much riding meant to you, and I wanted you to have it back. I wasn't going to let some damn bull rob you of something you loved."

Caleb was quiet. It hadn't just robbed him of his ability to walk or ride, it had robbed him of Addison, and he wasn't going to let that happen ever again. She'd become his whole world, and he couldn't wait to share his life with her.

25

The next day, Addison arranged for massages on the cottage patio under the tiki hut so they could hear the water lapping in the distance. She knew he might be sore after yesterday's sunset ride on the beach, so the massage was the perfect gift. Her heart had welled with pride at seeing Caleb ride again. It hadn't been an easy step for him, and he'd given her some resistance, but in the end, he'd done it.

During the ride, she'd glanced over and seen him in his glee as man and horse became one. Caleb belonged there, and she hoped that he would continue to ride once they returned to Dallas and later when he visited Golden Oaks.

After their ninety-minute massages, they decided to take a dip in the pool, but it didn't take long for their afternoon of swimming to lead to another aerobic activity.

Caleb led her to the pool steps and then pulled her onto his lap. He cupped her face with his large hands and kissed her deeply. His invasive tongue was like molten lava and incited hot flames of desire to shoot through her. And when he brushed his lips across her ear, along her jaw and back to the corner of her mouth so he could tease her lips, she moaned, quivering with need for him. When she felt his hands tugging at the straps of her bikini top, she didn't protest. She just watched it float away in the water. Her breasts were bare to him so he could feast on them. And that's exactly what he did: He made a meal of her.

He twisted her nipples into points until she let out a satisfied gasp. Then he bent his head, drew one hardened peak into his mouth and began suckling. Her breathing became loud, and her eyelids fluttered closed as she enjoyed Caleb's ministrations. He cupped the other breast and gave it the same treatment. Addison moaned, desperate for more.

Caleb obliged by changing positions so Addison was sitting on the steps. That's when Caleb lowered his head under the water and caught her bikini bottom between his teeth and pulled the thin fabric down her legs. Then he set about an exploration of the place between her thighs, which were spread-eagled on the steps. He grasped her buttocks and then his tongue darted inside her wet folds. He set her on a course of pure ecstasy, and Addison's moans grew louder with each stroke of his skillful tongue. As it went deeper, she began to writhe, and she couldn't help releasing a scream as Caleb brought her to one helluva an orgasm.

"Caleb!"

The sound tore at his soul, but he didn't stop. His tongue continued its assault, sucking on her clitoris until she was convulsing and screaming as her second orgasm hit her with full force. She arched her back off the steps, and Caleb hauled her to him, kissing her hard as he settled his jutting erection between her legs and plunged forward into her wetness.

"Yes!" she yelled.

Addison didn't know why she was surprised that Caleb would make love to her out in the pool, out in the open. From the start, everything about him was out of bounds and went against the grain. Caleb was a no-rules kind of guy. And after being so long without him—without this—she was now a no-rules kind of girl.

She clutched him to her chest as he kept ramming into her. "I love you." The words escaped from her lips as her pleasure rose. Her mind warned her to retreat, but there was no way she could when he was buried deep inside her, filling her completely and invading her womb as she accommodated him in a viselike grip. His movements grew more and more frenzied as he rode her hard, giving her the friction she craved until his orgasm hit him, and he detonated inside her. She felt it too, and it wrung yet another climax out of her.

"I'm sorry, Addison," Caleb murmured against her cheek as he collapsed on top of her and both their breathing returned to normal.

Sorry? That was the best he could offer after she'd just said she'd loved him. Why hadn't said he loved her? Was it because he didn't? The magnitude of his omission made Addison slowly extract herself from his embrace and climb out of the pool.

"ADDISON, WAIT!" Caleb yelled. After they'd separated, she'd rushed from him, reached for a towel to cover herself and shot inside the cottage. Caleb was seconds behind her, wrapping a towel around his middle as he followed her.

He didn't reach her in time. When he made it to the bedroom door, it was locked.

Dammit. He should have said he loved her too, but in the heat of passion, all he could think about was how tight she was, how her folds were milking him of everything he had to give. Her words of love, although not a shock, had caught him off-guard, and just as he was about to repeat them, his orgasm had hit hard and strong … and that's when he'd realized he hadn't been wearing a condom. Thus the apology.

He didn't want Addison to think he'd done it on purpose. This entire week, they'd practiced safe sex, but just minutes ago he'd gotten so caught up, he'd made a mistake. One which he'd compounded by apologizing instead of saying the three words she'd wanted to hear.

Caleb sat with his head between his hands as he waited for Addison in the living room. He didn't know what to say or do to make things right. He could only take his cues from her. She emerged thirty minutes later, fully dressed and holding a suitcase.

"Addison—"

"I think it's time we head back," she said, not looking at him. "We already stayed longer than I anticipated. This was only supposed to be a long weekend, and I need to get back to work."

That was utter bullshit, and he damn well knew it. Addison hadn't been thinking about work a half-hour ago when he'd been buried to the hilt inside her.

"We need to talk," he replied, coming toward her.

When he reached her, she tried to ignore him and sidestep him, but she wasn't getting past his six-foot frame.

"Let me pass."

"No, not until we talk about what just happened outside."

"Why? It won't change anything."

"Everything has changed," Caleb said. "We just made love, and we could have created a baby. And if we did—"

She cut him off. "We'll deal with it. But right now, I just want to get home, so kindly get dressed."

He glanced down at the towel he was still wearing. He was naked underneath it. And despite how cold she was being to him, he knew if he dropped his towel and took her back to the bedroom, he would reach her. But again, sex had never been their problem. It was communication.

He sighed. He would do this her way, but he intended on having a serious talk with Addison Walker. She needed to know that she was the only woman for him and he wanted her for his wife and not because she could be carrying his child, but because he loved her.

He was ready in less than an hour, dressed in a blue button-down shirt, denim jacket and Levis. Addison was waiting for him and from the looks of it, she'd already done some preliminary cleaning and was airing out the cottage because it had returned to the coastal environment it had been, instead of their love nest with flowers, candles burning and the scent of their lovemaking permeating every room.

Several minutes later, the town car was outside, so Caleb wasn't going to get the opportunity to speak with Addison. It was clear to him she'd wanted it that way. She'd wanted as little interaction with him as possible.

He was hoping to talk to her on the short plane ride, but instead, once he'd turned on his cellphone after several days, he discovered his uncle had left several urgent messages within the last twenty-four hours. They were about an accident on the HE oil rig. Caleb had no choice but to call him from the jet's phone. He discovered he was going to have to get over to the rig as soon as he got on land.

As they were touching the tarmac, he ended one of the many calls he'd had to make during the flight to find out exactly what had happened on the rig. "Is everything okay?" Addison asked.

"So you notice I exist?" She'd barely spoken two words to him since they'd left the cottage.

She rolled her eyes.

Caleb sighed. He knew he'd hurt her when he hadn't said he loved her, but after everything they'd been through, shared, how could she doubt him? Yet despite their personal relationship, they still had a business one. "As you probably surmised from what you overheard from my phone conversations, there's been an incident on the oil rig. Could be some fallout afterward. So to answer your question, yes, HE is going to need our publicist."

"Of course." She returned to staring out the window.

Should he have said he needed *her*? Would it have made a difference? She'd already made her mind up, and at the moment, Caleb wasn't sure how to get through to her. He just hoped that he would.

ADDISON WAS in a sour mood the next day. Given that she'd just shared a week with Caleb in Galveston, she should have come back feeling ecstatic; instead, she was more confused than ever. During the trip, she hadn't been that happy since, well, since the last idyllic week she'd spent with Caleb four years earlier.

Then her mind wandered to that incredible lovemaking session in the pool. It had been one of the most intense times they'd shared, and subsequently, they'd been so enraptured that Caleb hadn't worn a condom, which meant she could be pregnant. It was much too soon to tell, but it could very well mean that they would finally have a long-term connection. But she hadn't wanted it like this. Not without love, and it was clear that it was one-sided. She loved Caleb, but he didn't love her. Although she'd said it during lovemaking, she'd meant it and he'd known that, which is why he'd wanted to "talk." Had he been blowing smoke about wanting marriage and babies?

She'd never felt that connected to a man before and that free without anything between them. So she certainly hadn't been prepared for a talk so he could blow her off. No, thank you. She wanted to lick her wounds in a drink, but that was going to be impossible. As soon as she had arrived back at work, a pile of papers had beckoned from her desk, not to mention she had been waiting on a call from Caleb on a potential media firestorm that was about to hit Hart Enterprises.

It was a long day, and when she made it home, she really wanted a glass of wine, but she settled on tea instead. She was making herself a cup in the kitchen of the Walker mansion when Collette joined her.

"Well, look who's returned?" Collette said, giving her a kiss.

"Hey, girl." Addison gave her a one-sided hug.

Collette stepped backward with her hands on her hips. "Wow! Don't sound so excited to see me."

"Sorry." Addison smiled half-heartedly. "How the heck are you?"

"I'm on cloud nine. I met this awesome guy at a gallery opening, and we're going out on another date."

"That's great, Collette. I'm so happy for you."

Collette frowned. "For someone that just came back from a getaway with her boo, why aren't you smiling from ear to ear? Girl, if I were you, I would barely be able to walk straight."

Addison couldn't resist a chuckle at Collette's bawdiness. "You're a ham."

"Of course, but that's why you love me."

"Always will," Addison said.

"So, what's the scoop? What's got your panties in a twist?"

"One word: Caleb."

"What'd he do now? Did he not put it on you right?"

Addison laughed again. "No, he's more than adept in that department. What he's lacking is in the love department."

"Are you sure about that?"

"What do you mean?"

"Have you seen the way that man looks at you?" Collette asked. "I mean, I haven't been around you two a lot in recent months, but the man's in love with you. He was the moment he saw you at that club in Vegas."

"What?" Addison wasn't sure she was buying it. "Collette, you're mistaken."

"Like hell I am. I know when a man's in love, and I know when he isn't, and Caleb, my friend, is most definitely the former."

Addison wondered if Collette could be right. She'd hoped that was the case, but he seemed afraid to share his true feelings with her. Or had she not allowed him to? Had he been about to tell her he loved her at the cottage, but she'd been too stubborn to listen because she was afraid of getting hurt?

"Excuse me, Collette." Addison rose from the stool. "I have to go."

"But I just got here."

"I know, and I'm so sorry. Truly I am." She squeezed Collette's arm. "But I have to leave."

"To find Caleb?"

Addison smiled and nodded.

"Do me a favor then? Listen and be open, okay? Love is staring you right in the face, if you let it in."

"I will." Addison rushed out of the room.

"Caleb, I need you to focus," Duke Hart said that afternoon in the executive offices of Hart Enterprises. "Your head isn't here, and we need all hands on deck if we're going to deal with this issue."

"I know that, Duke," Caleb said tartly. He was aware that he was a little off, had been the last twenty-four hours since he'd arrived back from Galveston. He'd immediately had to jump into action over the accident and help his uncle while figuring out what could have gone wrong on the rig. Consequently, he hadn't been able to speak with Addison and make things right between them, and he was pissed.

How could she think he didn't love her? He'd done everything she'd asked. When she'd told him she'd wanted to go slow and given them a sex moratorium, he'd complied even though he ached every time he ended one of their dates. His body knew what it was like to be buried deep inside Addison's tight heat, and he'd taken many a cold shower until Galveston, when she'd finally lifted the ban. His patience and taking things slow hadn't gotten him anywhere. Instead, he felt like after the trip, they'd taken two steps backward.

And where was she anyway? She was his publicist after all, and shit was about to hit them the likes of which Hart Enterprises had never seen. And he needed her.

"Well, get it together," Duke replied. "I need you at 100 percent, especially once we get on that rig. The men will be looking to both of us for answers, and we need to be on the same page."

"I agree, and we will be."

They continued to strategize for another hour before taking a helicopter over to the rig. From the air, they'd been able to see the damage, but it wasn't clear just how bad it was until they'd landed. That's when Caleb realized the extent of the repairs needed. It could have been much worse—people could have lost their lives, and while, thank God, that hadn't happened, still a half-a-dozen men had been injured when a platform had collapsed.

After they'd assessed the damage, they announced a meeting so that he and Duke could address the workers. There were a lot of rumblings in the crowd. A lot of the men were upset that something like this could happen, and they wanted answers.

"I can assure you," Caleb said from the podium, "we'll get to the bottom of this accident and make any necessary repairs."

"How does that help us in the short term?" one of the men yelled. "I have a wife and kids back home that depend on my income, and I can't afford to get hurt."

"Yes, Mr. Hart, can Hart Enterprises assure its workers of their safety?" a feminine voice boomed from the crowd.

"Who said that?" Caleb scanned the room for whoever it was that had asked such a damning question. The crowd must have sensed his distress because it parted ... and there stood Addison.

She looked sexy as hell in a white pantsuit and quite out of place amongst all the hard-working blue-collar guys. He hadn't been prepared to see her, and as a result, was at a loss for words. It was Duke who answered. "We are completing numerous safety checks on the remaining platforms and will be temporarily ceasing operations until such time as we can verify there is no further damage and your safety is assured."

"What about our pay?" several men yelled.

"Every man on this rig will be paid their normal salary," Duke continued, "until such time as the engineers deem it safe for your return. In the interim, several choppers will be coming to escort you back to the mainland."

There were cheers amongst the crowd as most men looked at it like a paid vacation. Caleb could hear Duke speaking a few more words to them, but he couldn't take his eyes off Addison. What was she doing here? Was she here just as HE's publicist? Or was she here for him, to salvage their relationship?

After Duke ended his speech, most of the men dispersed. "Are we done?" Caleb whispered in his ear.

Duke glanced down at Addison standing on the platform and then back at Caleb. "Yeah, we're done. Go talk to your woman."

Caleb nodded and then jumped down off the podium and headed straight for Addison.

~

ADDISON'S STOMACH flip-flopped as Caleb approached her. He looked handsome and sexy. He had that effect on her. Even when she was angry with him, she still wanted to make love to him. It was like their bodies were in tune with each other.

She gave him a half-hearted smile. "Hey."

He returned it with an easy smile of his own and slid his hands in his pockets. "Hey."

"You're probably wondering what I'm doing here?"

He nodded, but didn't speak.

"Is there someplace we can talk?" she asked.

He began walking toward the end of the platform, away from a few workers still mingling around.

"I'm sorry about yesterday," she began. He remained silent, so she forced herself to continue even though her throat felt dry. Collette's words reverberated in her head. She was going to have to make the first move. "I may have overreacted."

He stared back at her, but again said nothing.

"I didn't give you the chance to explain or for us to talk. I just cut you off, and that was unfair. All I can say is that it was a defense mechanism. I didn't want to get hurt and—"

"And I hurt you," he finished for her.

She nodded and wiped an errant tear that slid down her cheek. "Tell me now," she said. "Tell me what you would have said if I'd given you the chance."

Caleb closed the distance between them and grasped the sides of her face. She closed her eyes at his touch, but he said, "Look at me."

Her eyes fluttered open, and she could see something in his, but she wasn't sure she could name it. Or could she?

"I would have told you that I love you too," Caleb replied softly.

Addison's heart began thumping. He *loved* her?

He sensed her disbelief because he repeated it again. "That's right, Addison Walker. I love you. I don't know if it was love or lust at first sight that night in Vegas all those years ago. I just knew I had to have you. And once I did, I became addicted to you. I wanted you whenever and wherever, and bless your heart, you were so young and naïve that you didn't resist me even when I was being possessive."

"I was falling for you."

"And I for you," Caleb responded. His hands left her face, and he grasped her hands. "I didn't know it at first, not until I spent those weeks without you. And then when I saw you at the rodeo that night, I planned on telling you that I wanted you back."

"You did?" She'd always wondered, but he'd never said it until now.

He nodded. "That's why I asked you to wait for me at the rodeo. Of course, neither of us had any idea that I would be severely injured."

"But even then, I was at your side, Caleb, because there was no other place I wanted to be."

He smiled. "I know, and I wish I could have appreciated it, but I didn't." He shook his head. "I was a fool, and I've regretted it ever since. And then three months ago, fate brought you back into my life. When I saw you at the country club, my heart truly stopped. I didn't think I could be that lucky again. I mean, I was already lucky once to walk again, but could I truly be lucky enough to have the greatest love of my life walk back into it? But I was. The only problem was you were with someone else, but I still wanted you back."

"Do you think it was easy for me?" Addison asked. "I never expected to see you again. I thought we'd had our chance, and if we couldn't get it right the first time, we were destined to be apart, so I tried to move on. But knowing you were here and free and that you wanted me back, there was no other choice I could make."

"I would have done anything to win you back," said Caleb. "I would have waited however long you wanted until you let me back into your bed, but more importantly into your heart again because that's just how much I love you, Addison."

"I love you too."

Caleb swept her up in his arms and kissed her mightily. He didn't care that they were out in the open in front of his men. He kissed her like he never wanted to let her go.

When their lips parted, he embraced her hand, bent down on one knee and said, "Addison Walker, will you marry me? Will you be my wife, my lover, my partner, the mother of my children?"

"Yes, of course, yes!" Addison cried. "Yes, I'll marry you, and let's hope after yesterday that I'm the latter."

Tears were brimming in his eyes as he rose. "I would be the happiest man alive if you were carrying my baby."

"And I would be the luckiest woman in the world if I were," Addison said. "I love you, Caleb."

"And I love you."

EPILOGUE

N ine Months Later ...
     Caleb looked down at the beautiful seven-pound and three-ounce baby girl Addison had just delivered. Ivy Hart was going to be the light of his life; she was already wrapping herself around his heart.

He couldn't believe all that had happened in the last year. After four long hard-fought years, he and Addison had found their way back together, and now they were married and had a beautiful daughter to show for it.

If anyone had told him five years ago that he'd be a married man and a father, he would have told them they were delusional. But the moment he'd seen Addison, the doe-eyed beauty had stolen his heart. Words spoken by the then groom-to-be Amar on their way to Amar's bachelor party had come back to haunt Caleb —that when he found the right woman, he would fall down on his knees and beg her to marry him. And he had.

"You have to share," Addison said from the bed, holding her arms out.

Caleb laughed. "Of course." He slid their sleeping baby into her arms.

"You know that might be hard for him," Rylee said from Addison's bedside. "Caleb has always had a way with the ladies."

"And I suspect his daughter will be no different," Noah said from the other side of the bed. "She will definitely be a daddy's girl."

"That's right," Caleb responded. "And I'll hurt the son of a bitch that ever hurts her."

"Well, let's hope they aren't as much of a bad boy as you've been," his mother replied from the foot of the bed.

"Mom!" Caleb laughed. He couldn't believe she'd said that.

"Hey, I'm not stupid," Madelyn Hart replied. "Your father and I," she said, turning to her husband standing next to her, "know you've been quite the ladies' man."

"A reformed ladies' man," Addison countered as she held their daughter. "Isn't that right, Caleb?"

"Of course he is," Benjamin Walker chimed in. "Otherwise, he'll have me to contend with."

Caleb walked toward Mr. Walker and shook his hand. "As it should be. How about a cigar?" He lifted one from his breast pocket and handed it to the proud grandfather. It had taken some time, but Addison's old man was finally starting to come around and give him a little slack. Caleb was happy he could make that happen, because Addison's and Ivy's happiness were all that mattered to him. They were his family.

"Love you, Addy," he said, returning to his wife's side and bending down to brush his lips across hers.

"Love you more."

BOOKS BY YAHRAH ST. JOHN

Connected Books

One Magic Moment

Dare to Love

Dirty Laundry Series

Dirty Laundry

Can't Get Enough

Stand Alone Novels

Never Say Never

Risky Business of Love

Hart Series

Entangled Hearts

Entangled Hearts 2

Untamed Hearts

Restless Hearts

Unchained Hearts

Chasing Hearts Pub Date

Captivated Hearts

Mitchell Brother Series

Claimed by the Hero

Seducing the Seal

Coming Soon in 2022

Guarding His Princess

ABOUT THE AUTHOR

Yahrah St. John became a writer at the age of twelve when she wrote her first novella after secretly reading a Harlequin romance. Throughout her teens, she penned a total of twenty novellas. Her love of the craft continued into adulthood. She's the proud author of thirty-nine books with Harlequin Desire, Kimani Romance and Arabesque as well as her own indie works.

When she's not at home crafting one of her spicy romances with compelling heroes and feisty heroines with a dash of family drama, she is gourmet cooking or traveling the globe seeking out her next adventure. For more info: www.yahrahstjohn.com or find her on Facebook, Instagram, Twitter, Bookbub or Goodreads.